088874

LP   Haycox, Ernest
      Long storm.

LONG STORM

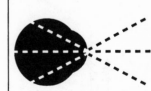

This Large Print Book carries the Seal of Approval of N.A.V.H.

LONG STORM

Ernest Haycox

Thorndike Press • Thorndike, Maine

Library of Congress Cataloging in Publication Data:

Haycox, Ernest, 1899-1950.
    Long storm / by Ernest Haycox.   *93 B6228*
      p. cm.
    ISBN 1-56054-699-9 (alk. paper : lg. print)
    1. Large type books.   I. Title.
[PS3515.A9327L6   1993]   93-7032
813'.54—dc20   CIP

17.⁹⁵

Thorndike Large Print® Western Series edition published
in 1993 by arrangement with Golden West Literary
Agency.

Cover design by Ron Walotsky.

This book is printed on acid-free, high opacity paper. ∞

CAST OF CHARACTERS

ADAM MUSICK . . . Rough-and-ready young captain of the steamboat *Daisy*.

LILY BARNES . . . She could have had any man in town.

EDITH THORPE . . . A genteel society girl, who wanted marriage *first*.

FLOYD RINGROSE . . . He hit the town stony broke.

BILLY GATTIS . . . Ringrose just didn't want him around.

EMILY VON GRATZ . . . She was a handsome woman with a wide experience of men.

WEBLEY BARNES . . . Lily's drunken father.

ELIJAH GORMAN . . . Ruthless promoter.

1

The raw southwester — bearing up the spongy odors of spring — came hard against Lily Barnes when she stepped from the house, plucking at the falls of her dark hair and winding her coat about her in sudden twists. The night's violent rain had stopped but sullen clouds rolled overhead like great sea breakers, whipped into ragged valleys and peaks by the upper air's storm. At middle afternoon there was little light in the day; house lamps were shining down Pine as she walked toward Front, and the town crouched in semidarkness and mist packed the timbered hills westward.

Front was a yellow muddy creek from the bend of A Street southward to Jefferson, bordered by shops and countinghouses and saloons and hotels crouched side by side, brick and wood and false front and board awnings tightly crowded together. Along Front at this hour was a crowded commerce of men and pack rigs and weary-bowed riders and great freight drays sallowly illumined by the street's gas lamps. It was spring once more; it was the beginning of another season of mining fever and on this day the steamer *Brother Jon-*

athan, seventy hours out of San Francisco, had arrived with its cargo and its thousand prospectors — and each week until fall came, another thousand people would arrive, by the *Brother Jonathan* or the *Panama.* Already there was a queue in front of the Steam Navigation Company's office, the arrived gold seekers anxious to book passage upriver to the Eastern Oregon and Idaho mines by way of the *Carrie* or the *Julia.* This day Portland town woke from its winter quiet and Marshal Lappeus would once again well earn his pay even though he, the possessor of one of the town's fifty-five saloons, had a tolerant eye.

Lily made her way across the uneasy intersection plank, noticing men step into her father's store, they being attracted by the sign he had put up: —

WEBLEY BARNES
Hardware : Tin Goods : Miners' Supplies
Agent for the
DAISY McGOVERN
Fastest boat upriver — and only
independent boat
TICKETS
HERE

She moved along the west side of Front, on through the little pools of odors thrown out by the adjacent shops, liquor, leather and bread, Dekum's confectioneries, the dry faint fragrance of Julius Kohn's cotton goods. At Oak there was a dense jam of drays locked hub to hub and the usual brawling of teamsters. Mr. Gorman, wearing his habitually cool expression, saluted her with his stovepipe as he passed by; at the corner of Stark she turned half a block up to read that the Willamette Theater offered Mr. and Mrs. Pope's Troupe in *The Lady of Lyons,* with Professor Sedlick's local pupils furnishing the orchestra. She turned the corner of the Pioneer Hotel and stepped into Burgduff's for a steelhead.

Mrs. Burgduff, a bulky woman made bulkier by various layers of sweaters, cleaned and wrapped the fish. Mrs. Burgduff had a pink, smooth face pressed square by her unchangeable, acquisitive thoughts.

"How many boarders you got now, Lily?"

"One."

"You could squeeze six into that house somehow."

"Six would be uncomfortable."

"Think of comfort later. Get the money now. When the gold rush has gone, Portland will be dead. The fish is twelve pounds — dollar twenty."

Lily continued her round of shopping, crossing the intersection plank again to the

City Bakery, to the Empire Market, to Failing's. She stopped a moment at the *Oregonian* office to read the latest announcements, by wire to San Francisco and by boat to Portland, and retraced her homeward route without haste, rather glad to see so many people livening Portland. A boat whistled for landing, the tone of the whistle identifying the *Claire* in from Oregon City. At Washington she paused in front of Dennison's Opera House: "Minstrelsy, Burlesque, Extravaganzas, Ethiopian Eccentricities. Nothing done to offend the most sensitive taste. *Honi soit qui mal y pense.* Parquette 50 cents. Orchestra Chairs $1. Private Boxes $3." John Green, coming by, found her thus interested.

"Lily," he said and plunged his hands into his front pockets, "you show a wicked curiosity."

"Very lively music comes from this place. What's an Ethiopian Eccentricity?"

"Something for miners, male citizens and assorted characters. It would be more proper of you to see Mrs. Pope."

"I don't like lavender sentiment," said Lily. The wind ruffled the edges of her hair and a smile made its small break along her lips. Mr. Green's glance remained on those lips. "Dennison's music is so brisk," she added. "I shouldn't mind being an assorted character

10

for one evening."

"Well," said Mr. Green, "too bad you can't see it." Then he added with a wry humor, "I enjoyed the show myself," and passed on.

A group of young men paused near her, seedy and callow Eastern city boys off the *Brother Jonathan,* and their remarks became audible to her. She moved on over the intersection of Oak and looked out upon the river to observe the steam ferry bring spray above its bow. Dekum's confectionery again blew its sweet breath on her and she halted with some indecision in her, and at that moment Edith Thorpe came out of Dekum's with Helen Bidwell.

Edith stopped and by the pressure of her hand drew in Helen Bidwell who meant to go on. "Why, Lily," said Edith in a voice which ran lightly up and down the scale of correct surprise. "I do believe it's been a month since I've seen you. Have you been away?"

Lily Barnes thought: Her manners were more natural ten years ago in Mr. Doane's school. She's been reading *Peterson's Magazine* lately. But she said aloud: "No — nowhere. The house keeps me close."

Edith said: "You weren't at Bishop's party."

"No," said Lily. (She knew that without

11

asking. Now she will mention what a nice time she had.)

"It was amusing," said Edith Thorpe, her voice pitched to casual drama. "Tyler Stone brought a bottle of rye and the boys went outside to do their drinking. Tyler always does that. Then a quarrel started and Adam had to stop it. I don't believe anybody wanted to stop, but they were all afraid of Adam. Then we drank too much coffee and it was three o'clock before we got home. Will you be going to the Willamette tonight?"

"No," said Lily.

Edith was smiling, Helen Bidwell was distantly calm. Both were watching her with their clever attention. Edith said: "You should go. I've cried at every performance."

"If I wanted to cry," said Lily, "I'd find a cheaper kind of tears."

Edith said: "I forgot. You don't cry, do you? The other day I was thinking when we were girls at Mr. Doane's school, Mott like to tease you. But you never cried."

"No," said Lily, "I never did. I fought back. Finally Mott grew afraid of me. It never took much to make Mott afraid."

The slightest flaw showed in Edith's pleasantness; the remark had touched her. "We had nice times. The town was such a nice place, but now there's five thousand people and I really don't think I like it."

Helen Bidwell spoke in her indifferent way: "We've got to go, Edith."

A sudden bright charm came to Edith. "We must do something together, Lily. When summer comes —"

"That will be nice to think about," said Lily. But she knew as she watched them go that such a summer would never come; they had grown up and they had grown away, and there was a difference between them which would never be less. She kept her eyes on the two as they moved so gracefully along the street. Edith's head dropped near Helen's and something was said between them and then Edith laughed and the two turned the corner at Oak. A final gust of rain came along Front Street, pushed forward by the hard wind. Lily looked down at her basket and shifted the weight, and again glanced toward the corner of Oak. Her face settled, becoming slightly puzzled and slightly sad as she turned homeward.

From the window of his office directly across the street, Webley Barnes had observed the meeting. He had a group of prospective passengers for the *Daisy McGovern* in the office at the moment, but he ceased to be interested in them and he watched the three girls as long as they were together, Edith and Helen Bidwell arm in arm, Lily standing opposite them. He knew what was happening; he had long watched it come — this break between youngsters who, starting in a rough settlement together, at last found their own levels and moved apart. Portland grew up and the old cruel story repeated itself. The bitterest of feelings came to him, for he realized the scene across the street was largely of his own making; he had started with the rest of the crowd in this new town but he couldn't keep the pace. Other men, more aggressive, were going beyond him, taking their families to a secure place and position; he fell behind and his place was his daughter's place. There was no hurt like the hurt which he brought upon his daughter, and he ground his teeth together and cried out in silence: "Damn 'em for their shabby pretensions and their cold hearts!"

He shook this out of his head with effort and turned to the nearest prospector. "The ticket is five dollars to The Dalles. You'll ride the *Daisy McGovern* to the Cascades, walk around the portage and catch the *White Swan* to The Dalles. You will book separate passage on the *Spray* at The Dalles for Lewiston?"

"The Dalles?" asked the miner. "What's that?"

"A town at the foot of a bad spot in the river. You get off there and take horse railway fifteen miles around the bad spot, and get on another boat."

The miner said: "The Navigation Company will sell a ticket straight through to Lewiston. Why can't you?"

"Ah," said Webley Barnes, "the Navigation Company is a monopoly that has made its connections. We're independent and do the best we can. But you're not likely to get on the monopoly boat tomorrow. It's full up, and will be for a week. You want this ticket or do you want to cool your heels in Portland until the monopoly is charitable enough to find room for you?"

"I don't see," said the miner, "how one outfit can tie up a river as big as this."

"The old story, my friend — the story of the strong and the weak."

Four days of miserable travel from The Dalles — along the drowned thickets of the river's edge, across rock cliffs, and through the everlasting jungle of fir — brought Floyd Ringrose at last to the edge of the Sandy at a point which seemed to be a ford. By river boat this journey was only a matter of a day's comfortable riding; but by boat it was also a matter of five dollars' fare, which Floyd Ringrose did not possess; moreover, he had left The Dalles in some haste, standing not upon his dignity. All his luck there had been bad; in Portland he hoped to find money waiting for him via Wells-Fargo draft from the East, and in Portland he hoped to get at his major business.

The day was gray and weeping, the sullen clouds pressed down, the roundabout timber exhaled a clammy dismal fog, the river lay dimpled by fat rain; and as he studied the additional discomfort before him, his face displayed a very raw temper. It was a bold face with heavy cheekbones and nose, accented by restless eyes and a full fleshy mouth above which a straw-yellow mustache — which was also the color of his hair — lay carefully trimmed. A great overcoat thickened him, and this he removed and tied to his saddle cantle to reveal a round muscular body, big wrists, big hips and heavy thighs. Having given the ford the shortest of studies, he issued a sudden grunt, raked the horse with both spurs and sent it immediately into the river.

The horse dipped under at the first plunge and came up struggling. Ringrose sat jockey style, prepared to leave the saddle, but a short effort of the horse brought it to a gravel bar in the stream's middle. Afterwards man and beast made the passage of the slack water beyond the gravel bar and came ashore in the midst of a gloomy grove of trees. Slightly ahead of him on this obscure trail Ringrose saw a fire burning. He moved directly toward it.

A single man crouched over the blaze, drinking his noon coffee as he warmed himself. His face, when it lifted to Ringrose, was young and seasoned behind a full beard. Ringrose said, "I don't suppose you object to my sharing your fire?" and stepped to the ground at once, water spurting from the tops of his boots. He crouched across the fire from the young man, spreading a pair of broad smooth hands. The young man stared at those hands; he looked up to Ringrose's face and caught the latter's sharp-cracked smile. "I have not been warm since leaving The Dalles," said Ringrose. "When does the sun shine in this country?"

"Don't know," said the young man. "Just coming in myself."

"From the mines?" asked Ringrose.

The young man was of a secretive disposition. He finished the coffee in his cup and handed the cup to Ringrose, pointing to the black pot bedded on the fire's coals. A puff of harder wind brought down sheets of rain from the overhanging skies, the water singing in the fire and drenching both men. The young man took no notice of the additional discomfort but Ringrose, wanting some target for his temper, suddenly kicked at the fire.

The young man silently observed this.

Ringrose sucked at the hot coffee and held the cup between his hands, soaking in its warmth. The young man, he realized, had not answered his question and did not propose to. He finished the coffee, put down the empty cup and smiled in a way that displayed the whitest and heaviest of teeth. This smile also brought his lids together until nothing much could be seen of the actual quality of his glance.

"How far to Portland?" he asked.

"About fifteen miles."

Ringrose stood up to stamp life into his legs. Water continued to run from his soaked clothes. "Well," he said, "it will be a bad ride. Much obliged for the coffee." He turned to his horse and took his overcoat from the cantle thongs and slid into it. He buttoned it and brought the collar up about his neck, standing with his back to the miner; and he remained that way a moment with his close thoughts, then swung rapidly on his heels. The young man had risen from the fire and had stepped over to his horse; he was on the far side of the horse, watching Ringrose across the saddle. He had his guard lifted and he did not intend to be surprised.

Ringrose showed his smile again. He said, "Good luck," and swung to his saddle, at once moving westward through the timber.

The coldness and misery of his body increased and he gave the horse a prompting with his spurs and went along the darkening trail at a faster gait. Occasionally the timber broke away to give him sight of a near-by farmhouse, and once he passed over a natural meadow and had some difficulty finding an entrance into another stand of timber where the rain fog lay so thick that he traveled as though a gray cloak were flung about him; the wet and rank odors of the forest were heavy around him and the sound of the wind was a steady humming above him. Late of that afternoon he broke out of the timber to come upon the junction of the trail with a road. Following the road downward he arrived at a broad river — the Willamette — puckered into whitecaps by the strengthening southwester. A ferry waited at the road's planked end; across the river Portland lay cramped within the hard semicircle of a forest, the lights of the town freckling the day's deepening gloom.

He rode upon the ferry at once and, since there seemed to be no other traffic the ferry put out upon the river, lifting and dipping to the choppy water. A lone man tended the engine within the deckhouse; half across the water this man appeared for his fare. "Fifty cents for you and fifty cents for your horse."

Ringrose stood at the head of his horse, watching the town take shape in the misty gloom. He seemed caught by his thoughts, for the ferryman had to repeat the question. Ringrose turned and presented the ferryman with his smile. "I shall have to ask you to trust me until tomorrow. I am stone-busted."

The ferryman was immediately aggressive. "Why didn't you mention that before you came on?"

"You might not have taken me," said Ringrose.

"I can still turn around and put you ashore."

"You could," agreed Ringrose, "but that would be a waste of time, wouldn't it?"

The ferryman said, "What have you got for security?" He stared at Ringrose, his glance finally touching the man's right hand. "That will do."

Ringrose gave out a short laugh. "It's worth more than your damned ferry."

The ferryman walked toward the wheel and gave it a spin. "You think I won't take you back? We'll see."

"My friend," said Ringrose, "don't do it."

The ferryman looked across his shoulder and saw his passenger with one hand plunged into an overcoat pocket and with his smile gone. Ringrose's lids were half shut and his

20

face had a stillness upon it. "I don't want to get in trouble with you," he said, "but I intend to cross this river. You shall get your money tomorrow." Then he let some of his temper slip out. "Keep going, you hear?"

The ferryman was angered at the situation and not unwilling to carry his share of the quarrel; yet, as in the case of the young miner, he saw something on Ringrose's face which appeared to warn him for he presently eased the wheel and sent the ferry on its proper course. A few minutes later the boat grated into the jaws of a slip at the foot of one of Portland's streets and the ferryman walked forward to make the boat fast. Ringrose mounted and rode off the craft without a word.

Beyond the wharf the muddy street began, moving westward up a slight grade between low buildings squatted beneath the slanted rain. Eight or nine blocks in that direction the houses faded into a kind of rough and stumpy land, which in turn broke against the black wall of a forest. Ringrose crossed three streets before overtaking a lone man plodding through the weather. "Where would Fourth be — where would Yamhill be?"

The man said, "Up two and five to your right," and kept going.

Ringrose rode the prescribed distance and

slowly cruised the block until he discovered a narrow two-story house flanked by a cabinet shop and an empty building. He continued along the street and found a livery. There he left his horse and returned to the narrow house; he gave a quick glance around him and rapped briskly on the door.

The door was opened by a woman of about his own age, which was twenty-five. The moment he saw her he lifted his hat, summoned his gallantry and made his bow. Her hair was a kind of brass yellow, a shade odd but striking, and lay extraordinarily thick on her head. She had a shapely, heavy body and her eyes were blue and looked upon him with something between reserve and doubt. They were the eyes of a woman, his well-experienced mind told him, who certainly had no fear of men.

"My name in Ringrose and I have just arrived from The Dalles."

"This is not a boarding house," she said.

"You are Emily von Gratz? I knew Jack Logan in The Dalles."

"Well," she said, "come in," and closed the door behind him. She faced him and gave him a going-over with her glance. "Did he tell you to come here?"

"If I needed to," he said.

"Well, you look as if you had need enough."

Then she added a casual afterthought: "His arm ever heal?"

He was impressed by her. She was a handsomer woman than he had expected to find and he did not hesitate to show her his admiration. The effect of that was to soften her expression.

"Didn't know anything was wrong with his arm," he said.

"Just wanted to find out if you really know him," she said. "He had any luck, or is he still in trouble?"

"He's all right. You know Jack."

"I do," she said dryly. "What do you want?"

"I'm going to set up a table in some high-class saloon," he said. "I'll need some advice about these people here and a loan of fifty dollars."

"You get run out of The Dalles?"

She immediately noticed the roughing of his temper, and she had some direct advice for him. "If you intend to gamble with the fashionable trade you'll have to hold yourself in. You can't pick trouble with the leading people. They're an odd sort. You can do business with them, but it's got to be genteel." Then she added, "Pretty broad of Jack to use me as an underground station for his shifty friends."

His smile grew thinner. He looked down

at his wet and shabby clothes. "I'm not as bad as I look," he said. "I am better than I now appear to be. What hotel should I put up at?"

"The Pioneer. Tomorrow get yourself a plainer waistcoat. These people here like a tame display." She left the room a moment, and returned with a stack of gold half eagles in her palm. He took these from her casually.

"Tame people?"

"No," she said. "They're tough enough to skin you clean in business."

He turned to the door and paused there. "I'm obliged for the advice," and as he stared at her he noticed the soft shadow of uncertainty come to her. When he saw it he was satisfied and left the house. Returning to Front, he followed it to Washington and stepped into the Pioneer. He signed for his room, crossed the lobby to the barbershop and made arrangements with a colored boy to take care of his clothes while he was in the bathhouse.

He had his bath, lying in it long enough to bake the day's chill from his bones, with a cigar between his heavy teeth and with a copy of the town's paper to pass the time; he got into his clothes when the boy returned them and he spent another half hour in the barbershop. Appearance meant much to this man and thus when he left the barbershop once more groomed, although his boots were still wet, he found himself in excellent spirits. He crossed the hotel's lobby, entered the saloon and pushed his way through the crowd to the bar. He had to wait for a drink and this made him restive, as any kind of delay did. Later, with a glass of rye in his hand and the smoke of a cigar making its screen around his face, he achieved the appearance of a man of thorough leisure.

He saw that he was in the town's best saloon, for he recognized the quality of the men around him, the sureness which was printed on them and the smell of money about them. He recognized also the accurateness of Emily von Gratz's description of them. They were sociable as they moved around to exchange news or to push their business ventures, but they were smooth, they were sharp and in their restrained way they were entirely certain of what they were after. They drank a good deal of liquor, which they bore well. In all this crowd he saw but one man he thought to be drunk; that man sat alone at a table with a bottle and seemed deliberately to be going about the business of drinking himself out. Presently he caught the man's name when a townsman stopped at the table and dropped his advice: "You ought to go home, Webley. Lily's probably got supper on the table."

Smoke and talk and ease filled the room. The talk was of business and politics and war. Ringrose heard the rebellion mentioned. "Grant," said somebody, "is the only general worth his salt. Lincoln had better recognize that pretty soon."

Ringrose gave the speaker a pointed stare and afterwards he looked around the room to see how the sentiment was taken by others. Apparently it was the prevailing opinion, yet he did observe one man who stood aside and made no contribution to the talk. This one had some faint mark of the Southerner on him and Ringrose, having finished his rye, strolled over the room and paused near the man. He made a show of lighting his cigar. Over the tip of the match he said: "Damned foul weather."

"Usual spring rain," said the man.

His talk had a Southern swing to it, not pronounced but still noticeable. Ringrose drew a long draft of smoke from the cigar and breathed it out. He looked directly into the man's eyes. "Any stars in the sky?"

The man stared at him. "Stars?" he said. "For the love of God, that's a bad joke on a day like this."

Ringrose gave the man an agreeable nod and returned to the bar for his second drink, continuing his survey of the crowd by means of the back-bar mirror. A boy — an undersized boy with a solemn and sharp face — came through the crowd in a ducking, turning way and squeezed a place for himself beside Ringrose. The boy caught a barkeep's eye and said: "A bottle of brandy, two lemons, and a cup of loaf sugar."

"That game still going on in Number Nine, Billy?"

"Yes," said the boy.

Ringrose stared down at this Billy and found nothing on the lad's face he liked. "You're damned young to be in here," he commented.

The boy had the liquor, the lemons and the sugar in his hands. He gave back to Ringrose a stare which was as pointed and cool as the one Ringrose gave him, and slipped through the crowd. The barkeep observed this small scene with amusement. "You got a match there, friend. That kid's the best businessman in town."

"Brash," said Ringrose.

"He's stropped his wits on some mighty hard stones," said the barkeep.

Ringrose laid down his glass, paid for the service and swung about with the notion of leaving these quarters which were becoming increasingly cramped as the night came on. Rain drummed the building wall insistently, raw air poured into the saloon each time an additional discomforted Portlander entered. Men's wet woolen clothes began to send up their steamy rankness in the room's warmth, and smoke got thicker and voices made a kind of foolish babble. This place was for the town's leading characters, Ringrose decided. They, having property to protect, would naturally be Union men. Eventually he would become acquainted with them and play his part among them, but meanwhile he wished to locate the quarters of the rougher sort. Therefore he pressed his way toward the door.

Near the door, and having some difficulty in securing a passage through the crowd, his turning glance touched a face in the smoky background of the saloon — a square, stubbornly built face with a full curly covering of beard, out of which stood a massive nose, a fleshy set of lips, and a pair of bright, black eyes. It was the face of just one more man in the crowd, yet some kind of memory jogged Ringrose's attention and he stared at the face with a moment's complete interest. The man gave him a most casual return glance, raised a glowing cigar to his mouth and swung his head as if to observe something else. The pressure of the crowd shoved Ringrose through the saloon's door into a wet and darkening night.

★ ★ ★

Billy Gattis never walked; he was always a boy on an errand, a boy in a hurry, and his habitual way was to travel the town's streets at a shuffling run, his body bent, his head down and his face turning from side to side in a manner to see whatever was around him. It was not only a sharp face but a face drawn to the point of being pinched, an unsmiling face on the dangerous edge of furtiveness. He was fourteen, and small, and as quick of mind as any man in town; he did any kind of chore that any man might ask of him for whatever rewards men might choose to give him, and he had been doing this since he was eight. He fetched lunches for late playing gamblers in their hotel rooms, he sold papers and lugged baggage and carried notes — sometimes with instructions to be secretive in his manner of delivering them; he was in and out of saloons and he knew the town's back rooms and he could find any of the town's characters on sudden notice. By consequence he knew more than he should have known, and all of this he kept to himself; he had early learned to think for himself and keep his mouth closed.

With one more night done, he moved uptown at his usual half run until he came to Emily von Gratz's house, made a circle of it

29

and went in through the back door with a small knock to announce himself. Emily lay on the couch, reading some late magazine from Driscoll's bookstore; she wore a Chinese silk wrapper and had her hair done up and, thus released from the confinement of her day clothes, she looked like a placid and fat and self-indulgent housewife.

"Milk's on the kitchen table, Billy. Those sandwiches are blackberry jelly."

He ate his late supper and poured himself extra milk from the quart can with the bill on it and returned to the front room.

Emily said: "You're tired."

"No," he said, "I'll spell."

"All right," she said, and began to pick words from the magazine she was reading. Billy stood by the room's center table, spelling the words she gave him. This went on for ten or fifteen minutes. Then she said: "Your eyes are half shut," and put the magazine away. "Anything happen in town today?"

"No," he said. "Maybe we don't have to spell any more. Maybe I'm good enough."

She sat up on the couch. "Tired of it?"

"No," he said, "not if you say not."

"People who grow ignorant," she said, "are like people who have no arms or legs. Look at Ben Crowley."

"Ah, he's lazy," said Billy.

"You watch the smart ones. They never stop learning things. Look at Mr. Gorman. He's always learning. Look at Adam Musick. You like him?"

"Yes," said Billy, "I like him."

"Be like him then."

"I like Ben Crowley, too," said Billy.

Emily von Gratz nodded her soft, unthoughtful face.

"That's fine. Like everybody. It don't do any good to hate anybody. You go to bed now. You're not getting enough sleep."

He went through the kitchen and left the house. He threaded the narrow between-building spaces of the block, once more at a trot, heading south through the wet and black night toward Harrison Street. There was a block here covered with scrub brush and fir timber, through which a muddy trail led to a shack long since abandoned. He let himself into the dark room, found his way to his bed, and undressed. He fell back on the bed, thinking of the town and Emily von Gratz, and spelling, and the white-haired gambler in Room Nine of the Pioneer, and the *Oregonians* to be picked up at five o'clock in the morning; and these things formed a series of moving images before his eyes and gradually dissolved into blankness as he fell asleep.

2

Adam Musick whistled for the Oak Street wharf at three o'clock and brought the *Daisy McGovern* softly against the piling. Lou Bradshaw and Emmett Callahan made the lines fast and the down-river passengers left the boat; then George Pope came from the engine room and the four men hustled a short load of freight ashore. Afterwards Musick took the *Daisy* across the river and nosed into the bluff at Pierpont's to take on wood for the next day's trip. It was six o'clock before the *Daisy* returned to the Oak Street landing for her night's berth.

Musick descended from the pilothouse to record the day's business in the purser's office while George Pope finished his engine room chores and Bradshaw and Callahan washed down the decks. The four of them made a partnership in the *Daisy McGovern* and they all worked extremely long hours rather than spend money on extra help. This, Musick thought as he posted his books, was the way it was generally in Portland; the country was still young and everybody was in a fever to become rich by seizing the chances around him. They could wait until they were older to slow down and enjoy themselves. Then, in the back of his head, a thought had its way with him: If we're able to enjoy anything by that time.

He moved into the saloon where Callahan and Bradshaw were arguing over supper. George Pope presently came up to join the argument. These three lived on the boat and did their own cooking, and seldom agreed on what they wanted to eat. Callahan said: "I'll go get a chunk of fish."

"Get meat," said George Pope. "We had fish last night."

Bradshaw said, "Good trip today," and a brief pleasure warmed his eyes. He was lean and dry and preoccupied, with a narrow face and small eyes set deep. "How much we taken in?"

"About nine hundred dollars," said Musick.

"It'll be like that all summer," said Bradshaw. "If that's our freight in the shed we should wrestle it aboard tonight."

"Hell with it," stated Callahan. "I'm going to Dennison's for some fun tonight."

"You're a fool with your money," said Bradshaw.

Callahan's smile roughened his cheeks. "I like a drink and a laugh and a woman once in awhile. Don't you?"

"Four bits admission," said Bradshaw, "a round of drinks for a dollar — and maybe the woman's expensive. Ain't worth the price."

Musick half listened to this invariable argument and half read the day's copy of the *Oregonian*. George Pope nursed a cigar in silence, neither amused nor interested. He had his mind on the *Daisy*'s machinery.

"Well," said Callahan, "it is few enough years that a man can get drunk and wake up next mornin' feelin' fine. And it's only when a man's young that he can catch the fancy of a woman. I'm an ugly scoundrel anyhow. I'll be a damned sight uglier five years from now. I'll be good and save money when women stop smilin' at me."

He stepped to the bar at the saloon's far end and brought back a bottle of whisky and four glasses; he poured the drinks around and lifted his drink toward the light and regarded it with warm interest. Musick, reading down the paper's columns, said aloud: "Dolly Rawl and her troupe of entertainers leave Portland for the mines, via the *Julia*, tomorrow morning."

"That will draw passengers to the *Julia*," said Callahan.

"Why?" asked Bradshaw.

Callahan burst into laughter. "Ah God, Lou,

is there no blood in you at all?"

Musick, continuing with the *Oregonian*, had come upon an editorial which interested him. "Listen," he said: —

"We have communication from the East to the effect that the Knights of the Golden Circle — that despicable secret tool of the Confederacy — is again resurgent after a period of inactivity enforced by some excellent detective work by the Government's Mr. Pinkerton. One crop of Knights having been harvested to prison, another crop now has arisen. As an organization it never has been extinguished. It has its chapters throughout the north and enrolls as members those disaffected people who are outright Southern sympathizers, or belligerent Northern States' rights believers, or those gentry who have no honest faith but who stand to profit politically or otherwise by a breakup of this Union, or those who hate Mr. Lincoln. To all of them the issue is clear: This Union must be dissolved by any means.

"Citizens may suppose we are exempt in Oregon from such an organization. They are mistaken. There are Knights in this state, and Knights in this town.

Of that we have been privately assured. This state is Union, and will demonstrate that fact at the June election. But let nobody suppose there are not men desperately working to effect a separation of the coast state from this Union. Senator Gwyn's idea of a separate Pacific Republic is still a glittering charm to foolish eyes; and there are enough Southerners up and down the coast to wish for an actual alliance of the coast states to the Southern cause. Either event would be the final disaster to this Union, and none know it better than those who seek such dissolution. The stakes are high, the men bold. This is another battlefield and we must expect trouble. Its nature we cannot know, but its eventual appearance we must look for and resist."

"And who would such men be, walkin' our town?" wondered Callahan. "I do not know anybody who is not Union. If I found one I'd break his damned head."

"We might come to that," said Musick.

Bradshaw said: "Keep out of politics. It's not good for business. It makes enemies. We got trouble enough running this boat against the Navigation Company. It would be foolish to add any more trouble."

36

"Lou," said Callahan, "if you cut yourself you'd bleed vinegar."

"You know what we've got here?" said Bradshaw. "We've got a million dollars if we can stick it out. The mining boom is good for five years. We've got a fortune, if the monopoly don't squeeze us."

Callahan, having heard all this many times before, shrugged his shoulders. "I'll get steaks."

"Thick ones," said Pope.

Musick left the saloon with Callahan and paused on the dock to run his glance along the *Daisy*'s hull and superstructure, observing that there would need to be some patching presently done on the forward deck. They had bought her cheap from Collins and Thompson in San Francisco who had found her small size unprofitable on the Sacramento. She was half the size of the *Carrie* which lay at the dock below; she was narrow-beamed and of small carrying capacity and sometimes handled roughly in the short rollers which chopped up the river in bad weather. But since she was small she was not regarded as serious competition by the Navigation Company, which was jealous of its monopoly; so far the Company had not troubled the *Daisy* by the usual device of lowering freight and passenger rates to the breaking point. Thus, for carrying the surplus traffic up the river — that traffic which the monopoly could not immediately handle — the *Daisy* was ideal; and on the run between Portland to the Cascades she could at any time beat the *Carrie* or the *Julia* by a full twenty minutes.

Callahan murmured: "We've had enough of her for one day," and moved on.

Musick followed, saying: "We'll have the graveyard filled by fall." The graveyard was what they owed Collins and Thompson for the *Daisy*.

"It will be a blessing," said Callahan. "We're working longer days that I like. But we'll never make Bradshaw's million. The monopoly will let us eat and make day wages. It will never let us get any bigger."

"There's another way of looking at it," said Musick. "If we stay small they can wipe us out whenever it suits them. If we get big they might not like a fight."

They crossed the levee and came into a yellow pool of lamplight lying before the Nugget Saloon. Rain came steadily on and wind rushed heavily over the town's housetops; night's blackness squeezed down with its weight and its loneliness. Stragglers moved along the street, roving in and out of the town's fifty-five saloons, and already there was music in

Dennison's Opera House. Emmett Callahan stopped as though a hand had seized him and he laughed in the softest way, his eyes turned toward a woman emerging from the darkness. It was Emily von Gratz, an umbrella tipped before her. She gave Callahan a glance, and then she stared at Musick and held his attention a moment. She said, "You both look dog-tired."

Callahan's smile grew brilliant. "Not now, Emily, not now." He had been a homely man until this moment, but suddenly he became buoyant with what was in him. There was nothing mean on that roughly built face; there was only a stirred gentleness.

"You're a hard Irishman," she murmured, and went on.

Emmett laughed and stabbed a thumb into Musick's chest. "We work too much," he said and moved toward The Shades Saloon.

Musick continued north, following Pine's black lane. House lights formed crystal squares at wet windows but none of this light reached the dismal street. The rank odors of Pounder's delivery came through the building's open arch, as well as the sound of drunken men idly arguing. At Seventh he turned through the Barnes's gate, now catching the rough and tumble report of the wind in the timber at the edge of town. He let himself into the front room's warmth and heard Lily's voice come from the kitchen. "That you, Adam?"

"Yes," he said and moved over the room, to pause at the kitchen's doorway. He had both hands plunged in the front pockets of his jacket and his hat shadowed his features — the meaty, creased lips, the heavy nose and mouth, the gray-blue eyes: He had been up since four that morning and he was tired; he had Callahan on his mind: Callahan's warning that they were all working too hard, Callahan's laughter when looking upon Emily. He watched Lily's hands move over the pans on the stove, the turning of her body, the evenness of her expression. Abruptly he had a picture of her lying in bed with her face against the black background of her unpinned hair.

"Was it a good day, Adam?"

He walked on to the back porch. He hung up his hat and jacket and rolled back his sleeves. "Best this year," he said and brought the wash basin to her. She filled it from the teakettle and gave him her first moment of undivided attention. Her eyes were as gray as his own, and they had for him a certain impersonal interest. As long as he had boarded here — six months — she never had varied that manner.

He took the basin to the rear porch,

spraddled his legs and washed in a noisy thorough way. He combed his hair, had a look at himself in the cloudy porch mirror, and stepped back to the kitchen. He stood by the stove, liking the warmth against his muscles.

"You need a haircut."

"I'll have to bring the *Daisy* in early some day."

"The *Daisy*'s a hard woman," she said.

"That's what Callahan said tonight. He wondered why we worked the way we did. Emily von Gratz came by and Callahan got philosophy when he saw her."

Another woman, Edith Thorpe for instance, would have made some sort of a gesture to cover up the indelicacy of the subject. Lily was neither shocked nor pretended to be. She had either a charity or an indifference in the matter which was probably the result of her father's training. Webley was an educated, defeated man whose views were unlike his neighbor's views.

"Did she look at you, as well as at Callahan?"

"She looked at both of us," he said. "I suppose it made no great difference to her."

"A woman can't look at two men without having a preference."

"She's past the point of choice, isn't she?"

"Unless she moved to another town and started fresh."

"It would catch up with her," he said.

She glanced at him, murmured, "Are you sure?" and turned from him to push her pans to a cooler part of the stove. "Dad's not home."

He heard the change of tone and he knew what it meant; he went to the rear porch for his coat and cap. "Where'll I look first?"

"The Pioneer, probably."

He returned to the night's hard fat rainfall. The wind once more had gathered itself, moving up from the southwest in storm force and creating a destructive racket of the timber west of the town's edge. A wash basin fell from somebody's porch and rolled erratically along the walk, and at the intersection of Front and Pine he observed all sorts of debris — paper and chunks of shingles and snapped-off fir stems — floating in the loose mud. The gold seekers who this day had arrived via the steamer *Brother Jonathan* now crowded the saloons and billiard rooms and hotels, passing restlessly from one place to another. They stood in dismal groups beneath the streets' occasional board awnings; he heard them cursing both the weather and the country as he went by.

At Washington he crossed over, entered the

Pioneer's overcrowded saloon, and discovered Webley Barnes alone at a table. He sat down opposite Barnes. Liquor had shaken Webley Barnes loose from his restraint; it had brought him to that stage where his vision was too clear, to the point where he saw the world and himself too well. He was not more than forty and inoffensively vain of his appearance; he was a handsome man, his features flexible and sensitive rather than rugged, and he took care to keep himself well-clothed and well-kept.

"I know," said Barnes, "I should go home. Have a drink first."

Musick rose and fetched an extra glass from the bar. He poured his whisky and refilled Barnes's glass. He made a gesture at Barnes, drank his liquor straight down, and sat back in the chair to give the other man time to pull himself together. There was nothing new in this scene. For as long as a month Barnes might maintain his pose as a brisk business-man; then, as though he had forced himself too long, his vitality ran out, strangeness came upon him and he turned to the Pioneer to drink himself into the blackest kind of a tunnel. It was a cycle which never failed.

"What about tomorrow's passengers?" asked Musick.

"Half a load."

"I'm pretty hungry, Webley," said Musick, rising.

Barnes looked regretfully at the whisky bottle. "Don't suppose you want another drink?" He stood up and remained still until Musick came around and got his arm. The two pushed through the crowd to the street, crossed the intersection and made their way beneath the densely driving rain. Most of Barnes's weight was against Musick. Suddenly his odd fancies began to pour out of him.

"Barbaric land. Dark — deep — wet land. Siwashes sitting in a log house, naked and unclean by their fire. You see their red eyes through their rotten hair. You smell 'em. They crouch and eat their dog meat with their fingers and itch their flea bites. They sleep in their dirty blankets. Some kind of a pagan god threatens them with thoughts of punishment, but they don't believe it too much. They've got some kind of a happy land hereafter with plenty to eat and a lot of sunshine. But they don't believe that too much either. We white people eat better and keep cleaner, but we don't believe in our gods much more than they do. It is a beast of a world. There's no difference in their lot and ours, except we are not bitten as badly by the fleas."

"Sure," said Adam. "Sure."

"Life's not much to them. They go out and

44

kill each other. We think that's savage but we kill each other in slower ways. They buy a woman with a horse and a blanket and a string of beads. We think that's indecent. But the string of beads works for us, too, if the beads come from Amsterdam and flash in the light."

"That all there's to it, Webley?"

They went across Second, across Third and Fourth, before Webley Barnes answered.

"Well, there's a beautiful light in the world, but nobody will see it. We are miserable, stupid, cheating, senseless animals."

The wet, wild night should have sobered him, but it did not. He had taken in too much whisky; his mind functioned, his muscles failed. At Seventh and Oak he was no longer able to walk. Musick lifted him like a sack of potatoes in his arms and carried him the rest of the way. It had happened like this before, and Lily, knowing what it might be like, waited at the door for them. Musick climbed the stairs and laid Barnes on a bed. Lily came in with a lamp, and the two of them stood over the bed, looking down on Webley Barnes, whose face had turned pale and loose. He opened his eyes. He said: "Don't feel bad, Lily. Don't ever let anybody get inside you and hurt you. Keep everybody outside. Don't love too much. Don't hate too much. Don't hope too much." He stared at them and he added in an exhausted, futile voice, "You are better than they are. God damn their pretensions and their snobbery and their cat claws. You're better."

He closed his eyes and was dragged down into a partial sleep whose wild visions shook him and made him whimper. Lily put a hand on his forehead. She bent over him, her voice dropped to a whisper. "Nothing's wrong — nothing's wrong." Adam Musick watched her face, arrested by the heavy softness of her lips, by the affection so clearly there. But there was no softness in her eyes. They were distressed, they were dark.

"I'll put him to bed," he said. After she had gone he pulled off Webley Barnes's wet clothes and rolled him under the cover. He opened a window to let in the raw wind and he lowered the light until Barnes's face was a white and wondering mask in the shadows.

He went down to supper in the kitchen and sat across from Lily. The calm remained with her and he had the feeling that nothing he could do, or any man could do, would break it. She was a mystery to him and perhaps she meant to be — locking herself away from those things which had destroyed so much of her father. The handsomeness of her father had come to her and he suspected she possessed

a love of life as strong as her father's. Somewhere and somehow Webley had been
betrayed and disillusioned by it; she meant
not to be betrayed.

"Whose cat claws?" he asked.

"I don't know."

"Something bit him. Too bad."

"He's asleep. He's happy."

"No way of changing him?"

"Why try? His life's been sad. He had a
good education but never found a way of using
it. He inherited money and lost it. He loved
my mother, but she only lived two years after
they were married. Everything he touched
went bad. Now he's afraid to touch anything.
I'm all that's left, and he's afraid he'll do
something that will hurt me. That's what he
was talking about. Let him drink, if it helps
him. I don't mind. It's his life."

"Who would want to hurt you?"

She had no answer; she remained beyond
the reach of his curiosity. He helped himself
to fresh coffee from the stove and ate his pie.
He sat back to enjoy the fragrance of his pipe
and to feel weariness comfortably loosen him.
The heat and the meal made him heavy-lid-
ded. He spread his heavy legs under the table
and relaxed on the chair. Light set up a metal
glitter on his day's growth of whiskers.

She said: "Better make your call and come

back to bed. Your day is too long."

"Callahan said that. He said he had to hear Dennison's minstrels."

"I'd like to hear them too."

"That place is not for you."

"Is it wrong to sit where people are laughing?"

He opened his eyes fully. "Would you go if I took you?"

"Yes."

He got up and was not pleased with her. "I wouldn't take you."

"I knew that."

He stood by, watching her body sway and turn as she moved about the room. He watched the slight changes of her face, the quickening, the loosening, the small expressions coming and going. She kept at her work, but she knew he was watching her.

"I don't know you," he said, "when you talk like that."

"What good would it do you to know me? Better go make your call."

Musick put on his jacket and cap, listening to the rising beat of the storm. He walked to the door, filled his pipe and discovered that he had no great desire to go out; yet he was restless.

Lily said: "Don't you want to see her?"

"Maybe it is Dennison's I need tonight."

"That's for those who have no other place to go. I'm surprised at you."

He turned about and found her watching him. In another woman, and once more he thought of Edith Thorpe, right and wrong were like the well memorized rules of a game. Edith knew the rules and was quick to call them. Lily seemed not to care about rules, but he could not be sure, since he could not penetrate her guard. He thought she was lonely and that many warm things stirred and unsettled her; but neither was he certain of this. Turning, he left the house.

Half a minute after Ringrose left the Pioneer's bar, Mr. Perley McGruder — whose glance had struck up a fragment of memory in Ringrose's head — moved from the bar-room to the hotel lobby and let himself into the street by the hotel's main door. The street lamps had recently been lighted to give some relief against the onset of a squalling nasty night; a few townsmen walked abroad, muffled and bent against the southwester's violence. Ringrose was by that time halfway down the adjoining block, traveling toward the northern quarter of town. Mr. McGruder observed him for a moment, lifted his coat collar, and set out on a discreet job of shadowing. He crossed Washington, turned and crossed Front and walked along the dark face of the buildings on the west side of Front, in this manner having a better observation of Ringrose diagonally over the way.

At Stark Mr. McGruder settled against a building wall, noting that Ringrose had wheeled into a saloon farther along. This appeared to be a matter of waiting under extremely disagreeable circumstances; for no matter how he turned and slanted or hitched his short broad body, he could not keep the wind-driven rain away. It trickled down inside his collar, it fell from the brim of his hat as a miniature waterfall, it collected on his beard and spread inside his shirt, it soaked his boots until they were as soft as moccasins. Mr. McGruder experienced a mild form of outrage at such weather; it was the sort of thing which deserved mention in a letter to the editor of the local paper. Absorbing the bitter nourishment of his sodden cigar, he was phrasing such a letter in his mind when Ringrose came from the saloon, retraced his way to Stark, stopped to have a look around him, and went up Stark to another saloon.

He was obviously making a tour of the town's bars for particular reasons. Mr. McGruder gave up the job and returned to his room in the Pioneer to wring as much of the night's moisture as possible out of his clothes and his beard. Then he descended to supper, detouring by way of the bar to insure himself against the chills; following supper, he climbed to the room and sat down to compose a letter.

ALLEN RUSK
SANSOME STREET
SAN FRANCISCO, CALIFORNIA

HONORED SIR:

Our Subject left The Dalles via horse two days ago. I judged he would go to Portland and, acting upon that Decision, I took boat for this town. My Decision was correct. He is here, now touring the various saloons with the intent of making connection with other Knights. In the bar of this hotel I overheard him drop the Password but make no contact.

You may infallibly trust my discretion and energy in the Matter. There has been no public Act of his in the past thirty days which I have not witnessed. As soon as he establishes connections I shall certainly know of it. I am convinced that his major business will be here. I do not know what is afoot but I believe it to be Grave and shall bend every effort to ascertain it. I flatter myself that I shall succeed in this instance as I have in the past. You may inform Washington telegraphically of my whereabouts and efforts. There is an Election here in June and I am certain all things must boil before then. It would be a good thing if Washington might check that end to discover how great are the Sums of Money being supplied our Subject. The greater the Amount, the greater their Intentions here undoubtedly will be. I am, Sir,

> Y'r Ob't H'mble S'v't.
> PERLEY MCGRUDER
> *Agent*

He sealed the communication, placed it in his coat pocket and gave a great belch; then he drew his chair to the room's window so that he might command a view of the nearest intersection, drew and lighted a cigar, and settled to his watch.

3

When Musick left the Barneses' house he paused on the porch a moment to turn his coat collar; a cloud, more heavily swollen than usual, burst above the town and the wind-whipped rain came down upon the housetops with such force that it sounded like fine gravel being flung out of the sky. His usual way took him up Seventh Street, but he had a chore to do before he paid Edith Thorpe his customary call and so he walked down Pine's black gut, literally pushing his way through a wall of weather. House lights were early dying and eave and wall and roof poured steady sheets of water upon the walk. He made his way cautiously across the intersection planks; at Fourth he heard some kind of a commotion in front of him — a shout and a running of feet and a challenge. Out of this entire blackness appeared a man who laid the flat of a hand roughly against Musick. "Who are you?"

"Musick," said Adam, and recognized Marshal Lappeus's voice. "What's up?"

Marshal Lappeus's voice lifted and faded in the great wind's racket. "Pass anybody?"

"No."

"Been a slugging," said Lappeus and moved away.

At Front Street the gas lights made a wan row in the glittering, foggy rush of the rain, and seemed like luminous toy balloons gently swaying. There was little life on the street, even under the shelter of the board awnings; citizen and transient alike were indoors, the transients making considerable noise in the saloons as Musick passed them. He crossed at Washington and entered the Pioneer.

"Miss Rawl?" he asked the desk clerk.

"In One, Captain."

Musick went up the stairs and turned to One, which was the corner room. He knocked and waited, and after some pause he heard a woman's slow voice say: "Come in." He opened the door and stepped through. She was accustomed to men, of course; the entertaining of men in one town or another and in one mining camp or another was her business. Nevertheless he left the door slightly ajar behind him as he removed his hat and made his bow. "Miss Rawl," he said, "I am Adam Musick, Captain of the *Daisy McGovern*. You and your company are going to The Dalles tomorrow on the *Julia*. I'd like to persuade you to change to our boat."

She had apparently been resting; she had the air of having roused herself from half a

54

sleep as she stood across the room from him. She was small and a little older than he had expected, and she was plainly tired. Her eyes were large and her face expressive enough, but loose in repose. She apparently thought him safe, for she said: "Please close the door. There's a draft."

"I regret I missed your performance at Dennison's."

"I had thought, from the crowd," she murmured, "every man in town must have been there."

"The *Daisy* leaves at seven-twenty. We connect at Cascades Portage with a middle-river boat. You will get to The Dalles as quickly with us as with them."

"They were kind enough to take care of all arrangements."

He smiled, and the smile gave him an entirely different appearance. "Naturally they'd be kind. It is to their advantage to have you on the *Julia*. Properly advertised it will give them a full boat tomorrow."

"That is a compliment, isn't it?" she said. "Would you have a full passenger list if I went on your boat?"

"That's it."

"You are nice. You are honest. But do you understand that our passage is free on the *Julia*? That counts a great deal with actors."

"It would be equally free on the *Daisy*." said Adam. "How many are in your party?"

"Seven." She had been polite and perhaps idly curious; but in watching him and listening to him she seemed to acquire some amount of interest. "Business is always sharp, isn't it? But if you are the captain, why is it your concern? It is your agent's business, isn't it, or your owner's?"

"Four of us own the *Daisy* and we furnish whatever competition the monopoly has."

"Is it hard?" she asked, and then he saw her interest grow.

"It is a matter of considerable work," he said, "and some wits."

"Well, Captain," she said. "I know about work and wits, too. I shall be glad to take the *Daisy*." Her face lifted from its weariness and became somewhat lively. "If you do not fill your boat it will be a reflection on my drawing power, won't it?"

"It will be filled," he said. He stood with his back to the door, hearing water from his hat and coat drip steadily on the room's carpet. "These men out here, uprooted from their people, are lonely. Maybe you don't know the extent of that loneliness."

She ceased to smile, but the following expression had an effect which came across the room to him. He felt it and was stirred by

56

it. "We are all lonely, Captain."

"I'll see that your luggage goes aboard, and I'll have somebody here in the morning to take care of you."

He opened the door; half through it he turned to smile at her and he saw that she was still interested. She had her head slightly tipped and her lips were pleasantly formed. "It will be a nice trip, Captain. Good night."

He went down the stairs and saw Billy Gattis coming from the saloon with a tray of lunch. He said, "Wait a minute, Billy," and brought the boy to a stop. Billy's too-wise, too-sober face lifted and he said, "Yes, sir," and waited.

"When you get through with that chore," said Musick, "run around to the saloons and ask them to soap on their back-bar mirrors the announcement that Miss Rawl and her troupe will go upriver on the *Daisy* in the morning."

The wind, when he left the Pioneer, was a shrill yell around the town's housetops, and the wind sent great waves of rain along a street turned into a running creek. At the corner of Yamhill he saw Phoebe McCornack and Perry Judd, mate of the *Claire,* standing in the sheltered doorway of Oare's Restaurant, both laughing at the weather. He paused a moment, made unexpectedly hungry by the fragrant odors coming out of Oare's.

"If you wait for this to clear up," he said, "you'll be here all night."

The two seemed to find the remark amusing; they were a happy couple and everything pleased them. They made one of the nicest stories in Portland, these two, always together and always contented. Judd looked toward the girl and he said: "That would be hard luck, wouldn't it?"

She said: "Would it?" And then both of them forgot Musick. He grinned and went on, knowing he was wholly outside their world. They didn't need him, they didn't need anybody else. It was a fine thing to see.

He walked west on Yamhill. The gas lamps died behind him and he was alone in Yamhill's vaporous gloom, the store lights and the house lights making no impression on the night. Portland was a shelter in which five thousand people enjoyed their warmth and thought themselves secure. In that they were mistaken. The seas could rise, the wind could grow and the earth open up — and then what good were man's feeble little mounds of wood and brick, or his engines, his gold, his pictures and books and fireplaces? I'm in a low state, he thought.

He had reached the part of town in which the better houses sat on their block squares, fenced around by pickets; he turned through a gate and walked toward the Victorian front of the Thorpe house whose angular house edges reminded him of a homely, passionless widow. He knocked at the door and stamped the mud and water from his feet until Edith Thorpe came to the door.

She said, with some coolness, "When nine o'clock came, I gave you up."

He swept his hat in a half circle to remove the water from it, and stepped into the comfortable front room to find that the other visitors had preceded him — Elijah Gorman apparently to talk a little business with Thomas Thorpe, and Mott Easterbrook who was faithfully making his usual evening tour. These two spoke to him and he answered, and afterwards he made a bow to the family proper — to Grandmother Thorpe who sat shadowed in the room's corner, to Mrs. Thorpe who gave him an absent-minded nod, to William Thorpe whose teeth flashed white behind a cropped and curly beard.

"I hear," Mr. Thorpe said, "Webley was in no shape to eat his supper tonight."

"We put him to bed," said Musick.

From his station in the center of the room, Musick saw Grandmother Thorpe bend with interest, and he observed Mrs. Thorpe's glance of dignified warning go to Grandmother. Grandmother sat back with a gesture of repressed impatience.

"What started him off?" asked Gorman.

"Why," broke in Easterbrook, "he had his dry spell and now has to have his wet spell." He grinned at Musick, and let the smoke of his cigar trail upward across the light ruddiness of his face and across the blue eyes which were usually amused and never troubled. He strained himself at nothing, not even at his pursuit of Edith. Courtship to Mott was a parlor game which had its rules; among the genteel, the rules had to be followed.

Gorman said: "I see you've got some freight on the dock. You'll get it no farther than the portage. The Navigation Company has got stuff stacked up there an acre deep. If Ruckle or Bradford can't get our freight over the portage road, how do you expect to get yours over?"

"Shipper's risk. I tell them all that. Don't you?"

Gorman said: "They know that without being told." He had a smooth face except for slight whiskers along the edge of his jaws; he was genial in this company, but it was a genialness stiffened by an extraordinary character. He was another New Englander who, coming to a new community for the chances it offered, had seized his chances and meant never to let them go. He was one of the driving forces behind the Navigation Company; by patience or power or subtlety, whichever best suited, he and his partners had joined the individual river-boat owners into one group and the group had become a monopoly which, fattened by the traffic to the upriver mines, was on the way to great wealth. Other river men, competing for this traffic, had been bought out, or frozen out by a sudden cut in fares and freight rates which they could not long afford; and Musick well understood that he could be likewise frozen out. But Mr. Gorman and his partners, always quick to discern any possible threat to the Navigation Company, appeared to see no risk in permitting the *Daisy McGovern* to profit by the overflow traffic which the company could not handle.

"You'll do well all summer," said Gorman, "the traffic won't stop." Then, in a display of interest, he said: "Lay your money by. There'll be other ventures. I hope you're thinking of them now."

"Yes."

"Solid ventures, I hope," said Mr. Gorman, flicking Musick with his glance.

"Yes," said Musick, and added nothing to that.

William Thorpe was a quiet spectator and Mott Easterbrook sat back in his chair with amused comprehension. They realized, Musick observed, that he was playing his little stack of chips against Mr. Gorman's formidable strength; for that matter, Mr. Gorman understood it too.

"That's good," said Mr. Gorman. "There is fortune here for everybody, but everybody won't get fortune. There is a good deal of nonsense abroad about equality. You can't give eyes to the blind or energy to the weak."

"True, so far as it goes," said Musick. "But even the blind have got to eat and the weak have got the votes to destroy you any time they wish."

Mr. Gorman straightened, for this touched his basic beliefs. "Then who will build and risk and make the cities and create the trade? It is no good to cry at the fortunes which the able make for themselves. That's why the able work and thereby create better times for everybody."

"Better times never reach everybody," said Musick.

"They will not save, they will not work. If a man spends his wages at Dennison's every night, who should cry about that except himself?" He slapped both palms against his knees as though the subject irritated him. "It is Cain and Abel again. The argument never ends."

"Cain," said Musick, "would have enjoyed Dennison's."

Mrs. Thorpe softly said: "Politics is not a

good after-dinner subject."

Somebody's boots tramped up the steps of the Thorpe house and somebody's knuckles vigorously rapped the door. Mr. Thorpe rose to answer it, and a vague face showed through the doorway. "I should like to speak a moment, privately, to Mr. Gorman." Mr. Gorman rose and walked to the porch.

Edith's voice came from the kitchen. "I've got coffee for you, Adam."

He went into the kitchen and watched her step behind him and close the door. "You should not bait Mr. Gorman. It is like the little boy teasing the tiger. You look very tired. Why didn't I see you yesterday evening?"

"Had to work on the *Daisy*'s engines."

She searched the cupboard for a saucer and cup, poured his coffee and found him sugar. Knowing his tastes, she offered him no cream. "You troubled Mr. Gorman with your talk. Papa says Mr. Gorman can starve you out any time. You should not risk it."

"He won't do it now," said Musick. "The company's got more business than it can handle. All we take is the overflow. It is a matter of profit. Mr. Gorman is very practical when it comes to profit."

"Papa says he could stop you another way. He could have the Bradfords and Mr. Ruckle refuse to let your passengers go over their portage roads to the middle river."

"They're in it for money, too. The more traffic, the more profit. They will not shut off the dollars."

"Mr. Gorman might persuade them."

Edith was repeating her father's views, and her father was close enough to Mr. Gorman to know what the latter thought. Adam drank his coffee down. "What else does Mr. Gorman think?"

"Papa says Mr. Gorman thinks you very clever, but that he always watches clever men when they are competing against the Navigation Company."

She was not entirely pleased with him; she liked dignity and she liked manners, and he knew it troubled her to have him appear here dressed in his wet work clothes. Her people would no doubt call her attention to the difference between his appearance and Mott Easterbrook's.

He said: "I'm sorry I look like a laboring man. It has been a long day."

"I said nothing about that, Adam."

She wore a new dove gray dress from Mrs. English's dressmaking shop. It was firm around her shoulders and drew discreet attention to her breasts. Her face was smooth and perhaps would always hold its smoothness, for she had her mother's evenness of temper. What she most wanted was a house standing on its square block somewhere in this part of town, with all the security and pleasantness it meant. She disliked intemperate emotions and once when he had kissed her with considerable roughness she had sharply rebuked him. "Don't bring Front Street up here, Adam! You're not a miner off the boat hunting for a woman!" He unsettled her, and she hated to be unsettled. Now and then he thought he had wakened some feeling in her which she wished let alone.

"What is it, Adam?" she asked, showing some impatience at his silence.

"Too much work today. I guess it's time I went to bed."

"What did you mean when you said that you and Lily put her father to bed?"

"I put him to bed," he said, knowing what was in her mind.

"It sounded differently, as you originally said it."

The materials for quarrel were all here, his own weariness, her resentment, and the mention of Webley Barnes. This was his woman. The long days he put in were for her, for the house she wanted and for the way of living she wanted. Her wishes kept him at his chores and made him discount these moments when, tired of work, doubt came upon him. Yet here they were, Edith and he, looking at each other as strangers. He said: "Good night," and turned away.

"It isn't late."

"I don't want to play a game of endurance with Mott tonight. He's fixed for a long stay."

Her head lifted, the corners of her mouth deepened. "Is it necessary for you to lodge with the Barneses? It is not a conventional family."

"When you speak of sin, don't be delicate. Use the words you're thinking of."

He turned away, but her voice swung him back. She was watching him as if she wondered what she must say to erase the unpleasantness of the moment. Her will was strong enough to make it difficult for her to bend, but she put away her resentment and smiled, and in the smile he saw the charm which had always drawn him toward her. "Well, Adam," she murmured, "we've had our quarrel. Let's not stay angry."

He put both arms around her and kissed her. The edges of her lips were firm when he kissed her, neither opening nor softening for him; she was conceding just enough to forgive him for his rudeness but not enough to match the feeling lying within him. Her body had its resistance, its fear of what might happen; it was a barrier between them which he hated, and therefore he held her lips until he felt the resistance leave her. Then he stepped away.

There was a cloudiness in her eyes. She looked away from him, drawing a deep breath. "You shouldn't have done that. I don't know what to think of you, or of myself. I think you have lived too hard and rough a life."

He had broken through her reserve, and this she disliked. She had meant to close the evening gracefully, to erase the odd antagonism between them; she had not intended to mean more by her kiss. It was to have been a small gift, a half promise, a way of making him anxious to come again tomorrow night. Well, maybe he was wrong. Maybe he was Front Street destroying a fineness he could not understand.

"When," he said, "does a kiss turn from proper to improper?"

"Adam, let's not discuss it."

The evening was ending as so many other evenings had ended. She had drawn away. She was watching him with a restored certainty, and seemed to disapprove of that which he offered.

He said, "Good night," and turned from her.

"You must be more diplomatic. Mr. Gor-

67

man is very powerful. He can do you much good or harm. He likes flattery. All powerful men do. You must be agreeable to him. It is so simple."

He returned to the front room. Mr. Gorman, having finished his interview with the messenger on the wet and windy porch, now stood with his back to the room's stove, his hands holding up the tails of his coat. The messenger's news had ruffled him and though he smiled at Adam, it was more the wry smile of a man who had found himself bilked.

"Understand you are taking Miss Rawl and her troupe upriver."

"Seems to have been promptly advertised."

"Was it the lady's own choice?"

"Yes," said Adam, returning the smile in better measure, "after the matter was presented to her."

"You work fast," said Mr. Gorman. "It will of course fill your boat."

"I expect so," assented Adam.

The Thorpes listened with interest and Edith's face mirrored strong disapproval. In the background Mott Easterbrook was once more an amused spectator.

"I admire resourcefulness," said Mr. Gorman. "Up to a degree."

"To what degree?" asked Musick.

"A man must learn what is wise and what

is unwise," said Mr. Gorman.

"A study of the Navigation Company," said Adam, "seems to show that anything is wise if it works." He bowed to the people around him and left the house. He realized he had stung Mr. Gorman. When the polished manners were scraped aside, it became evident that Gorman was like the roustabouts who worked for him; he would fight rough-and-tumble and he had no liking for defeat. Musick smiled into the rain-gorged night and felt much better than when he had stepped into the Thorpe house. A little taste of action sweetened the end of a long day.

Easterbrook and Mr. Gorman presently left, and somewhat later Mr. Thorpe rose and went upstairs to his bed. A great change came over the three women as soon as his upper door closed; it was as if they had each a life and an interest which could at last be brought into the open. Grandmother came from the corner shadows and took the chair Thorpe had vacated. Mrs. Thorpe dropped the last pretense of mending and lifted her face toward Edith.

"Did you quarrel with Adam?"

"I am never sure how I ought to manage him."

"Promise a little," said Mrs. Thorpe, "but not too much. Then he will respect you. A woman must not destroy the ideal of purity she represents to a man."

"Ah," said Grandmother, "that is so silly. I never taught you that, Gertrude. You've been married so long that you don't understand men any more."

Mrs. Thorpe said: "There was a period of silence in the kitchen. I hope you didn't let him kiss you. Never let a man taste his delights before marriage."

"Oh, foo, foo," said Grandmother.

"I wished to punish him for being late," said Edith. "It didn't help. I let him kiss me, to make up."

Grandmother stared at Edith in her bright, warm manner. "You're too cold. If I were your age, I'd have that young man crazy wild."

Mrs. Thorpe protested. "Don't speak like that. A man has to be brought out of his baser nature. It's what he expects. He looks to a woman for it. She must not be improper."

"Ah," scoffed Grandmother, "there is no such thing, in love."

"Mother," said Mrs. Thorpe, "you must not say that. You really must not."

Grandmother's face was coarse and warm with the memories of her early days. "We have become well-to-do people. The well-to-do always forget what things are like. When I was young we had nothing. When I met Jake, he had nothing. So we weren't ashamed of anything. Some ways he was a thoroughly bad man. I always had to be on guard against him. But I kept him busy every minute. I never let him go. Men are savages, so they are. But women are no better. A woman wants a man, and she wants him the same way he wants her."

"You shouldn't speak of your past," said Mrs. Thorpe. "You were wild."

"Had the best time ever," said Grandmother. "I'd of turned from Jake in a minute if he hadn't had what I wanted. He'd of turned from me if I hadn't been what he wanted. We had to stay together, even when we hated each other. Well, if you're cold, Edie, you're like to get Mott Easterbrook. My, my!"

Mrs. Thorpe said, "I prefer Mott."

"That Adam's got the devil in him," said Grandmother.

"I'm not cold," said Edith, quite suddenly.

"Then you're afraid."

Mrs. Thorpe rose and gave Grandmother a killing glance. "Edith is not a Siwash woman, waiting to give her self away to the first man who comes along the trail."

Grandmother's knowing smile remained. She watched Mrs. Thorpe climb the stairs, and then she turned her attention back to

Edith, her moist bright eyes running over the girl's shape. "You've got a good figure. A man ought to look more than once. You should see to it that he wants to look more than once. A woman oughtn't fight against a man when he wants too much. She should make him fight against himself. You put your body against him when he kissed you?"

Edith's glance wavered. She looked at the floor, her breath running faster. But her color did not deepen, Grandmother observed. There was no blush of modesty from this Edith who was supposed to be a modest girl. Grandmother launched her pointed question: "You got desire, Edie?"

"A woman has her nature to fight against. It's dangerous to let a man rouse her."

"Always dangerous to be alive," said Grandmother. "You won't be safe till you're dead. But dead's dead, and what good is it? You'll be in the mud with your man a lot of the time. That's better than being nowhere." She sat still with her thin hands lying upward on her lap, a very old woman who had not grown mellow. Grandmother had seen the devil and knew him well, and sometimes had loved the odor of brimstone which surrounded him; she hated age and was vainly proud of her lusty youth and never wanted to forget it. Life had meant so much to her that she still grew warm at the mention of the town's scandal. So she watched the strained attention on her grand-daughter's face and the cloudiness in her granddaughter's eyes.

Edith suddenly said: "I wonder if I'm a bad woman?"

Grandmother got up from her chair and made her pointed remark.

"Good or bad, a woman wasn't born to be wasted. Anything's better than nothing."

4

Musick went down Yamhill to Front and paused beneath a board awning to light his cigar. The gaslights began here and marched northward, shapeless blurs behind the rain fog, scarcely touching the gloom of black shop wall and dead store window. The Willamette Theater had finished its performance, Dennison's was at this moment letting out its patrons, and hotel windows were turning black one by one. There remained only the saloons, those fifty-five warm and noisy harbors for Portland's foot-loose men. He continued north on Front toward The Shades, observing the wiry shape of little Billy Gattis dart from The Pioneer and go along the street at half a trot.

It was still the shank of the evening for the crowd in The Shades when he entered, nodded at Tom Gaween guarding the door, and found a spot at the crowded bar. The tables were in full play, and men stood around the place in close groups while white-jacketed floormen hustled for business and hallooed their orders back to the bar. Smoke hung down from the colored gas chandeliers and steam rose with its fragrance from the lunch counter. Some casually hired musician sat in a corner and plucked music out of a guitar, making little impression against the noise.

The Shades belonged to Ed Campbell, and Campbell had a reformed sport's notions of elegance and dignity; therefore all the enormous paintings scattered along the walls were masculine — a stag, a solitary Indian staring into a valley filled with emigrant wagons, a mountain sunset, and a portrait of Ed himself — done by an itinerant artist who had worked out his board and his whisky bill. "By God," Campbell had often explained, "he never drew a sober breath but he had all kinds of medals from Paris. He had to have a model for that Indian picture so I got Tom Gaween. It was all right until this artist told Tom to strip. Then we had trouble with Tom. I had to get him drunk and keep him drunk. So they was both drunk, this artist and Tom, me proppin' up the artist and a couple of the boys holdin' up Tom. Never say an artist is delicate. This fellow was wonderful. He could outdrink any five men."

His own portrait fascinated Ed more than the others. It hung on the saloon's south wall, full length against a darkened background, the swarthy face and the black and cold close eyes standing out in a startling style; there was, too, the suggestion of smoke rising from the earth around him. It was Ed Campbell forever set down for posterity, a thing he could not get out of his mind. "Think of that. A hundred years after I'm dead I'll still be there. Wish he'd left out that smoky business, but he outtalked me. Said I ought to recognize the smoke and identify the smell. He sure was an artist."

Campbell spotted Musick and came forward, a stocky body in a fine broadcloth suit and hard white shirt. He caught the nearest barkeeper's eye. "Don't take Mr. Musick's money. Adam, you see that fellow playing at Ned Barton's table — the one with the damned fancy vest? Ever see him before?"

"No. Maybe he's off the steamer."

The indicated man — it was Floyd Ringrose — sat flushed and handsome in his chair, idly playing and idly drinking. Musick shook his head.

"You think he's a gentleman? It's the vest. If I thought he was a sharp I'd run him out. Would a gentleman wear that vest?"

Musick stood braced against the bar, smiling down at Campbell.

"A man might wear that vest, yet be capable of stealing the silver off the Pioneer's table. A gentleman for thirty years can go bad in ten minutes. Who knows? You don't know

me and I don't know you. Nobody knows anybody."

"Adam," said Ed Campbell, "you talk like
the artist. I understood that fellow. He was
a bum and he knew it. He didn't have anything
left. But you're no bum, so what's it mean
when you talk like that? You're gettin' what
you want."

"You getting what you want?"

"Always said I'd have a first-class saloon.
I got it."

"Satisfied?"

"You mean should I want two saloons instead of one? What the hell would I do with
two saloons?"

Meanwhile he had kept an eye on the trade
and his roving glance now fell on a man entering the saloon. He made a slight signal to
Tom Gaween who stood near the door.
Gaween stepped up to the newcomer and with
a smooth skill turned the man out. "The artist
asked me that once. What'd he mean — and
what do you mean? Well, I know. Every man
wants maybe one certain thing he ain't ever
going to get. The trick is not to let it break
you." Then he added: "Don't forget, the
drinks are on me," and walked away.

Observing a seat at Ned Barton's table to
be vacant, Musick moved over and took it.
He paid for a small stack, nodded at Barton

and gave the other players an incurious glance. The yellow-headed stranger — Ringrose — had a pair of powerful eyes, which, touching Musick, struck hard enough to leave a bad effect. It was no doubt unintentional, but the result of the glance was to irritate him. He signaled the floorman for a drink and a sandwich and settled to a casual playing which interested him so little that he wondered why he remained.

He was tired enough to sleep the clock around, yet the odds and ends of a lot of things in his mind kept him awake and restless. He had Elijah Gorman on his mind, for one thing. The *Daisy* so far had not been threat enough to disturb Gorman, but it was only a question of time when Gorman, who resisted any kind of competition, would make up his mind to put the *Daisy* out of business; that was the constant threat hanging over the *Daisy*. He thought, too, of Callahan and wondered what fun the Irishman had found for himself this night. It never required much for Callahan; he got drunk and burned away whatever it was that festered within him, fell asleep, and woke happy.

He called a bet, and lost, and discovered he had gone through his stack. He shook his head at Ned Barton and sat out of the game. His own cure should lie in the Thorpe house;

this night it had not. He had gone there with indifference and she had met him with plain resentment, and from that point onward they had engaged in some kind of silent struggle over a cause he didn't understand for a victory which seemed to be important. Where was the music a man ought to hear when he stood before a lovely woman?

His thoughts, so idly moving, went unaccountably backward to his earlier years and he had a sharp, fair, unexpected picture of Edith as she had been in Doane's school. One day, newly enrolled in the school, he had seen her — and the shock of that discovery returned to him and was as keen now as it had been then. Maybe that was what tied him to her, that first sight of his first girl, that image which had struck him so hard and had remained so fixed through these years. First things left the deepest mark. Even now when he looked upon the mature Edith and was puzzled and sometimes rebuffed by her calm aloofness, he remembered the warmth of her hand as a girl, her pleasant smiling, her quickness in coming to him when they walked homeward; and the image of this girl lay before him when he faced the grown-up Edith, and produced its hope that the young Edith remained in the older woman. That was his steady hope. It was the young Edith he wanted to see again; it was the young Edith he loved.

The stranger opposite him said: "Anything in the sky tonight?"

Ned Barton answered. "No sky to be seen, friend. The rain washed it away."

"No stars of any kind?" said the stranger.

"No sky, no stars," said Barton.

The stranger suddenly smashed a palm full down upon the table, creating a racket. Adam Musick found himself looking into the man's round and heated eyes. "My friend," said the man, "you have been staring at me a hell of a long while. What are your intentions?"

"Why," said Musick, "I'm thinking of something else. Looking through you, not at you."

He made it as an explanation, but the scene had attracted attention and it embarrassed him to be playing the soft part.

"Then take your damned eyes off me," said the stranger. The rest of the players drew back, deliberately indifferent, while Musick laid both of his broad hands upon the table and sat still and counted his knuckles. It grew very hard on him, the pressure of those who waited for him to make a fight and the easy insolence on the stranger's face. But he thought to himself: To hell with it, and got up. Then he said aloud, staring down at the man: "I shall accommodate you," and walked over to the bar. He nodded at the barkeep and waited for his drink, and he realized he had made a mistake; not because of what others might be thinking of him, but because of his increasing dissatisfaction with himself. He drank his whisky and he filled the glass again and downed it. Now it was near twelve and he had four hours to sleep and wake to another day's work.

Why did men work? If for bread and butter, why should they work so hard? He looked back across a year's time and he thought about his days and could not remember one day which had been wholly free. He was a horse, plodding a trail with a wisp of straw ahead of him; and so were the other men in this saloon. They would presently go home to sleep, and would wake and work the day through, and time would run on until they were old and all the hot fancies had died out of them.

Callahan's voice came over his shoulder, "What'd you eat that tastes so bitter?"

He turned to see Callahan laughing at him. "Emmett," he said, "at this hour you ought to be lying in the gutter or in jail."

Callahan wiggled a finger for a glass and helped himself to Musick's bottle. "This last crop of pilgrims off the *Brother Jonathan* are a weak lot. I tried three saloons, and no fights offered."

"Here's to fortune," said Musick, and lifted his glass.

"Not that," said Callahan. "I've seen men with fortune. They're a sad lot. If we make our million we'll be sad, too."

Musick caught the guitar player's eye beyond Callahan and ducked his head. The guitar player came over and said, "Which one, Adam?"

"The one about the boat," said Musick. "But we have got to have a tenor." He was looking at Ned Barton's table and he saw the stranger's eyes fixed on him. "Ned," he called, "come on over a minute."

Barton left his cards to make the fourth man in the huddle. The guitar player ran a thumb across a chord and listened to the voices of the three search for the pitch. He said: "You're sour, Callahan," and tried again.

"Now make it nice," said Musick.

"Here we go," said the guitar player and brushed his hand across the strings.

"The bow went up, the stern went down,
The captain cried, 'We're goin' to drown.'
The mate said, 'No, we've got to try
To drink this river wholly dry.'
The captain said, 'I'd rather sink,
For water's a thing I cannot drink,'
So he drank his whisky and swam ashore

And the mate took water and was seen no
   more.
Listen, boys, to the moral we tell,
There's a lot of ways of goin' to hell."

"Beautiful," said Musick and patted both
Barton and the guitar player on the back as
they walked away. Callahan stared at him
closely.

"You're primed," he said. "But you ain't
happy yet."

"We're going to make a million and be big
citizens with twenty-dollar beaver hats. Then
we'll be happy."

"By that time your belly will be out of order
and you can't drink and you can't have fun
— and you're a dead coon," said Callahan.
"None of it for me. Think hard, boy. What're
we drinkin' to?"

"A long life."

"Nah — after forty, all your troubles come
home to stay."

"Name it yourself, then."

"A bit of sweat, a good steak, a sound sleep
— and a woman."

"What woman?"

"Don't be particular, boy. One drink don't
last, and neither does one woman, one meal,
or one life. Take 'em as they go. That will
do to drink on."

"Now I've got you pegged," said Musick. "You don't know. You're just talking."

Callahan laughed in his throat and gave Musick his sweet, homely Irish smile. "What the hell else do you think a mick would do?"

Musick had his glass of whisky lifted in his hand. "Never mind —" That was the end of it; somebody, coming into the bar, gave him a deliberate shove and threw him against Callahan. The whisky spilled from the glass and ran along his fist; he put the glass on the table, knowing even then that the push had been no accident, and he came about to find Ringrose there.

Ringrose had a flushed, good-looking face; but his eyes were the quarreling kind and his glance was a rough-and-tumble thing as it came at Musick. He had one hand idle on the bar and he stood exactly as a man would stand who expected trouble.

"You're pushing right at it," said Musick.

"I want a little room here," said Ringrose.

He should have fought this fellow back at the table, Musick thought; for the man was the sort who took softness for weakness. He was one of those who loved to harry a straggler, to make his sport out of those who gave ground. He stepped slightly away from Ringrose, creating a space for the latter; and he observed the little streaked reactions of arrogance spring up here and there on the man's florid face. Tough, he thought, but not too smart. Callahan, behind him, gave out an irritable grunt; the men around Ringrose had drawn off, and Gaween, posted by the saloon's door, watched this scene with his practiced eye. Musick said: "That room enough for you?"

"If I want more I'll take it," said Ringrose.

"I can see that you like to push," said Musick.

Ringrose lowered his head and watched Musick from this odd angle; he was interested, he was alert, he was slightly warned. "Maybe you're dumb, but maybe you're laying it on me."

"You smart enough to know that answer?" asked Musick.

"You want a waltz," decided Ringrose. "I'll give you a waltz."

Callahan had reached the bitter end of his patience as a spectator. "By God, Adam, take him or give him to me."

"Go get your own man," said Musick. "This man thinks he can lick me. I'm going to let him try."

"Too damned much talk for a decent fight," complained Callahan.

"You Oregon jays are nothing but talk and haggling," said Ringrose. Then, still arrogant, he announced his conclusion. "I'll pound your head in and show you who's the turkey around here."

His right hand had been lying loose on the bar; it closed and swung off the bar, low-aimed at Musick's stomach. Musick knocked it aside and came in against Ringrose. He was laughing and he had no anger in him; he was pleased at the sight of the sudden rash temper on Ringrose's face and he side-stepped as Ringrose, off-balance from his missed blow, fell against him. He wrapped an arm around Ringrose's waist and, with the man thus on his hip, he bent aside and got Ringrose's feet off the floor and made a full fast turn and flung Ringrose out from him into the center of the saloon.

Ringrose never got his feet properly under him. He struck Ned Barton's poker table with the small of his back, fell onto its top, tipped it and went down with it landing on his shoulders. Musick, looking on with his continuing good humor, heard the table crash through the saloon's stillness.

Ringrose rolled like a cat, kicked at the table with both feet and was up at once. He made a complete circle before he located Musick; he stared at Musick with a face discolored and disfigured by the sudden intensity of his anger. The sight of that unrestrained emotion sobered Musick, for now he knew this was to be a bad fight with no fun in it. He balanced himself on his toes and watched Ringrose come slowly at him. "I am going to cut you up, my friend," said Ringrose.

His arrogance had left him, his coolness came back. One hand rose for a guard and the other hand began to punch out, light and swift and tentative. He ducked and drew back, and moved in; he swayed his shoulders and took short side steps and his green, fixed glance came up through the slanted edge of his brows. Tom Gaween, himself a professional, called: "Watch that guinea. He's a pug."

Musick turned on his heels to match Ringrose's steady side-stepping. He received the man's searching punches on his arm, he batted them away with his palm, he let them slide along his shoulder, he began to feel their sting. Of a sudden he found himself too slow. Ringrose quickened the pace, broke through his guard and landed a hard smash on the chest. It unbalanced Musick and made him drop his guard and at once Ringrose came in and struck him twice, to the neck, to the side of the face. Musick pushed against Ringrose to smother this attack and felt Ringrose's knee slam at his crotch. Heat went through Musick as he turned and grabbed at Ringrose. He was struck again under the chin and as he wheeled slightly back, Ringrose's thumb, held like a knife, slashed him across the cheek.

He had been trying to match Ringrose's cleverness, but the try for his eyes roused him; temper tumbled through him and he ducked his head, catching a blow there, and got his hands on Ringrose and heaved the man across the floor to the saloon's wall. He laid his weight against Ringrose and beat the man on the side of the head. Anger continued to heat him; he jammed the butt of his palm into Ringrose's chin, slamming Ringrose's head into the wall; he did it repeatedly until Ringrose whirled and ducked down. Musick caught him at the neck, locked an elbow around his throat and again threw him toward the center of the saloon.

Ringrose fell, rolled and came up. He turned the wrong way and checked himself and swung around. Musick chopped him in the belly, forcing him back. Ringrose brought up his guard and began to feint out with his right hand; he tried to make a stand but could not match Musick's steady pressure. Musick tore down Ringrose's guard. He was fully aroused and he had forgotten that this fight had been meant for fun; he struck the man on the face, caught him in the kidneys, spun him half around. Ringrose righted himself and launched himself into one final violent attack, throwing aside his caution and his skill. Musick got through the man's carelessly moving arms and stunned him with a short punch to the cheek; and at that moment Ringrose dropped his hands and was a wide open target ready for the kill. Musick stepped back. He watched Ringrose's eyes a moment, and shook his head.

"That's enough of this," he said.

Ringrose stood with his knees bent and his legs spread apart. He drew both hands down across his face and he closed and opened his eyes and stared at Musick. He shook his head, pulling wind into his chest rapidly. Sweat sparkled along his forehead and stains began to show on his light skin. He felt the saloon's silence and looked around at the crowd, too spent for curiosity or resentment.

"Now let's have a drink," said Musick.

Ringrose got out his handkerchief and began to pat it across his cheeks. He put away the handkerchief; he pulled his shoulders up, shrugging his coat into better shape. He lifted his hands and inspected his knuckles.

"How about that drink?" said Musick.

"You go to hell," said Ringrose.

"Both of us will, maybe," said Musick agreeably. "You crowded me and I took you up. That's settled. We'll wash it down and forget it."

"No," said Ringrose.

Musick smiled. He walked forward and laid a hand on Ringrose's shoulder. "It's not that bad —"

Ringrose knocked Musick's arm aside and turned and left the saloon.

Musick went to the bar and took himself another drink. His head was clear and he felt loose and fine and comfortable. Nothing troubled him, nothing weighted him. Callahan came up, grinning. "Now you're happy," he said. "See what I mean? But it won't last. That fellow picked you out, Adam. It wasn't an accident."

"Why?"

"He wanted to make himself a reputation."

"Why?"

"I don't know," said Callahan.

"Well," said Musick, "he didn't make it."

"He might of done it," said Callahan. "You were slow startin'. He was a fine fighter until you hit him in the belly."

The crowd around the bar listened to him. Ben Crowley stood close at hand and took in the talk, and near by, too, was a short, broad man with a coal-black set of whiskers whose eyes seemed unusually inquisitive. Musick put down his glass and walked to the doorway with this stranger's eyes reminding him of something he could not place. When he got to the street he saw a shadow against the saloon wall near by and guessed it to be Ringrose; but he was no longer interested in Ringrose, and so he turned homeward. The rain was slackening and the wind had fallen away from the peak of its violence, but all the eaves along the street were making a great racket with their spilled water.

A light still burned in the Barneses' house; when he got inside he found Lily in the kitchen, seated at the table with her elbows on it and her chin cupped in her palms. The warmth of the room burned on his cheeks and the sight of her sent a current through him, like the smell of ammonia or the taste of ginger.

"It's fine outside," he said. "The wind blew our sins away."

"You went to Dennison's instead of paying your call."

"I paid my call. Then I went to The Shades and got in a fight. I feel fine."

"I knew you'd drink tonight," she murmured. She rose and found a cup and poured hot coffee into it, and handed it to him. "Take it black." She sat down and watched him; her spirit brushed him and her lips were soft when they thought of him. "You didn't need whisky. Isn't she better than whisky?"

"Why does a woman fight a man? A man's

not a horse to be broken. Faith comes first, not argument. Maybe, after forty years of marriage the light goes out and people hate each other. But in the beginning it shouldn't be that."

"How is she to know what you are? You don't tell her anything. You don't tell anybody anything."

"People don't talk themselves into love." He made a gesture with his hand. "It comes and goes. It's a lot of things, but it's never words."

She again had her chin on her palms; she was listening to the sound of his voice, but not to his words.

"Tell that to her, not to me." She grew restless with his glance and rose and found another cup and filled it with coffee. She stood sipping at the coffee. "You're wild. I can imagine how you kiss her. It would scare anybody."

"You talking for her?" he asked.

A clear dislike sprang to her face. "She can talk for herself."

"Guess I said something wrong," he murmured. He took his bedroom lamp from the kitchen shelf and lighted it. He climbed the stairs and turned at the landing. She was at the front door, locking it. Afterwards she swung about and her glance reached him. Her face was heavy and carried an expression he had not seen before.

"Adam," she said, "don't make too many pretty pictures about women. You'll get hurt."

5

Floyd Ringrose stood with his back to the saloon wall, too roughly handled to go after Musick when he saw the latter come out of The Shades and stand momentarily in the doorway's light; anger was in him, but no force. He watched Musick disappear up the street and then he got sick, and stood still to weather the sickness through. Somebody else came from The Shades. He paid no attention until a voice spoke close by.

"You were careless."

"Get on," said Ringrose.

"I saw a star tonight," said the man.

"Where was the star?"

"In the Southwest," said the man, and offered his hand. Ringrose accepted it and a grip was made. The man stepped back to search his pockets; he lighted a match and revealed a rough, wedgelike face, bordered by ragged whiskers. The light soon died in the windy blast. "My name is Telliver. What is yours?"

"Ringrose. I've been at The Dalles. But I come from the East."

"Follow me," said Telliver. "Been watching you all day."

He walked on to Front, with Ringrose beside him. He had a long, fast-reaching stride which presently annoyed Ringrose. "Pull down," said Ringrose, "before I break a leg on this damned rattletrap walk."

"Musick," said Telliver, "scrambled your wits. I saw you start that fight. Better leave him alone."

"What's his politics?"

"His politics," said Telliver, "is like most men's politics around here — to make money as quick as possible. I guess he's Union."

"We'll have to remember him."

"Better forget him," suggested Telliver and turned across the intersection plank at Stark. Ringrose missed his footing, plunged one boot entirely up to its top in the mud, and nearly lost the boot before he gained the far walk. He followed Telliver up Stark, cursing as he went. "I do not know that such a miserable country is worth the trouble. It is a land of perpetual weeping."

Telliver laughed and swung into a stable's dismal arch.

He murmured, "Put a hand to my back and follow," and went confidently through the stable's ammonia-reeking blackness. He turned into a corner murmuring, "Larkin?"

"Yes," said somebody. "What's the word?"

"Mr. Ringrose," murmured Telliver, "you

give the word for the outer door."

Ringrose came forward and touched this Larkin whom he could not see. He bent his head, whispering the word. Larkin said, "Go right in, brother," and opened a door which led into a single room twelve feet square. There was a box in the room's center and a lantern on the box, whose sallow shining touched nine men standing around the walls. Telliver said to these men: "New brother here — Brother Ringrose. From The Dalles — and from the East."

The men in the room considered Ringrose in entire silence. Presently one of the group stepped forward. "I'm the inner door," he said.

Ringrose said: "There are two sisters, and one is beautiful and oppressed."

"Where does she live?"

"In the South," said Ringrose.

Another man said: "Glad to see you, Brother Ringrose," and there was a little shifting around this confined place, men taking stations according to some kind of ritual. It left Telliver alone on the room's south wall.

"Brother," he said to Ringrose, "we been waiting for somebody from the East. What brings you here?"

"I must say," said Ringrose, "these are miserable quarters. Is this the best crowd you can drum up?"

"Why," said Telliver, "if I called for Southerners on the street I'd draw five hundred in ten minutes. I can step into some of the town's best houses and get a proper answer. They'll come when needed. Now what do you bring us?"

"We have got to take the Pacific Coast out of the Union this year. Should have been done last year. If it is not done now, it will be too late. That's the word from the top."

"And what," said Telliver, "is the top doing for us? We've had damned little help."

"Five hundred guns arrived here last month on the *Brother Jonathan,* crated as machinery. They're stored in a barn down the valley."

"What barn?"

"I'll tell you when the time's right."

"When's that time?"

"After the election. We have got to win the election first. How does that stand?"

"The Union people will caucus this month at Eugene City. I don't doubt they'll put up Gibbs for governor. The Southern Democrats meet at Corvallis in a couple of weeks. We'll name a full slate for the legislature. John Miller's to be our man for governor."

"Who's arranging this at Corvallis?"

"You go see Allen down there."

"A Knight?"

"No, but he is against Lincoln and for States' rights. He'll serve us. We'll use any instrument which cuts our way, brother."

Ringrose said: "Take care the instrument does not later cut you."

"Later will be time enough to take care of that," said Telliver.

This Telliver was a deceptive kind of a man, laughing and unmoved and with some insolence in him. His bottom was undetermined, nor was it certain that he knew the risks of this game, which involved a gallows for all of them if caught. It occurred to Ringrose to sober this group to its dangers.

"I should warn you," he said, "there's a Federal agent in this town."

Telliver's brows showed fine, interested creases. "How do you know?"

"I've dealt with Pinkerton's men before," said Ringrose. "You'll see him around town, short, well-fed, close black beard. Looks like a businessman until you give him a sharp watch. Now — do we win this election?"

"The southern half of the state without doubt. We'll take up the eastern counties. Portland and the valley is debatable, but if we get a majority in the legislature we shall have enough to do what we're after. What are we after, brother? A Pacific Republic or a joining with the South? Our line is not clear."

"It'll be clear enough when we elect our men," said Ringrose. "Now listen carefully. Jeff Davis looks this way. California is ready. We have got to be ready. First we win the election and put our people in key places. Then we wait for Lee to give us a victory in Virginia. Then we bring the guns from the barn."

"Suppose we don't win the election?" asked Telliver.

"In that case," said Ringrose, "the rifles come out of the barn sooner. One way or another, we'll use those guns. How many Circles have we got in this state?"

"There has not been much correspondence," said Telliver, "but we think there are eight."

"I can see we are not organized here," said Ringrose.

"Not necessary," said Telliver. "Our friends will rise when the time comes."

"You don't know how uprisings are made," said Ringrose. "You don't need a majority in a community to perform your purpose. Ten men, working as close as the fingers on your hand, are better than a hundred who do not know what they're doing. In the border states we swung many a district when the majority was against us. I can tell you now that you do not have a majority in this town. I can look at the town and see it. But you do not need a majority."

"Brother," said Telliver, "these people here are not easy to persuade or scare."

"You don't know," said Ringrose. "You have not tried. These people are loyal to the Union because it is profitable and because it is easy. If it were not easy to be loyal, a lot of them would change. If they thought they could make more money under the Confederacy, they would change. This town is a tree full of fruit. Shake the tree and the rotten fruit drops. But you must know how to shake the tree. I'm here to tell you how to do it."

"You shook the tree tonight," said Telliver, "and the apple didn't drop."

Ringrose stared at Telliver with his straight, affronted glance. Telliver met the inspection with his assurance, wholly confident that he was as hard a man as Ringrose. But the silence grew long and the force of Ringrose's eyes became a difficult thing to match. As with the young miner out on the trail, and as with the ferryman, Telliver at last saw something on Ringrose's face which disturbed him, and eventually he dropped his glance.

Ringrose said, quite softly, "I'm here to tell you how to do it. There are some people here who do not think at all; who can be led by anybody. To them you speak boldly. You put doubt in their heads. There are some who are afraid. Those are the ones you threaten. Then there will be a few left who will resist you in any event. They are not many, but they're important. They lead the cattle. Those we handle differently." He gave Telliver his rough glance. "Our friend is one of those. What's his name?"

"Musick."

"I didn't know his style of fighting," said Ringrose. "Next time I'll know it."

"Why try him again?" asked Telliver.

"I'm here to destroy any man who stands against us, to put the fear of God into him, to shut him up. I'm here to see that you also shall do it. Your easy days are over. There's not much time. We are expected to take Oregon out. It is one more battle for the South, and it may be the deciding battle. That's why I came here. When I order you to fight a man or kill a man I want it done. If you're not prepared for it, don't come to this meeting again. I want no weak stomach in this Circle."

"Brother," said Telliver with visible curiosity, "you don't sound Southern to me."

"No," said Ringrose, "I am not."

"What are you in this for?"

"We'll be powerful," said Ringrose. "We'll have property and we'll have influence. When we conquer this land it belongs to us. Tonight we meet at the back of a stable. Before the year is ended we'll be out in the open. We'll be in power. This is a bigger thing than you think, brethren. There's gold and there's purple in it for all of us. Good night."

He had dropped his bait and now he turned from the little room.

Ben Crowley, having witnessed the fight in The Shades, slipped from the rear door of the saloon and made his way between buildings to Oak Street, moved down to Second and stood back in the shadows. He waited here, with three other saloon doorways visible to him in the windy night, but presently, like a fisherman weary of an empty pool, he crossed Second, went along to First and halted across from another of the town's saloons. A buggy came around the corner, bound uptown, and by the momentary light of the gas standard he saw a merchant of the town and a woman, both drunk. Early that morning, before daylight, he had seen them drive down the White House Road; and now as he watched them pass by, he thought: "I'll bum him for ten dollars tomorrow. He'll know why — and he'll give it." Then the thought left him, for he saw a man come out of the Lotto directly across the street and go toward Second at a wavering gait. At Second, the man turned the corner; instantly Ben Crowley crossed the street's deep mud, placed himself in the shadows of the building walls and patiently followed. He turned the corner and had a small view of his quarry half a block ahead; he rose on his toes and softly came up behind the man, made his jump, closed his heavy, muscular arm around the man's throat and jerked him down to the walk. He dropped with the man and laid his chest over the other's chest, riding through a short interval of struggle. There was always this shocked moment of resistance with a drunk, but that usually passed; it passed with this one, he lying exhausted and uncertain while Ben Crowley ran through his trouser and coat pockets, found a bit of hard coin, and rose up and rushed away. Behind him he heard a small cry, the sound of which turned him down another between-building space.

He came out at Front and Oak, got under the gas standard and looked at the coins in his fist. He said, "Ah," in disgust and heard feet trotting along the walk. He put both hands in his pocket and stood by the lamp standard, closing his eyes partially, letting his body sag, putting an indifferent expression on his face. Billy Gattis came forward. Billy saw him and pulled down from his trot.

"Hello, Kid," said Ben. "Pretty late."
"Yes."

"You don't get much sleep. Can't grow without sleep."

"I get enough."

"You're all right," said Ben Crowley. "You're goin' to get somewhere. Don't waste your money, Kid — and don't drink. Look at me."

"Need a dime?" asked Billy.

"I had supper. Goin' up to Emily's tonight?"

"Why?"

"Good woman," said Ben Crowley. "I like her."

"Better get out of the rain, Ben," said Billy, and went forward at his trot.

Crowley watched the boy's figure fade down toward Pine Street. Marshal Lappeus swung from The Farmer's Palace, slowly traveling. He said, "Hello, Ben," and moved on without waiting for an answer. Crowley moved up Stark, turned into the heart of the block and came to the rear of Ryan's stable. He had not slept here for several weeks and he was not sure of Ryan's welcome; therefore he let himself into the stable with caution, crept forward until he found a big box stall wherein Ryan kept his bedding straw, and laid down on it, bringing the straw around him.

"A dollar and a half," he said, thinking of the money he had got from the drunk. "Hell of a note." He heard voices near by and could not place them. He sat up and he saw a thin crack of light coming under a door opposite the box stall; that was Ryan's tack room and maybe Ryan had friends in there. He had the notion of going over to the door to listen and was on the point of rising when the door opened and he saw — for the single moment the door remained open — a shape against the doorway and a blur of faces inside. The man coming from the room was Ringrose; the other faces could not be identified. Then the door closed and he heard Ringrose move down the stable and leave it.

6

The rain had stopped, the wind had died. At five o'clock of the morning Portland lay spent and dreary, exhaling a mist which touched Musick's face and remained upon it as a kind of sweat. The building corners were ugly shadows before him, the shopwindows looked upon him with dismal eyes and all around him lay the unkind odors of this town, the rotted mud, the soured refuse beneath the sidewalks, the stagnant stables, the humid bitterness seeping out of the Nugget Saloon, the greasy sewage along the river's edge. Asleep, the town lay sprawled out like a cheap and dirty woman.

Musick's footsteps ran before him in woody echoes as he walked down Pine to the levee. A long line of drays and wagons stretched along Front, waiting turn to board the *Julia* and the *Daisy;* as the season went on that line would come to be a permanent part of the street. The *Claire,* on the Oregon City run, lay directly above the Daisy.

Crossing Front, Musick saw a small shape come trotting along the sidewalk. This would be Billy Gattis delivering the morning paper, and, without looking at his watch, Musick knew the time would be ten minutes after five. Billy's face was pale and sleepy and thin as he came forward and he murmured, "Hello, Mr. Musick," and handed Musick a paper and went on.

George Pope had the *Daisy*'s boilers already warm, and the fine smell of breakfast came from the galley. The partners took their breakfast and fell upon the freight waiting on the dock for them. The wagons next came on, all but one. That one Musick turned back. "Full load."

The driver swore without much animosity. "Tomorrow, then?"

"We lay over on Sunday. You'll go up on Monday."

At six o'clock day crept through the fog, lightening it but not dispelling it, and the *Julia*'s whistle broke over the town. This was the hour's warning signal. From the pilothouse of the *Daisy* Musick saw the *Julia* as a phantom shape in the mist though it was but a block below him; the river's far shore was invisible, while the houses of the town above Front were only half revealed. By six-thirty Portland was fully awake, wood smoke curling from tin chimney tops and the smell of this smoke strongly lacing the air. Billy Gattis came aboard with his pack of papers and took stand at the gangplank: within a few minutes the passengers began to arrive, their baggage slung about them in various fashions. The hotel hacks appeared with the more luxuriously inclined travelers, including Miss Rawl and her troupe, and a few townsmen assembled on the dock to witness a scene which never lost its attraction.

Exactly at seven the *Julia* gave out another long whistle blast and over the distance floated the subdued ringing of the *Julia*'s signal bells and the soft breathing of her machinery as the big Pittmans thrust her paddles around. The *Julia*'s bow came abreast the *Daisy* on her downstream turn, so that for a moment Musick saw the crowd of passengers on her decks and heard their cheering. High in the pilothouse the *Julia*'s captain, Dave Bain, lifted a hand to Musick. Briefly she stood in the river, swinging; afterwards the mist took her and there was nothing of her except the hard and faithful rushing of her paddles. Her swell came back.

The *Claire* soon pulled away and from his viewpoint in the pilothouse Musick saw a scene which, daily repeated, never failed to warm him. Perry Judd, the *Claire*'s mate, walked slowly along the starboard side of the boat with his cap lifted toward Phoebe McCornack who stood along the side of the wharf building and blew her kiss to him; then turning, she walked slowly up Front Street. There was such a thing as fidelity, Musick thought, and for that one moment he had a sudden hopeful insight. It went away almost immediately; it was like a flash of light on the rolling crest of a river swell, so briefly viewed that the image of it never made a print on his memory.

He stepped from the pilothouse and looked down upon the dock. Miss Rawl's published passage on the *Daisy* had drawn a crowd and Emmett Callahan was having his difficulties at the gangplank. He saw Webley Barnes work his way through the crowd and cross the gangplank, and in a little while Barnes and Bradshaw climbed to the pilothouse. There was no mark on Barnes to show his night's fall from grace. He was shaved and neat and he was cheerful; he had burned the acid out of his soul.

"We're four tons under our load limit," said Bradshaw. "We can take fifty more passengers."

"Take 'em," said Musick and looked at his watch. "Ten minutes, Lou."

Lou and Barnes went below. Musick watched the extra passengers come across the gangplank with their luggage; and he looked beyond them until he saw Lily standing against the wharf building as a spectator. She wore a dark coat against the raw morning but no hat. Her hair rose back from her temples, made its mass on her head, and was caught into a fall behind. She wasn't smiling, but the thought of a smile hovered around her mouth. He looked at his watch again, nodded to her and stepped into the pilothouse, ringing down the stand-by signal; suddenly beneath him the *Daisy* seemed to gather her power like a horse at the barrier. It was an illusion, of course, but it pleased him to feel that the *Daisy* answered.

He let go a short blast of the whistle and swung the *Daisy*'s wheel slightly to port and heard Emmett Callahan's voice come hallooing up, "All gone!" The *Daisy*'s nose gently swung out and a strong April current caught her, and the dock receded into the mists. The *Daisy* came to her heading. Dimly Portland stood to the left, shapeless in the unsunned mist; to the right was the ragged border of the river's other shore. A little after eight o'clock the boat came to the Willamette's mouth — the turbulent spring current here seizing the *Daisy*'s hull — and reached for her new course up the Columbia.

A westerly wind lifted the fog. Fort Vancouver lay against the Washington shore, the military post on its high ground, the fragments of the old Hudson's Bay post still showing near the water. The *Julia* was fifteen minutes ahead, a lively lady kicking up white petticoat ruffles of water with her paddles. The Navigation Company never liked the idea of the *Daisy*'s greater speed; therefore Dave Bain would be pouring on the wood to keep the *Julia* out front.

A lone gold seeker, a brash youngster with a curious, callow face, climbed to the pilothouse door, opened it and entered it with the freedom he would have used in his own home. "Cap'n," he said, "you got a view here, ain't you?"

"Get the hell off this deck," said Musick very gently and watched the lad depart. The smoke of his cigar drifted around him, and the smell of the river came through the open window. He stood with his feet apart, his hands easy on the wheel, softly correcting the *Daisy,* and his eyes watched the river's marks and the river's fat yellow-gray surface.

These hours of running the river gave him time to think, and his thoughts sometimes went far; yet those thoughts never had the sting and the doubt and the darkness which they had when he was an idle man ashore. At the wheel he might dig deep with his wonder, but the wheel was beneath his hands, giving him the reassurance of being active — and to be in action was as near happiness as anybody could come. Men were not meant for peace. Their minds, so filled with incessant wonder, would never let them alone, and their bodies were racked by feelings which eventually destroyed them; there was a form and a substance and a meaning somewhere, no doubt, but men died before they knew what any of it was. What was a man that he looked into a woman's eyes and searched for things he wished to see, and could not see? What was in the man himself, that he should never be satisfied? Maybe, he thought, nothing but her body for the little time it lasts. Maybe for something the two of them make which, when joined together, goes on longer than I think.

Lou Bradshaw came up and took his relief at the wheel while Musick stood momentarily by to watch the river. There would be no sun, but the mist had drawn aside and the clouds hung a thousand feet off the ground so that he saw the river's reach all the way to the foot of Lady Island. They had gained somewhat on the *Julia*.

"Adam," said Bradshaw, "this traffic to the mines ain't goin' to stop. Time to think about a second boat. If we play it right, we'll be big."

"Ever think of getting married, Lou?"

112

"What would a woman see in me now? Wait until I have got a stake. Money changes the way a woman looks at a man." Bradshaw's thoughts jumped to another track. "We are not charging Durfee enough for the bar privileges. He's hip deep in customers."

Musick descended to the passenger deck for his usual rounds and paused to look into the saloon where Durfee, who ran the bar on a concession basis, labored alone with his land-office business. Men lined both sides of the boat, they sat aft, they prowled the freight deck, they gathered for poker games wherever space permitted, and one foolish spirit had gotten himself out on the rounded, slippery housing of the paddle wheel. Musick called to him: "Get off there," and continued his circuit. Turning forward on the port side he found the door of Miss Rawl's stateroom standing open. Miss Rawl lay on the room's small bunk, kept company by another young lady of the troupe.

Musick said: "It is a full boat, as I told you it would be."

Miss Rawl said: "It is nice that you have had luck, Captain," and her eyes touched the young lady with her; that young lady rose from the chair, gave Musick a brilliant smile, and left the cabin. "Step in, Captain," said Miss Rawl.

Musick tossed his cigar over the railing, removed his hat and took the chair, turning it so that he might see not only Miss Rawl but also command a view of the shore.

Miss Rawl drew a comforter over her and turned her head, the better to watch him. Her life appeared to be a thing of contrasts, in which an hour of extreme energy and charm before the footlights was followed by periods such as these when she rested, quiet and loose, and made no attempt to charm anyone. She was around thirty and no doubt had been on the stage since early girlhood. Against the pillow her hair seemed very black and her face was the actor's supple face, trained to register whatever expression was required of it.

"Well," she said, "we have got to wear ourselves out on one thing or another."

"How's that?" he asked, not knowing what was in her head.

"You with your river and I with my trouping — and these men hunting their gold. I don't suppose many of them will find their gold. But perhaps neither will you nor I. Are you married?"

"No."

"You're young to operate a boat."

"We're all young on this river."

"Don't let the river spoil you."

"Could it?"

"A captain is law on his boat, isn't he? And I'm the star of my show. That could spoil both of us. People are a little afraid of captains and stars because they think we're different — and that makes us lonely, because we really don't wish to be different."

She had not moved, but while he watched her he saw change lightly go over her face; it made her face longer and her lips heavier, and a warmth began to illumine her eyes. She made a gesture with her hand and brought the quilt higher around her throat. "Your boat," she murmured, "is cold."

"You wish me to close the door?"

"Yes."

He rose. He stepped to the door and put his hand on the knob. He looked across the river to the shore willows; the *Julia* was ahead of him, pointed at Rooster Rock. He stood long still, watching the *Julia* but not thinking of the *Julia*. He gripped the door's knob quite hard; then he stepped outside the cabin and looked back at her, tremendously embarrassed because he might be causing her embarrassment. Probably she would regard him as a fool. She was smiling a regretful but not unkind smile. "You're nice, Captain," she said.

The remark struck him in his pride and his face, normally ruddy from sun and weather, showed a greater ruddiness. She saw it and at once explained herself. "I didn't mean it that way. Some things keep you young. Then you lose them and you're no longer young."

He watched her with strong curiosity, understanding her a little better and enormously liking her. "Why is it you're lonely? You've had men enough to pick from."

"I've already told you. Captains and stars are different. People are afraid of them."

He put on his cap. "Shall I shut your door?"

Some private and ridiculous thought amused her, for he saw the effect of it dancing in her eyes. "No," she said. "Not now."

Musick walked forward, climbed to the upper deck and stood a moment by the pilot-house rail, watching the *Julia* come down upon Rooster Rock and swing over to run the new course past Reeder's Island toward the black wall of Cape Horn. Below him, on the freight deck were fifty passengers, all of them with their dreams of gold making them brave. Maybe two or three would make a decent strike; the others would do no better than day wages and would spend it as they made it in order to live. By fall some of them would be dead, and some would drift back East empty-handed, their time lost and the world marched a year beyond them. The rest would never return; they would be the drifters of unknown whereabouts and their people would seldom again hear of them.

He narrowed his eyes and he saw these men age before him and he saw their dreams die. It would go in such stealth, little quantities bled away by successive failures, by tragedies, by the lessening of that fire which made them men. A wonderful and merciful blindness now hid this from them; but one day the knowledge would come to them in their respective revelations. One man would repeat the old words of faith to himself and suddenly those words would be empty. To another it would be the impact of a stronger man's arm, making known to him his own vanished strength. A mirror would tell the story to some, or a slow and rising pain, or the realization that coffee and meat no longer had the old taste; and to many men, always thinking of bright tomorrow, there would come the most cruel of all realizations — that the tomorrows were nearly done. And thus to each in his time the dream would end.

Between his narrowed eyes, he saw them aged in his imagination, with nothing to show for their hopes. The fire of youth had hotly burned in them and had driven them, but nothing had come of it; they lay as shadows on the deck and their lives meant little and their passing would not be noticed. If the fire

117

were divine, why should this be?

He stepped into the pilothouse and took the wheel. The *Daisy's* nose lay dead on Cape Horn which stood as a great block fortress on the Washington shore; the *Julia* was a quarter mile ahead. The jaws of the gorge were here — that massive crack in the earth by which the Columbia River passed the Cascade Range on its way to the sea. On the Oregon shore the gorge's rim stood two thousand feet high, its face darkened by timber; and over that face, at intervals, lace-like ribbons of water fell whitely through the sunless air. Musick studied the timber and had his thoughts about it, and those thoughts made a half-formed notion in his head.

"Fine place for a sawmill," he said to Bradshaw. "The logs could be skidded down that slope with no trouble at all. Fishers Landing would be a good place. There's land enough along the river for a good farm."

"Wild as hell up here," commented Bradshaw.

"That's all right for me."

Wind and current began to work down the river; waves broke against the *Daisy's* bow and came aboard as thin spray. "Time to pass the *Julia,*" said Musick. "Better go down and fire for George."

Bradshaw said: "Have we always got to

make this race? No use rubbing salt on Gorman's hide all the time. Someday he'll take no more of it, and close the door on us."

"He would have done it before now," said Musick, "if he knew of a good way."

"You like these damned races," said Bradshaw, and left the pilothouse.

Musick had the *Daisy* in the wake of the *Julia*, and he watched the *Julia* carefully, waiting the time when Dave Bain swung her off the Cape Horn marks. The great black chunk of Castle Rock stood directly upriver; compressed by a narrowing channel, the river pushed harder against the *Daisy*'s hull. He felt that force all through the boat's frame. A quicker, colder wind drove in the spray and the group of men lying on the forward freight deck rose and retreated from it. Bain, he observed, was taking the *Julia* closer in to the Washington shore than usual. There were submerged rocks directly below Cape Horn and about thirty feet from shore which Bain — who was as familiar with the river as with his bedroom — knew, but either he planned to shave them extraordinarily close, or he counted on high water to carry him over. Bain wanted all the slack water he could find and put the *Julia*'s nose practically upon the beach before he swung. The moment the *Julia* came around, Musick brought the *Daisy* out of the

119

Julia's wake, crossed the *Julia*'s stern wave and called down through the engine-room tube. "Let's have that pitch wood."

The two boats were now traveling parallel, with the *Julia* three lengths ahead of the *Daisy*. Bain still held the *Julia* as near the shore as he dared, whereas the *Daisy* bucked the full force of the current in the middle of the channel. The result was that the *Julia* now began to increase its lead.

Musick watched the *Julia* with the sharpest attention. Her bow was even then coming over the submerged rocks and Bain was no doubt spending this moment in prayer and sweat. Musick felt the tension of the moment himself, for if there was not water enough — if the rocks were too near the surface — those sharp edges would split the *Julia*'s thin hull like a knife slicing across stretched paper. He watched the *Julia*'s bow bring up flashing streams of spray from the wind-roughened current and he waited for that sudden, jarring halt which would mean that the *Julia* had struck. Then, letting out a breath, he said to himself, "She cleared," and felt his relief.

Bain pulled a long blast from his whistle and opened the pilothouse door and waved a hand across the water. Musick gave Bain an answering whistle. It was close navigation and Bain knew it, and knew that he — Musick

— knew it. Then the *Julia* passed abreast the sheer black wall of Cape Horn, and against this blackness her superstructure seemed very white. Big a boat as she was, she was like a toy against the hulking mass of rock.

Bain had won this maneuver and was well in the lead; but now he was out of the easy water — the current against the Cape Horn rocks being as powerful as in the midchannel — and he would have no more easy water until he passed Cape Horn and again began to crowd the sandy beach above. There was another maneuver meanwhile in the making, and one that Musick and Bain had played a hundred times. Out in the middle of the river and slightly to the right of the channel stood Boca Rock which, breaking the flow of the current, created a half mile of slack water below it. Into this slack Musick now edged the *Daisy*. The moment he struck it he felt the *Daisy* surge ahead.

There was a strong southwest wind blowing upriver and this brought the smoke from the *Daisy*'s stack forward around the pilothouse. The *Daisy* was laboring and she had reached a certain point of strain which shook her, but she had not come to full power yet. Not until the window in front of him began to rattle in its sash would he know that he had all he could get, or dared to get, out of her. He called down to Pope: "A little more, George."

The race had drawn the passengers of the *Daisy* to the port side as enthusiastic spectators, and it had drawn the passengers of the *Julia* to the starboard side in equal enthusiasm. Across the interval of water men shouted their cheerful insolence, which the wind whipped away, and some man on the *Daisy* brought out his gun and began to shoot at the *Julia*'s stack. Musick saw Callahan hoist himself up from the freight deck and push his way through the crowd in search of that man.

The *Daisy* came abreast the *Julia* which had the full current off Cape Horn to buck; but the *Daisy* was approaching the shoals and the reef which stretched out from the foot of Boca Rock and now it was Musick's gamble as it had been Bain's earlier. He felt the river bottom grow shallow beneath him; that shallowness telegraphed itself through the *Daisy* in sharper reverberations like a wagon rolling over a rough road. He took a sight on Boca Rock and he took a sight on the shore, identifying his position in relation to the reef. Maybe there was water enough to go over the reef, but listening to the racket throughout the boat, he made his decision not to risk crossing the reef. He had a load of passengers to think about, and if he struck he could not beach the *Daisy* in time. Callahan climbed up and stood at the pilothouse door, saying nothing, but obviously bothered. Musick again sighted the shore and Boca Rock, delaying a turn as long as he could; when he could no longer delay, he swung to port. As soon as he passed from slack to full current an arresting arm seemed to seize the *Daisy*'s bow; but the noise died out of the boat and Callahan, much relieved, descended to the passenger deck.

The *Julia* had dropped behind. Bain, now clearing the palisade of Cape Horn, turned his boat toward the shore, once more hunting easy water. She was a pretty sight, the spray of her wheels whipping around the stern like a white cloud and pillow-shaped rolls of smoke crowding out of the stack and streaming forward in the wind. Bain drove her and enjoyed every minute of the driving.

"George," said Musick down the tube, "give me some more."

Ahead lay Prindle Landing, at which point the river's channel swung right and made a long diagonal crossing to the Oregon shore. Coming up to the Prindle turn, the *Julia* would have the outside — and therefore the long side of the turn to make; if the *Daisy* reached the turn first, Bain had no recourse except to drop back and give the *Daisy* the channel and follow the *Daisy* across; he could not dispute the

Daisy's right-of-way, and once more he would be twenty minutes behind the *Daisy* when they reached Ruckle's Landing.

Therefore Bain forced the *Julia,* approaching nearer and nearer the shallow, weedy water of the shore — close enough, Musick thought, to throw a hat to the beach. But the *Julia* liked this water and came charging up over the distance until her bow was on line with the *Daisy*'s stern.

"Goddammit," said Musick down the tube, "give me some more push."

The rattling of the window before him told him he had all he would get. Heavy rollers, built up by tide and wind, lifted and pulled at the *Daisy*'s bow. The boat began to heel and drop and rise, and streamers of water sprang up like white flares and struck the boat's bulkhead with a buckshot rattle. The foredeck was wet and the pilothouse window beaded over. He watched the *Julia,* suddenly interested in her. Bain, coming to some swift decision, had turned his boat out from the shore; he meant, Musick thought, to make his shoot at the river crossing from this point, very low down, and cut behind the *Daisy*. He meant to make another gamble with the river and put the *Julia* on the inside of the turn.

Coming around, the *Julia* faltered and the *Julia*'s bow rose and rode high a moment and fell, and her bow wave died and she lost way. She had struck.

Musick rang down for half speed, and in a moment he rang again and let the *Daisy* drift. The *Julia*'s bow continued to turn with the current and the current carried her back; then Bain reversed her paddles and pulled around and went full ahead toward the shore. All this had carried her a greater distance downriver from the *Daisy*. Musick, knowing Bain meant to beach his boat, turned the *Daisy* and ran in.

He saw the *Julia* strike the beach and rise high and come to an awkward halt. Men along the deck fell down; they rose and rushed forward and the deck crew began to work a gangplank ashore. That, Musick observed, was unnecessary. The hole in the *Julia* was high on starboard bow and now out of water. She had struck a deadhead.

He eased the *Daisy* toward the shore, brought her nose around and came up to the *Julia*. Callahan heaved over a line which was secured. Bain walked aft from his pilothouse and faced Musick across the short distance. He had both hands in his pockets, a cigar slanted in his mouth and great disgust on his face. He began to speak, but the *Julia*'s safety valve popped and set up a tremendous racket which Bain waited out. Bain's mate arrived and when the steam quit popping, the mate said: —

"Hole forward big as a hog, and a hole on the bottom twice that big. Both dry — on the beach. Two frames busted."

"We're here all night," said Bain. "You can patch it, but we'll need a pull to get off the beach. Bring in that plank. Don't want these fool passengers to get lost in the woods." He turned to Musick. "How many can you take upriver?"

"Seventy-five, if they stay in one place."

"All right," said Bain to his mate. "Put the plank over to the *Daisy* and count out seventy-five customers. Stop on your way downriver, Adam, and take the rest back to Portland."

"Bad luck for you," said Adam.

"Ah," said Bain, "to hell with it. I was watching you. Ten feet more and you'd piled up on Boca Reef."

"That's the ten feet I stayed away from," said Musick. "What were you aiming to do — cross behind me and put me on the outside of the Prindle turn?"

"It would of worked," said Bain.

The two of them stood by, watching the *Julia*'s passengers transfer to the *Daisy*. There was an argument between the *Julia*'s mate and some men of the crowd who could not go.

The mate had the plank brought quickly in and he threw off the *Daisy*'s line. The *Daisy* drifted off until she got steerageway. Straightening for the upriver run, Musick gave the *Julia* a whistle salute but got none from Bain.

At one o'clock, coming inside Bradford Island, Musick blew for Ruckle's middle landing on the Oregon shore. There was a flimsy wharf, from which a wooden trestle ran back to the timber; and here on the edge of the timber, horses stood hitched to a car mounted on a wooden track which, skirting the unnavigable rapids of the Columbia, reached a place where the middle-river boats waited to carry their freight and passengers onward to The Dalles. The low slate light of day remained constant in the dark gorge but ahead, far ahead, was the brighter color of sunshine. Up there the mountains lost their somberness; up there the river passed into the dry, desert basin of the interior country.

The lines were thrown out, the gangplank lifted over — and then the hurried passengers stamped ashore, running for the waiting portage car, shoving and cursing and infected by anger as they ran. From the pilothouse Musick watched them go, and watched Miss Rawl's troupe quietly follow. Eager gentlemen already had bid for the favor of carrying the troupe's luggage.

Miss Rawl tarried a moment on Ruckle's dock and turned and lifted her glance to the pilothouse. Musick stepped outside; he removed his hat and looked down with his smile. "Captain," she said, "may the nicest things happen to you."

"Luck," he said. But he was remembering what she had told him — that when good things went away, youngness went with them — and he spoke to her of this, knowing she would understand. "Nothing dies, does it? Whatever was good will always be good. I'll think of you."

"Why, Captain," she said and her face remained upward-tilted a moment, as though she were trying to see him very clearly. Then she gave a little gesture and turned with her troupe and moved toward the portage car. Men jammed it and the remaining crowd made a circle around it, but the circle opened before Miss Rawl and her troupe, and one by one men on the car slowly surrendered their places to the women. Shortly, the car moved out of sight into the timber and as it vanished Musick felt regret run quickly through him; she had warmed him and had made him feel things not often felt.

A pack team came aboard, and an army officer with a cluster of children. Bradshaw called up, "All on, Adam."

Turning the *Daisy* in the narrow channel Musick observed the freight piled high on Ruckle's wharf. Across the river lay the Bradford landing with its equal quantity of freight. These two portages, one on the Oregon shore and one on the Washington side held this throat of the river in their hands. Even the Navigation Company with all its power had to pay their tribute, a thing which Musick knew offended Gorman's sense of power. Gorman would not rest until he had these portages under the control of the Navigation Company, but there was no way of controlling them unless he could bring Ruckle and the Bradfords into his monopoly. There was not much chance of doing this as long as those men made their excellent profits without need of Gorman's help.

But Gorman would never be easy about it. If the Navigation Company had anything less than entire control of the river, it had less than full monopoly. In the end Gorman would get his control; he was already operating on the jealousy which existed between Ruckle and the Bradfords and might have success in that line. One way or another he would eventually succeed, for his was the greater power and in business the greatest power always won. When that time came — when the Navigation

Company controlled the portage — all independent firms on the river would be out of business. The Company would shut them out by refusing them access to the portage.

Musick thought of this during the downriver run. It was on his mind when he stopped at the beached *Julia* to take aboard the rest of her passengers. Power was a queer thing. Men hated and feared power — in the hands of others. Men knew that power was a thing which corrupted the possessors of it; yet even as they knew it they struggled for power, believing that they could be pure in possession of it where others were not. But pure or impure, men were driven by the need of it and spent their lives seeking for it. They had to do it; it was a force in them, like the steam in the *Daisy*'s engines. When the engines died, the *Daisy* died; and when the fire went out of men they too died.

Bradshaw came up. "A hundred and eighty passengers from the *Julia*."

"Plus seventy-five we took up. That's two hundred fifty-five. Make out a bill to the Navigation Company for two hundred fifty-five passengers at two and a half each."

"All right," said Bradshaw, but he shook his head and was suddenly afraid of the idea. "Couldn't we ease it a little? We're hitting Gorman's pocketbook. He'll hit back. We live on his good humor. Be wise to charge him nothing. Make him feel kindly toward us. It would be harder for him to shut us out."

"Outside of business hours he would be grateful for a favor," said Musick. "Inside business hours he wouldn't let sentiment tie his hands." He recognized the dried-out, troubled expression on Bradshaw's face. He smiled. "Play easy with Gorman and he'll have no use for you. Hit him hard and he'll think twice before he hits back. He's no different than Tom Gaween. It's the big fist they both understand best."

Bradshaw shook his head. "There's a million dollars for us, just around the corner. We got to do it clever, or it's gone when we reach for it."

"You don't get a million by begging scraps. If you got it by begging, it wouldn't be worth having." He straightened the *Daisy* into the channel; he put the *Daisy*'s bow dead on Rooster Rock and felt the boat run. Bradshaw stood silent, half embittered from the suspicion that the money he so badly wanted was slipping away. He said finally: "By God you'd do anything to get in a fight," and left the pilothouse.

Musick renewed the light of his cigar and brought the *Daisy* gently back on her marks. "Maybe," he thought, "a doubled fist is all

131

I understand, or any man really understands." The *Daisy*'s sounds came to him familiarly, each sound rising from its proper place, reaching its proper pitch, establishing its own characteristic vibration. He listened carefully; the whole boat was singing as it ought to sing.

Late of the afternoon the *Daisy* touched the Pine Street wharf, discharged its passengers and crossed the river for wooding-up. Returning, Musick saw Mr. Gorman waiting on the wharf. Musick descended to the passenger deck and went into the saloon where the other partners had gathered. Durfee had left a bottle and four glasses for them. Callahan was filling the glasses. They stood around the table while they drank and were in this stage of comfort when Mr. Gorman came in.

"What happened to the Julia?"

"Struck a deadhead above Cape Horn and beached," said Musick. "The holes are out of water. It is a patch job, but you'll have to send up the *Carrie* to pull her off. We took some of her passengers on to the Cascades and brought the rest back here."

"He hit midstream or close in?"

"Close in."

"Racing, I suppose?"

"We always race," said Musick. "Aren't those your orders to Bain?"

Mr. Gorman gave him a strong glance. He

132

said, "I'm obliged for your help."

"Lou," said Musick, "have you got the bill?"

Bradshaw walked into the purser's office and returned with the bill in his hand. He was nervous and he was worried over what might come of this; he passed the bill to Musick who in turn gave it to Gorman. The moment he touched the bill Mr. Gorman grew harder and more careful. Musick saw the man's eyes race back and forth across the paper, but he saw no reaction on those firm, closed lips. This was Mr. Gorman looking at bad news. Mr. Gorman lifted his glance and placed it on Musick.

"You shall have it," he said very dryly, and turned out of the saloon.

Callahan said cheerfully: "He didn't like it."

Bradshaw slapped a hand on the table. "Neither do I. We lost money on it. We may lose the river on it. By God, Musick, you push too much."

"Never back up," said Musick. "If he finds he can push you an inch he'll push you a mile."

"And how can we stop him," asked Lou, "if he starts pushin'?"

"Knock him off balance. Step aside when he hits, and clout him as he goes by."

"Oh, hell," said the exasperated Bradshaw.

"What with? We're small and he's big. We got a slingshot and he's got a cannon. Don't be a damn fool."

The three partners were watching Musick — George Pope with his round and incurious face now touched by slight interest, Bradshaw in open resentment, and Callahan with his smiling doubt. Musick lifted his cap and scrubbed the scum of a long day from his forehead. He was tired, he was dull, he was restless. Whiskers blackened his face and the shadows lay heavier in the flank of his cheeks. His cheekbones were flat and high, and with weariness upon him, his features tightened and his lids dropped until he seemed to be staring upon the world with antagonism. But he smiled back at Callahan, and the smile erased this hostile surface appearance.

"Think of Gorman for a minute," he said. "He's sure of himself — he never doubts he'll get to the top. He'll brush aside whatever he can. Well, he'll brush us aside if we are afraid of him — if we're willing to believe he's bigger than we are. That's the old story. The strong think they're strong, and the weak think they're weak. The weak whip themselves by thinking so. The minute we think the Navigation Company can lick us, we're licked."

None of them understood him. Pope and Bradshaw stared. Callahan, idly chuckling, shook his head. "It sounds fine, Adam, but what's it mean?"

"A million dollars," said Bradshaw, unable to get it out of his mind. "A million dollars right beyond our fingers."

7

Webley Barnes came into the *Daisy*'s saloon, appearing cheerful. "You're filled up for Monday. Passengers and freight."

"Well," said Callahan, "go ahead and make a million dollars. I don't care. I was born in the gutter and I'll die there. But it would be nice, sleepin' in the gutter, to know I once was rich. Wouldn't mind knowin' how a woman looks at a man with a lot of money. When he throws a thousand-dollar bill in her lap, would she show him anything he never saw before? Would a thousand dollars bring something two dollars wouldn't? When he paid for it, would it be worth it?"

Webley Barnes said: "I have taken on a venture of my own. The Fleming Brothers wanted to sell out an old line of tinware and crockery. I bought it on ninety days' time. It occurred to me that with all the freight blocked at the Cascades, there must be a great need in eastern Oregon for cheap stuff."

"How'll you get your freight through?"

"Ship by the *Claire* to Oregon City and pack it muleback over the Barlow Road. Ellison and Chaunce at The Dalles are buying."

Musick noted the optimism on Webley Barnes's face. The man had failed so many times that he had lost faith; now there was the prospect of success, and this made him respectable to himself again.

"Webley," Musick said, "is it a sure and certain deal?"

"It's sure," said Barnes.

Musick poured whisky around and lifted his glass. "Luck, Webley," he said.

"Sure," said Barnes. "Adversity is supposed to make a man. What fool said that? Failure couldn't touch anybody if it were only himself; it's when somebody else close to him suffers for his failure that he feels the knife in him."

"Luck," repeated Musick, and turned to Callahan. "Going to the rally tonight?"

"What would that be?" asked Callahan.

"What's your politics?"

"What'd you think," countered Callahan, "me being an Irishman? A Democrat, of course."

"There's two kinds this year," said Musick.

"I thought there was but one kind of tom-cat," said Callahan.

"The Republicans and the conservative Democrats are all one party this year — the Union Party. The Southern sympathizers are the second kind of Democrats. They have taken the Democratic label with them."

"I'm no Copperhead," said Emmett Callahan. "I'm a Lincoln man. If the secesh have taken the label, where have they taken it? We'll bust their heads and take it back. Is that what the rally is for?"

"No. Just to hear the candidates make speeches."

"Ah, that," said Callahan and dismissed the idea. "There will be promises and words. But I'll forget the words, and so will they, and we'll just have another set of lads to pay and feed." He looked sharply at Musick. "Why have not these men in office done what they said they'd do?"

"What'd they say they'd do?"

"How would I know? But why didn't they do it all the same?"

"Well," asked Musick, "how do you know they haven't done it?"

"Because they never do," said Callahan.

Adam walked out of the boat's saloon, Callahan and Barnes with him. Somebody had lighted a tar barrel before the Pioneer Hotel and part of a crowd was around it, although the rally had not yet begun. The promise of excitement was a magnet instantly drawing Callahan away. Musick and Barnes walked homeward past the saloons with their lush Saturday night trade. Supper was ready.

Webley Barnes sat down to the table with

his restored good humor. The effect of it went to Lily and changed her as well. Musick had observed the closeness of these two before, but it was never so noticeable as now. The grace which was in Lily came largely from her father; and from her father also came the inner laughter and the sense of tragedy so strong in imaginative people. Webley said: "I shall have to do a little work tonight. I have got men crating the goods for the *Claire*." He ate very little and soon left the house.

Musick listened to the man's feet go stamping down the walk. He observed the change upon Lily's face, the loss of gayness and the onset of doubt. "Adam," she said, "could he possibly fail?"

"Nothing's certain. He might fail."

He saw an expression close upon terror in her eyes; it was a fleeting thing, but raw and plain while it lasted. "One more failure would be too much for him."

"He takes things hard."

"He's not worldly," she said. "He's always so hopeful, and so punished when things turn bad. Then he goes down. You saw him go down last night. You heard how bitter he was. He never meant it. He wants the world to be lighthearted. He wants to live that way."

"Then it's a poor world for him," said Musick, "and he'll die disappointed."

"That's a hard way of looking at things, Adam."

"I'm like your father. I want the world to be what it isn't."

"No," she said, "you're not like him at all. My father could be hurt a thousand times, but never fight back. You'd fight until you were killed."

He got up from the table and lighted a cigar, and the meal and the cigar created a contentment which went through him. These were the rare moments which could be labeled happiness — secretly coming and secretly going. He helped her clear the table and then strolled around the front room, jingling the silver change in his pocket; he came back and paused in the doorway and watched Lily put the kitchen in order. The weight of his glance was on her. She felt it and ignored it until she reached the far end of the room. Then she turned and met his glance, and grew still. Across the room's width he saw her to be alert, but with an expression in her eyes that stirred some old memory he could not identify.

He said: "You don't need to lift your guard, I'm not dangerous." He went to the front room, got his cap and left the house, drawn toward the sound of the crowd now gathered on Front Street.

When he reached Front he saw the yellow-crimson pulsing of the tar barrel's fire in front of the Pioneer Hotel, and the shifting and bobbing of men's shapes against that odd glow. This was four blocks away but a speaker's voice came toward him, sometimes with the full-lunged and insistent stridence of an auctioneer, sometimes with the pure musical baying of an opera singer on a high note. The crowd's approving yell rose up and the shapes of men swayed under the tar barrel's saturnine glow, like savages dancing out their tribal rites.

He was in front of Dekum's confectionery store. As he stood there he remembered a little girl he had once noticed paused before this window, wrapped in pleasant delight as she looked upon the candy trays, yet touched with a regret that moved him even now when he thought of it. The candy was before her, but she could not have it. He had gone in and bought a sack of it and had brought it to her; and he remembered the change of her expression.

He turned quickly about and went back to the Barneses' house. Lily was in the front room, standing before a window. She turned from it, with not quite enough time to lift her guard, so that he saw the shadow upon her spirit. "Lily," he said, "let's look at the town."

Her glance searched him for a reason and a reaction made its obscure print on her face. "Why, Adam?"

"Better for two to walk together than for one to walk alone."

"I'm not the one you should be walking with."

"I doubt if it would bother Edith."

He had said the wrong thing on the night before; he had said the wrong thing again. She gave him a short glance. "I wasn't thinking of Edith." She turned to the closet and got her coat and came back, smiling at the woodenness on his face — the look he usually wore when he failed to understand. "Never mind," she said, "it doesn't matter."

He helped her with the coat. He touched her shoulder with his hand, and felt the effect of it and stepped away. She turned, noticing the change on his face. "Adam," she said, once more doubtful. "I —"

He opened the door and took her arm. Pine Street's darkness closed around them as they walked and the sound of their feet went rattling onward. "Don't build a jail for yourself," he said. "That's what we all do."

"You're free."

"I don't know," he said. "Maybe I'm not. But if I am, what am I free for?"

"Don't you know what you want?" she asked.

"No. Do you?"

She walked along without immediately answering. The example of her father's life had made her careful; she would not open herself and be hurt as Webley Barnes had been. At the corner of Pine the light of the gas lamp came upon them and she looked up to him and smiled. "Find your own heaven. Don't borrow mine."

"You're not in heaven; you just dream of it."

"How much closer does anybody get?"

"That's a thing I'd say," he pointed out. "We're alike."

His interest came down on her like a rough hand. "No," he said, "that can't be right."

"What do you think I am?"

Somebody went by and said, "Hello, Adam," and Musick answered, "Hello," without looking up. She faced him, her coat drawn up around her neck against the night's raw air; she had her hands in her pockets and she was interested. She looked like a woman flirting with a man and drawing him on. He knew better. Her manner was light, but a hard layer was behind the lightness. Below the layer was a spirit he frequently felt yet knew nothing about. She was slow to condemn, so slow that he sometimes wondered if the actions and morals of people meant anything to her. He had the greatest impulse to use his words upon her like sledge hammers, to change the light in her eyes, to waken and shake her and to loosen the things within her. But he drew her on toward the Pioneer, saying nothing.

They came to the edge of the crowd. Old Colonel Delaney was speaking: a lawyer, a loyal Union man, a cool and tough character who knew when to be a firebrand.

"They are among us — perhaps even here now listening — these men of the maelstrom, who took their milk at the breast of the harlot Sedition. She is their true mother, malign and heartless and owning no scruples to the laws of God or man. Yes, and they are her true sons, come among us to spread the seeds of treachery whose flowers are more poisonous than mountain ash. Have you read the *Times* this morning? The editor of that paper — that sheet, that rag, that foul and bloody banner of indecency — is one of the breed. What did he say? He said that the Union Party was a corruption composed of black Republicans and backsliding Democrats — that the only true faith was the Democratic Party — that rump of a thing deserted by all loyal Democrats and now composed only of ragtag and bobtail, openly urging the destruction of this Union, openly advocating that this State withdraw and become a part of an Independent, slave-loving Pacific Republic. I say —"

The rising tumult of the audience stopped him; he stood good-humoredly patient while men cheered and their voices lifted shrill heated calls. The tar barrel's light laid a tawny, smoke-shot glow over the scene and its flickering created the illusion that men were swaying and gently capering to its tempo. Behind the Colonel stood a band which now broke into the "Battle Hymn of the Republic." The voice of the crowd thickened to a solid and continuous shouting.

Lily looked on, her eyes quick to see and her manner turned eager. The Colonel's words had brought up some of her own loyalty; now and then she lifted on her toes and put a hand to Musick's shoulder for support, and once when a near-by man blocked her view, she gave him a push with her arm.

The band quit and the Colonel's strong tenor voice renewed the attack. "Those men are traitors to this Union, openly and continuously and adversely. I say they were born traitors and their characters are such they could be nothing else but traitors. I say that when the election day of June seventh comes, we shall destroy their standing forever in this state, destroy them politically, and, if they persist in their machinations, then by God of Heaven, we shall destroy them physically —"

His remark touched off another demonstration. But a voice stronger than even the Colonel's began to be heard through the crying of the crowd and, lifting his glance, Musick saw Floyd Ringrose on top of the board awning of the building across from the Pioneer. Ringrose had gone into that building, ascended to a second-story room and had climbed through a window to the awning. Thus twelve feet above the crowd, he pointed his finger like a gun at the Colonel.

"Yield!" he cried. "You have said too much."

The crowd grew quieter. The Colonel, facing Ringrose, said: "Have I smoked out a Copperhead?"

"Listen to me, you windy mouthpiece," said Ringrose. "I am a citizen of this Union. I was born in the South and I am a Democrat. I am a free man and my politics are my own. I say to you that your words are the words of a liar when you brand Southerners as you do."

"What are you then?" challenged the Colonel. "If you are a Union man, you've got no sore corn to be stepped on. Or are you a Copperhead?"

"Whatever I may be, sir," said Ringrose, "you are a jackass."

"The braying I hear does not come from

my direction," stated the Colonel.

Ringrose looked at the crowd and made his appeal to it. "Men like that man," he said, pointing to the Colonel, "are dangerous. They inflame, they destroy. What is a Copperhead? Why, apparently any man who does not believe exactly as this fanatical bigot believes. I have affection for my country and so do we all. But you do not make Christians by fire or sword. You may take the South and rape it and gut it and lay it waste, but you cannot change its opinion. The South was a part of our country. It would still be a part of our country if reason had been used upon it, if men had been big enough to admit that other men may honestly hold to their own opinions. Upon this continent two kinds of beliefs can live side by side. But upon this continent you cannot have a prostrate South and a triumphant North. It will not work. What have we got for our war but tears and tragedy? Nothing more! No answer and no solution — nothing but Northern and Southern men fallen and rotting like cornstalks. Is that the answer? Never! The South may die but it will not surrender its ancient beliefs. It will not surrender its respect. It will fight to the last man, and the Northern armies will wilt away of bullet and disease in the Southern swamps and some day there will be nothing left of either North or South but skeletons upon the earth, and the buzzards will wheel over an empty and desolate scene, and they alone will profit from the insane machinations of men like this man who, pouring his bile and fury upon our quivering sensibilities, at last destroys our fortunes, our homes, our lives." He paused for breath; he paused in a heavy silence, and then in a softer tone he drove in his point. "Is it total destruction of everything you want? Or do you want to let the South go in peace, so that we may all survive? I say —"

Shoved on by an offended loyalty he could not control, Musick abruptly pushed his way through the still audience. This man was eloquent and he made vice seem pretty; this man was a pure Copperhead spreading his wares. Musick came up to a two-by-two post supporting the awning upon which Ringrose stood. He struck the post with a shoulder and felt it give. By then he was enormously angered; the feeling got into him and went bounding through him until he could stand no resistance. He backed off and struck the post again and carried it way by his attack. He jumped aside as the end of the awning collapsed. Ringrose slid down the sagging boards, feet foremost, hit the ground, rolled, and sprang up. He made a complete turnabout; when he saw Musick he halted and drew himself straight. The fall had jarred him. He was pale and his hair fell across his forehead in a yellow swirl. "By God," he said, "do you let me alone, or do I have to kill you?"

"You," said Musick, "are a Copperhead straight out."

"I warn you, sir," said Ringrose, "let me alone. I shall speak. I am free to speak."

"You're free to speak. But I do not want to hear you and I am free to shut you up."

"Take care," said Ringrose. An oldness, a wildness came to him; his face was scratched by long lines and his skin seemed of a sudden the same color as his hair. He threw back his head and he made a gesture with one hand toward his waistband. He had the edge of his coat shoved aside when Musick hit him across the arm and drove the arm from its downward swing. He waited a moment, and saw that Ringrose meant to try again; then he smashed him left-handed on the neck and tipped him into the crowd.

Musick said, "I won't hear that talk. You're for the Union or you're against it. One thing or the other." He waited and he watched Ringrose, and he had a hope that Ringrose would come at him again. He wanted this fight; the urge came out of nowhere and was something he could not help.

Ringrose looked at the crowd; he studied the surrounding faces carefully, and straightened to watch Musick again.

He was debating the fight and half inclined to renew it. The wish burned in his eyes and created that bright oddness which Musick had before observed in them; but in the end he turned on his heels and pushed his rough way through the crowd and disappeared in the darkness of Alder.

Colonel Delaney called: "You have cooled our friend, Adam. Now let me finish my pleading." He was good-natured about it and the crowd was good-natured; and in fact the Colonel, resuming the speech, had difficulty whipping up a proper state of emotion. Musick, returning to Lily, observed this and smiled at it. Oregonians were a different lot than Ringrose knew about. They were a steady and fairly mild people, they liked their politics rough but they could be amused later at their own intemperance. It was a rare thing to get them up to intense pitch; they much preferred easier ways.

"I'm glad you brought me," Lily said.

"I'm a plain fool," he said cheerfully. "Is it too cold for ice cream?"

"It would be nice." She took his arm and walked with him along the back edge of the crowd. They went half a block up Morrison, entered Coffin's Ice Cream Saloon, and sat down at a table; she was both pleased with him and concerned with him.

"I knew you intended to hit him," she said. "It was on your face. You're satisfied now. If you had whiskers, like a tiger, you'd be licking them."

"A man gets old and stale from too much thinking. Good thing sometimes to use his muscles and forget about his mind."

"He'll have to leave town. They'll tar and feather him. Who is he?"

"Ringrose. A newcomer. Portland's got a way of taking the swash out of men like that. Lappeus will cart him off to jail tomorrow and Risley will fine him twenty-five dollars for breaking peace. Afterwards he'll walk the street and nobody will give him a thought. We are a peculiar people."

The ice cream had the flavor of lemon in it and was very cold. Other young couples came in, and spoke. Perry Judd, mate of the *Claire*, sat near by with Phoebe McCornack, both of them so engrossed that they saw nobody else. As he sat there, not much interested in talking, Musick tried to describe Lily to himself, but had no great luck. She was pretty, but prettiness was an ordinary word. Perhaps she was beautiful. He had considerable reluctance in admitting that, for beauty was some-

151

thing the poets talked of in vague and often straining terms which meant nothing.

She was at present paying him for bringing her here, showing him an attention which women used on men, young or old, whenever it suited them; it was a little coin which they always found at hand. He watched her lips, which had seemed to him on occasion to be full of want. How hard did desire press her and with what grace did she surround it? When she looked up to a man, one day, and accepted him would that man see only a shallow brightness of desire, or would he see a glow that tied him to her forever? He looked down at his dish of cream. He ate it and continued to think about her.

"Adam," she said, "you didn't answer me. What am I?"

"Webley Barnes's daughter. A girl in a brown coat. No, not a girl. A woman."

"What's a woman?"

"Other half of a man. But a man has a level and so has a woman and neither knows if they'll match up right. They never know until it's too late."

"Want me to think you're wise, don't you?"

He enjoyed the light malice in her talk. He paid for the ice cream and they moved up Morrison into the street's darkness. Here and there lighted house windows made yellow squares against the night, and somebody near by played a piano stiffly and badly. In the damp air lay suspended the heavy odor of the firs crowding this town. At Seventh, Musick swung north. Lily seemed to be content with this, and paced with him. The mass of houses was dark and the town was dark; and blackness was a pressure upon Portland. Far up on the edge of town she checked him, saying, "It's late," and turned him back. He was happy at this moment and could not tell why. He walked down Montgomery to Sixth, and along Sixth, and presently passed the Thorpe house. He had given no thought to it but he felt a change in the girl beside him so that he unexpectedly knew she hated Edith Thorpe. The revelation astonished him. How much hatred was there like this, deep and still and hidden in the people he daily saw?

They walked on homeward with the ease gone. He opened the gate and stepped aside. She went through it to the porch and reached the door and turned to him; coming nearer her he caught the tenseness of her attitude, as though she had come to a crisis and had stiffened herself to meet it. She had no explanation to give him, yet she blocked the door and compelled him to halt and puzzle out what was in her mind.

He bent to catch a better view of her face

153

and when he saw the heaviness of her lips he thought he knew what she was telling him; and a pair of shears seemed to cut a restraining cord and he put his arms around her waist and drew her in to him. He was not yet sure and he felt a great dread of making a mistake with this girl. For a moment he watched her and saw no anger and felt no resistance; then he lowered his head and kissed her.

It was what she had wanted. She felt the luxury of it as well as he; and for him it was a need that he could neither check nor satisfy. A fine sweat broke out upon him. He knew the pressure of his arms and his mouth was too great for her, yet her own arms were tight around him, holding him as he held her. As long as it was this way, he felt he had his rights to her — the rights of any man in a woman who willingly met him; but in a little while there was no more force in her and she lay passive, waiting for him to be done. He no longer had her. He stepped immediately away; his knees were unsteady and there was a vibration all through him.

She was calmer than he was. Her voice revealed it. "You wanted to know," she said. "Now you ought to know."

"It was good. That's all I know."

"Oh, Adam," she murmured, and added: "I wasn't saying I was in love." She tried to read the little shifts of expression on his face, but got nothing from them; and her manner settled and she shook her head. "I thought I had been so clear," she said, and entered the house.

He remained on the porch for five or ten minutes, needing the cool night's air; then he went inside and crossed to the kitchen. She had found herself a cup and had poured herself coffee from the still-warm coffeepot on the back of the stove; she sat with her arms on the table, once more a girl who looked regretfully at something beyond her reach. He got another cup and took a chair opposite her. She wasn't what she had been before. He could not mark the exact change, but the change had nevertheless happened.

"And I wasn't trying to take you away from Edith," she said.

He finished his coffee and rose; he washed the cup and set it away and left the kitchen. He heard her call his name and he turned back to the doorway. "I'm sorry," she said. "I shouldn't have permitted it."

He climbed to his room, loose and confused; he sat on a chair and put his feet on the bed. Was she hating him now? Maybe he had left the print of brutality on her mouth. He wasn't certain of himself. Maybe the impulses which drove a man so hard were dirt-common, nothing better; maybe she wished for something else and hadn't found it. Well, the kiss should have told her all she needed to know about him. She held the information now.

He removed his feet from the bed and laid his hands on his knees. They had looked at each other for more than a year with a safe distance between them. In a moment's time he had crossed the distance. There was no backtracking from it. He couldn't again look at her without a feeling of ownership, and inevitably in his mind would be the question — when would he next possess her? It would be in her eyes when she looked at him, the knowledge of what she had given, and her intimate thoughts as to when she would once more give. A man could not walk into a woman, turn about and walk out; from here onward when he looked at her, across the table or across the length of a room, there would be a knowingness between them. Was it only male and female stalking each other? Or was there in all this the first sound of the angels singing? He stared at his hands.

8

Mr. Gorman had the habit of making frequent casual tours of the town, and thereby the town was always a concrete picture before him. He well understood that it was easy for people to make a devil out of an unknown figure, whereas it was difficult for them to hate somebody they knew well; and since he was engaged in the creation of a great business enterprise in a land which had a fear of largeness, he took care that he should never become a distant figure.

This night he made his rounds during the political rally and witnessed the turmoil with the eye of an undisturbed spectator. He noted Musick with Lily; he saw Victor Gwyn leave the Lotto Saloon and go erratically up Stark, a young man of some business brilliance but with unstable appetites which, Mr. Gorman concluded, would ruin him. It did not matter if a man drank or liked women, these being human appetites; the issue was whether or not a man could handle his appetites discreetly. There was a form in life which had to be observed and if a man did not keep this form he was not of sufficient character.

In Mr. Gorman's mind was a clear distinction between public and private virtue. A man had his proper obligations to his family and to his community; he ought to support his church, to labor personally for schools, for improvements, for welfare, for the hundred and one things which made a community better. All men were equal as human beings. But when he stepped into his business life, Mr. Gorman shut several doors behind him. In business there could not be equality, since there was no equality of ability. Business was a thing of power in which the able survived and the weak were sloughed aside; business was a stewardship of the able and the strong. If business were ruthless it was only because it had to weed itself of the incapable; the more efficient it was, the greater the benefits it shed upon the whole life of the people. The stewards of business would of course get greater rewards. That was the incentive for the able. As for the less able, they would find their stations somewhere along the line. A human being had his rights which could not be destroyed; but in business, which was the handmaiden of prosperity, the less able could not be supported beyond their own merit.

Mr. Gorman would have been the first man, upon hearing of a family's distress, to go personally to that family and supply its wants from his own pocket; and though he would have expected a word of thanks, he would not have wished the family to lower itself by making the thanks effusive. He would have gone farther. He would have found some kind of a job for the man and — though this began to touch his business code a little — he would have closed his eyes if the man were not a good worker. As against this, he would have applied all the power at his command to crush a business rival standing in the way of the Navigation Company. To him the company was an instrument in the working out of America's destiny; he was a prime mover in that destiny and he had a genuine feeling of his own part in it. Also he proposed to profit by it and saw no ethical reason why he should not.

He saw the light burning in Webley Barnes's store and stepped in to discover Barnes seated at a clerk's high desk, going over the ledgers.

"Working late?"

"I'm sending a shipment of tin and crockery by pack over to The Dalles."

Mr. Gorman's business mind began to work. "Cheaply bought?"

"Very good price. The Flemings are selling out their hardware line."

"Have you got a sound consignee?"

"Ellison and Chaunce at The Dalles."

"Yes," agreed Gorman, "they're good. But freighting is expensive."

"With goods piled up at the portage, I think my consignment will get through soonest by pack outfit. That's the point of the deal."

"Good chance, but don't gamble on it. Get a firm offer from Ellison and Chaunce. Let them gamble on it."

"Arranged that way," said Webley, and showed pleasure at having anticipated one of Mr. Gorman's objections.

"I hope you make a profit."

"I could use a profit," said Barnes thoughtfully.

There was a slight wishfulness in Barnes's remark which Mr. Gorman did not care for. A man in business needed to be tougher than Webley Barnes. A successful man had a star over him, a smell of success about him. Barnes had not. Barnes saw too many things in too many lights, so that there was not one single light shining out of him or one single desire driving him. In a sense he was built too finely; his mind was too flexible. Maybe he should have been a poet. Mr. Gorman had great respect for a poet's ability to dream, but none for a poet's ability to perform.

"The boys seem to be doing well," said Mr. Gorman. "Full boat Monday."

"Full boat all summer from the looks of it," said Barnes. He grew slightly reserved, for he thought Mr. Gorman was fishing for information.

"Should be good all year," admitted Mr. Gorman, "next year, too."

"That's what they think," said Webley Barnes. Then he let slip a piece of information he regretted disclosing. "They're talking about another boat."

"Well," said Mr. Gorman, still casually, "they're pushers. They'll get along. I'm fond of Adam. Headstrong, but sound." Then, honest in his wish to help Webley Barnes, he added: "See that your venture is pinned down on all corners. Think up every possible trouble and cover yourself."

He turned from Barnes's office and paused a moment to give light to his cigar, idly listening to the tail of Colonel Delaney's speech. Thorough Unionist and Republican though he was, Mr. Gorman had little respect for political speeches; he subscribed wholly to Colonel Delaney's view but he found himself picking holes in the Colonel's reasoning. Arguing a case before a judge, the Colonel's argument would have been as sound of texture as a Hudson's Bay blanket; before this audience he talked like a flannelmouth. It was a concession to the less reflective members of a democracy, as the Colonel himself would have been the first to admit.

About to turn into the town's upper darkness, Mr. Gorman observed a young small shape slip through the crowd — completely indifferent to its excitement — and come in at a trotting sort of a gait. It was young Billy Gattis, no doubt bound out on an errand. Mr. Gorman hailed him. "Wait a bit, son."

Billy Gattis came back with reluctance. It always struck Mr. Gorman that here was a gray-faced boy who had no boyhood left in him. Somehow Billy had been cheated out of boyhood laziness, boyhood laughter, boyhood friends. He was as thoroughly alone in this town as any human being could be, forever on a run as he went about his errands. He appeared to be driven by a mature man's ambitions but he had about him a slyly desperate and half furtive manner, as though he feared he would be stopped.

"School's soon out," said Mr. Gorman. "You'll have time for full summer's work." Then it occurred to him to ask: "Go to school, don't you?"

He observed the lightening of Billy's manner. "Gone as far as I'm going."

Mr. Gorman shook his head. "Without education you can't climb. Like trying to go up a ladder without arms."

"A lot of men in business here never had as much as me," said Billy.

Mr. Gorman pondered the answer, meanwhile noting the combination of uneasiness and determination in the boy. It gave him the uncomfortable feeling that he was persecuting Billy Gattis, and therefore he changed his talk. "There's a solidness in you, I believe you're bound to go far. I have got a place in my office for you."

"What pay?"

The offer of a job had seemed to Mr. Gorman something at which the boy should have jumped; the question did not please him. "Five a week."

The boy's face expressed a fleeting change; afterwards the strained watchfulness returned. He said: "I get that much a day now. People who stay at hotels, like miners and travelers — and others — don't regard money very much."

"They apparently don't," said Mr. Gorman dryly. "But it's a bad crowd for a boy to be thrown with."

Billy's quick mind had worked Mr. Gorman's offer around during this talk. "Could I work for you during the day and keep my other chores for night?"

Finding himself before a sharp bargainer, Mr. Gorman lost some of his goodwill.

"You've got a paper delivery in the morning. Then you'd work for me. Then you'd do chores until midnight. It won't do. I want a boy's best effort. You can't be three boys."

Billy Gattis said, "Thanks for the offer," and moved his feet as though delayed beyond his time. Mr. Gorman, priding himself on his persuasive powers, tried one more argument.

"In a good firm you might go a long way. Want to be rich someday, I suppose?"

Billy had never relaxed his vigilance. Suddenly he said, "Yes, sir, I want to be," and moved off at his trotting walk.

Mr. Gorman said to himself, "Well, by God." This boy had push and undoubtedly would be rich or be hanged. He watched Billy Gattis turn down Oak Street, and he had his silent admiration as well as a twinge of doubt.

After the scene in front of the Pioneer, Ringrose moved up Alder Street and made his way to the house of Emily von Gratz. He knocked and let himself in before she answered the door, and he saw in her eyes an expression of dislike for his abrupt entry. It amused him, as it always amused him to put his will against the will of others. He smiled at her and went on to a chair. "Have you got a drink of rye in the place?"

"What've you been up to?"

"Your Colonel Delaney was making a political speech. I did not like his gospel and I challenged him. Then I had some argument with another of your townsmen. Musick is his name."

"He put his knuckles on your neck," observed Emily.

"There's a bad horse," said Ringrose and dismissed it that way. But Emily, looking at him with her speculation, knew he had not dismissed it. He had an enormous amount of vanity and though he covered himself pretty well he could not quite conceal the resentment in his eyes, or the short expression of distaste around his mouth. As well as she knew men, Emily found this man odd. He was pleasant to her and he had manners, yet his manners were never stable, never very deep. She went into the kitchen for whisky and glasses and brought them back; she poured a drink for him and one for herself and stood by the table, still trying to discover what he was.

"You've got a lot of bluenose men around here," he said. "I have never met such a lot of watery, bargaining characters. They'd sell their own women if the price was right."

"What are you here for?"

"Business," he said, "and that's enough for you. The man who brought you this rye had pretty good taste and money to afford it. Who brought it?"

"None of your business," she said, "and that's enough for you."

He ceased to smile, and pink color ran around the back of his neck. He had not expected to have the cutting edge of his words turned against him by this big and seemingly easy woman. She had known he would react in this manner, had known that he loved malice for his own use but hated to have it used on him.

"You don't know my town and you don't know me," she said. "We're not that soft. You're no Southerner, either."

"You're a smart woman," he said. "What am I?"

"A rascal bound for trouble and sure to get it."

He looked at her with a complete, interested coldness, as though she had caught him off guard and had gotten some information out of him which he felt was dangerous for her to have; and for an instant he sat tense in the chair. Then he relaxed and he smiled at her. He reached into his pocket and produced five twenty-dollar gold pieces. He took her hand, put the gold into it and pushed her fingers shut.

"Where'd you get that?"

He watched her closely. "You like that stuff?" he asked. "You want a lot of it?"

"You talk like a drunk."

"Who comes here?"

"Suppose I told you? What'd you do — go make him pay you to keep still? You know what I call men who do that?"

"No," he said, "that's not my business. I've got more money behind me than any of your Portland boys."

"You still talk like a drunk."

He rose and filled his glass and walked over to the big couch in the room's corner. He sat on its edge to drink his whisky, and put the glass on the floor and stretched full length on the couch. His face grew ruddier; he looked at her, his teeth showing when he smiled. He made a motion to her. Emily von Gratz watched him a long moment, feeling her anger slowly go; she was suspicious and she was uncertain, but she stepped to the head of the couch and laid a hand on his head. "They did a good job of spoiling you," she said. "But they all got on to you after awhile."

"Who?"

"Women. I suppose some of them wanted to stay on, even when they knew about you."

He reached around and drew her to the couch. She sat on the edge of it, raking his face with her glance. She was critical and yet she was interested. She said: "You're no good — but a lot of women get stuck on bad men. They fool themselves about the man a long time, hoping they're wrong about him. And he's decent just once in awhile — and that keeps them going. Then some day they know they're never going to get anything back."

"Why don't they quit then?" he asked.

She shrugged her shoulders and now she was pretty — the lines of her face softened, the strain gone from her eyes. "Well, it gets lonely. Everybody's got to have somebody."

He laid a hand around the back of her neck and pulled her against him. She turned her head away for a moment, until he said, "That's not what you want to do, is it?" She lifted herself slightly and gave him one more heavy, searching look, and lowered her mouth to him. In another moment she drew back, confused.

"My God," he said, "you're not rattled?"

She shook her head but there was a loose and hopeful expression on her face; and out of his long memory of women he knew what was happening to her. She was setting him apart from the other men she knew and letting herself fall in love with him. Good or bad — they all fell in love and they all grew possessive.

He said: "Who's Musick?"

It took her a moment to clear her mind. She straightened and lifted one of his hands and held it. "You've got nice fingers. Ever do honest work? Musick's part owner of a boat. Let him alone. He'll break your teeth and flatten your nose and you'll look like a barroom bum."

"Bully boy?"

"No, but he won't stand much."

He drew his watch, saw the time, and lifted himself from the couch.

"You've got some sort of funny business," she said.

"What makes you think so?"

"I feel it," she said.

She got from him again a direct stare. "Don't get curious."

"Try to be kinder," she said.

"Why?"

"It's all right when we're young," she said. "We can be fools. We don't have to think too much about what's happening. We can try one man or another, or one woman or another, and there's always time left. But it don't last. We get older and everything catches up and the time's going too fast — and what's left then?"

"Well," he said, "what have you got left now, Emily?"

She looked away from him. "You didn't

169

have to say that."

"No," he said. "I guess it was a bad thing to bring up."

It was an unexpected kindness from him and she turned back with a certain amount of hope. "There's always something left. Floyd, if you stick to what you're doing — whatever it is — you'll end up dead. People like us are never wise. We wouldn't be here if we were. But sometimes maybe we get wise before it's too late. Let's leave here and try something else."

"I've got business here."

"The same old story."

"I'm enjoying my life," he said.

"You won't when you're old. You'll hate everything, and so will I." She leaned toward him with an unusual intensity. "We'll be sorry. Let's leave now."

"You're a sentimental wench. I —"

A sound from the kitchen brought Ringrose to his feet in sharpest reaction. The kitchen door opened and Billy Gattis came in and stopped at the edge of the living room. He gave Ringrose his inexpressive stare.

"Your milk's on the table," said Emily. She looked at Ringrose. "You know Billy."

"Yes," said Ringrose. He returned Billy's stare and he held it, beating at the boy with his eyes. "Knock next time," he said. "Knock

and wait for an answer before you come in."

"Never mind," said Emily. But she saw then that Ringrose hated Billy Gattis and, looking over to the boy, she also saw that he hated Ringrose. Ringrose took up his hat and coat and walked to the front door, and slammed it when he left the room.

"Billy," she said, "you been flip to that man?"

"No," said Billy and turned to the kitchen.

"You know what his business is?"

Billy delayed his answer until she thought he meant to say nothing. When finally he said "No," she realized he was lying.

Ringrose, leaving Emily's house, gave the street a careful inspection and moved north. At Stark he turned toward the river, entered Ryan's stable, and found his way to the pitch-black rear of the place. A voice challenged him: "Who's this?"

Ringrose tendered the password to a man he couldn't see, caught the man's palm in the proper grip, and was let into Ryan's tack room. The crowd had been assembled for some little time, for the place was thick with smoke. He had been discussed, he realized; and he sensed that these people were not pleased with him.

Telliver said: "What for was that fuss with Delaney?"

"To show you how it's done."

"You did nothing," stated Telliver.

"I've done enough of this work to know more than you do. Loyalty's an easy thing when it costs nothing. Your Portland men are fat and lazy, thinking no harm can come to them. I saw faces change when I said they'd lose property. That will stick in their minds. It will work like slow poison."

"You didn't scare Delaney and you didn't move Musick."

"Always a few leaders for a herd of cattle. We break the leaders. We destroy them. Then your cattle will wait for new leaders."

"How's that, brother?" queried Telliver. "Who do we destroy?"

"Those two will do for a start," said Ringrose.

"You're hell for talk," said Telliver.

Telliver was the tough one in this crowd. It was, Ringrose guessed, a matter of pride with the man. Telliver had been the leader and it sat poorly on him to have another come in and take his place. Ringrose, holding his silence, debated with himself. Which was the best way to handle him, softly or with violence? What would move Telliver — what did Telliver want?

"When we break heads, brother," he said, "I'll break the first one." Then he thought

he knew what would bring these men back to him, and he laid out his bright trinkets one by one to fascinate them. "Any of you ever had all the money you wanted, or the women you wanted? Any of you see a good piece of land you'd like to have? There's wealth in this state, but who's got it now? You have not got it. The fat Union boys have got it. When we take out this state, they won't have it. You'll have it."

Telliver said, uncertainly, "I don't know about that."

"You'll see," said Ringrose. "There were a lot of rich Union men along the border states. Where are they now? Dead or gone, brothers. Who got their land? The Knights did. That's what I mean."

"These people here," began Telliver, still doubtful, "might change their politics, but they won't change their pocketbooks. In or out of the Union, they'll vote to keep what they own."

"Vote?" said Ringrose. "They'll vote this month. That's the last time they'll vote. I told you that people are cattle. It is a silly thing to think a man who makes his living shining your boots has got sense enough to vote. We'll drive the cattle, brother. What are you doing here if you don't expect to sit in the saddle?"

He left the room on that note and found

his way to the street. He went softly along the walk, thinking to himself that Telliver would be his enemy when the Knights came to power. Telliver was ambitious and would not be happy with less than first place. Telliver was a good deal like Musick and Delaney, too stiff to obey. It might be necessary to put Telliver aside.

It was a risky game. Ringrose had his hopes for luck, but he knew the penalty if his luck ran out. The sense of risk balanced his headiness but it did not chill him. He had read a little history, just little enough to find a pattern for himself in the lives of the earth's unscrupulous conquerors. They were the ones he had admired long enough to convince himself at last that great risk for great gain was the only object of a man's life. He was not a Southerner by birth, yet he was more Southern than the Southerners in belief. He was not an aristocrat; he was a product of mean people who lived in dismal surroundings and his own career was checkered with failure and petty dishonesty and the contempt of others who had known him. This was a humiliation which burned within him and furnished the power which drove him; this and a quick mind which never could be content. He had joined the Confederate Army because, feeling that the North would lose, he saw a chance for himself. He was here in Oregon as a secret agent for the same reason. If the Union broke, this state was far from the center of either Northern or Southern authority. Oregon might be a part of the South, or a piece of a new Pacific Republic or — and this also he had in his head — it might be wholly independent. He had no certainty of its future, or his own; but he proposed to take advantage of whatever chance came along, and seize it and grow on it. More than that, he had accepted the possibility of failure, which was a charge of treason against him. He had visualized himself as a Western Napoleon; he had also visualized himself before a firing squad. It was the possible penalty which gave drama to his ambition; he was at present an unknown man involved in small intrigue, and his life had no distinction; but tomorrow he might be a great man, success covering his sins. It had happened often enough in history to be possible now.

Mr. McGruder was, as he had once admitted in a letter to his chief, the soul of industry; and during this day he had kept scrupulous account of Ringrose's actions. He had viewed the scene in front of the Pioneer, had followed Ringrose to Emily's house and, by devices of which he was proud, had successfully trailed his quarry to the entrance of Ryan's stable. His next step was to go to the adjoining street and lay a blind course through the heart of the block to the stable's rear wall. When he put his ear to the wall he made out the reverberation of talk; sliding his fingers along the wall, he discovered the stable's rear door, opened it, and let himself into the stable's alleyway.

Pencil-thin streaks of light outlined another door to his right, indicating a room, and voices made a faint undertone in that room. This was a satisfactory discovery and for a moment he was tempted to cross to the door, but was turned from that temptation by the memory of a prior occasion when such a maneuver had trapped him. His present location was scarcely less dangerous; swinging to his left, both arms extended, he touched the partition of a stall which seemed to be empty, and stepped into it. It occurred to him at once that this was an excellent point of observation — the doorway of the opposite room could be well viewed when it opened — and he took one more step into the stall, settled on his heels, and dropped a hand directly into the soft belly of another man.

He pulled back, but not quite in time. The man's arms swept up, closed around him, pulled him down. At once he was engaged in a furious, speechless struggle. He had considerable strength of his own, and a lifetime's practice in this sort of employment had taught him much; but the fellow below him had a powerful set of arms. He could not break their encirclement, he could not bring his own trapped elbows into play. The best he could do at the moment was to roll, bring the man above him and deliver a full blow of his knees into the other's belly. Once more rolling, and twisting as he rolled, he butted his head into the fellow's face hard enough to bring a brilliant shower of light across his brain, hauled one hand free and laid his elbow across the other's windpipe.

"Lad," he said, "stop this nonsense."

He got a sound wallop in the flank for an answer and he knew he was about to be unseated, for his victim surged about the floor with increasing violence; he let go and rolled to the other side of the stall, at once doubling his legs in preparation for attack from the unknown assailant.

It did not come. Instead, the door of the back room came open and a yellow light poured out of the place, turning the stable's gloom to a coffee-brown. One man came from the room, closed the door behind him, and passed down the stable toward the front. Mr. McGruder suddenly thought: "Now why is this other lad quiet as me?" He had thought himself betrayed by some fellow stationed as guard for the meeting; now it appeared the man had reasons of his own for remaining silent. He said softly: "My friend, maybe the both of us had better leave these quarters."

"Well, then," said the man. "I don't want no trouble. You one of 'em?"

"Not likely."

"Thought you was. Better move along. The rest of 'em will be comin' in a minute."

Mr. McGruder got to his feet and stepped into the spongy dirt of the stable's runway. He thought he had the man directly behind him but he wasn't certain of it until he reached the street. Then he saw the man's shadow close in upon him. "Doin' some listenin'?" asked the man.

"If I were you," said Mr. McGruder, "I'd not ask."

"Well," said the man, "I don't know," and before Mr. McGruder was aware of it, a match burst in his face and he stood identified. He made his own identification as well — remembering the face he saw — and quickly batted down the match.

"A very foolish thing, my boy. Where've I seen you?"

"Crowley's the name," said the man. "Have you got a dollar or so?"

"Pulling my leg a bit," said Mr. McGruder. "I don't like it. I'd advise you against such business. You'd not want law on your hands, would you?"

"Everybody knows Ben Crowley," said the man. "Lappeus is my friend. A dollar or so would tide me over."

"Lad," said Mr. McGruder, "you may be of use to me." He searched his trousers and found a pair of dollars and passed them over. "There's more of that, maybe. Who's in that room?"

Ben Crowley said: "No, I'll have nothing to do with it. It's bad business and not in my line. I thank you for the money, and I ain't seen you anywhere."

He disappeared before Mr. McGruder could ask him another question. There was a sound within the stable to warn Mr. McGruder of the meeting's breakup, and at once he strode to the street's corner, crossed over and made his way to the hotel.

He had his drink in the bar and went to his room, once more to draw a chair before the table and to compose a report: —

Our Subject has made a Connexion as I foresaw. There is a substantial Circle here whose Meeting-Place I have discovered. You may be certain that, with the usual despatch I flatter myself to own, I shall soon have a list of Persons belonging to this Seditionist Group.

It was my Intention to pay the Governor of this State a visit and apprise him of my Business. I find the more ardent Unionists here believe the Governor to be a strong States' rights man. As Evidence of such Temper, the Governor recently appointed to the Senate a Mr. Benj. Stark, whose political Views are strongly suspect. I shall not therefore see the Governor and risk All thereby.

Desperate Things are afoot here, among the Knights. Sedition will have its Way, unless thwarted by June 7, the election date. I assure you I shall be fully informed and will infallibly take Action before that Date.

I flatter myself the Business goes well forward.

I am, Sir,
Y'r Ob'd't H'ble S'v't.
PERLEY McGRUDER
Ag't.

9

Musick woke late on Sunday morning, having slept so long and soundly that he rose dull. On no other night did he get more than six hours abed, and this extra sleep on Sundays should have refreshed him; but it never did. There seemed to be a rhythm to a man's life which could not be broken without bad effect. He was like a horse turned out to pasture once a week; but he had been so long accustomed to harness that he stood at the pasture gate and waited for the empty day to end. A man started from boyhood free and irresponsible — and this was what he came to, of his own making.

He went downstairs to find Lily holding his breakfast. Webley Barnes had risen early in order to catch the *Claire* for Oregon City. Lily filled the wash basin with hot water for Musick and he went to the rear porch with his razor and mug. With whiskers as tough as wire, and growing in contradictory directions, shaving was always an eye-watering ordeal, a matter of stropping and cutting, and stropping again; and cursing either silently or openly from the punishment of it.

He came and sat down to hot mush, eggs, potatoes fried in butter, and two small pork chops. Lily sat with him to enjoy a second coffee, her hair very carefully done up for church. He looked at her through narrowed lids. "Beautiful job," he said. "How long did it take?"

"Forty-five minutes. It's like your shaving, except that I don't swear aloud."

"What swear words do women use?"

"Those they hear men use."

He looked at her lips and the sensation of the previous night came back to him and he wanted to kiss her again. This was the way he knew it would be. The barrier was down and she would never get it entirely restored. The effect of the kiss would be working at them and pushing them on. They were on the edge of the same mystery every other man and woman faced, none of them knowing what good would come of it or what tragedy would come of it.

He looked at her arms below the half sleeves of her dress. He looked at her idle hands, which the night before had been so insistent with their pressure. Her body had been temporarily his and he had his possessive feeling about it and could not help himself. He lifted his glance and saw that she had been reading him through the silence. She was sure of herself; the cloudiness was out of her.

He rose. "Let's get at the dishes."

"You go on."

He went through the back porch to the woodshed and got a file from its place on a rafter and sat on the chopping block to sharpen the ax. He had risen dull and he remained dull, and he began to wonder what he would do with his spare time if things were arranged so that nobody had to work more than a day a week. He could chop wood until there was too much of it chopped. He could fish until there was no fun left in fishing, or he could hike in the timber with his pipe and finally grow bored. He could build a boat or break a team for trotting or — as a last resort — read a book. But all these things wore out because they were extra. They were bits of play designed to kill time, not to use time. A man was made for action. When he ceased to act he wasn't anything; he was another Ben Crowley sitting on the side lines, alive but useless. He was no longer in the stream and he no longer mattered.

He took an armload of wood into the kitchen's wood box and washed the pitch from his hands. He put on his coat and combed his hair. Lily was upstairs; he stood in the front room, listening to her steps go back and forth in her bedroom. She came to the top of the stairs and stepped slowly down; she had changed into a long-sleeved mulberry dress which had a small flare at the bottom and came tightly against waist and breasts. She wore a small hat at the back of her head, of the same mulberry color, and carried a handkerchief and a Bible in one hand.

She stopped before him and he saw the faint dusting of rice powder on her cheeks. She had chosen the dress with care; she had chosen a mood to match the dress with equal care. The silence held on between them and she continued to watch him, apparently searching for certain reactions in him. But the silence grew too heavy for her and she broke it. "You cut yourself shaving. You'd better start. You'll be late."

He went to the door and opened it. Then he turned back to have another look at her, feeling that he had failed to say something that should have been said. She stood in the room's center, still watching him; she wasn't asking anything of him that he could make out, but he had the idea she was thinking of his sitting beside Edith in church, and that she was displeased with the thought. He left the house and walked up Seventh Street.

The metallic blast of church bells rocked the town's self-conscious Sunday stillness. The Thorpe family came down the walk in

formation, Mr. and Mrs. Thorpe, Grandmother and Edith. Adam lifted his hat and
received their various recognitions, and he observed Edith's little signal of displeasure at
his lateness. He stepped between Edith and
Grandmother — an arm for each — and set
out with the Thorpes on their Sunday parade.
From other quarters of town other families
trooped in similar parade, all of them meeting
at the church door for a moment's decorous
talk, and dropping their voices as they passed
into the church's dusty smell, into its hallowed
silence and somber twilight. Now, as on every
occasion he came here, Musick remembered
opening a trunk which had stood long untouched in the attic of his grandfather's house.
The dry odor of mortality had come from the
trunk and the clothes in the trunk were yellow
and pressed flat, yet in the stretched places
at knee and elbow and breast was the mark
of the round and firm and heated bodies which
once had filled them.

He sat on the hard bench between Grandma
and Edith. A shaft of sunlight slanted through
the church window, the dust particles within
it making a golden agitated fire. Grandma's
eager glance darted around the congregation,
hunting for traces of new scandal and remembering twenty years of old scandal. Edith sat
straight, her expression sweetened from

knowing that she looked well in her dress. Sunday was a ritual, and ritual pleased her. Musick watched her a moment and there came to him the same foresight of age by which he had watched the miners on the deck of the *Daisy* grow old before him. He saw Edith grow old, the sweetness slowly vanish from her lips, the roundness die out of her body; and age came to him as well and he sat here an old man remembering the things he might have done which had not been done, and he looked around at the people of the congregation and saw them all to be old, to be waiting in resignation for their release.

Grandma's brisk sigh brought him back and the beady brightness of Grandma's eyes reminded him that she had not grown old. He had a great respect for Grandma and doubted if she had left undone anything she had ever wanted to do. Grandma had lived her days with a loving and greedy fullness. Meanwhile the minister had begun to speak, a tired man at middle age; there were no trumpets in his voice, no fire in his soul. Musick listened to the minister's words and heard nothing and then he glanced at Edith's hands folded upon her lap, to the shapely line of her knees and lower body and a stream of interest moved through him. Why was not the minister's sermon like a woman's figure, evoking the desires of a man and filling his spirit? He sat still, suddenly rebellious, suddenly fearing he had missed his way.

At the end of the services he dutifully followed the Thorpes back into the mild day and stood with them while they chatted with others. Lily came out and joined the group, and at once Edith turned to face Lily. Edith's voice was pleasant and her face had its smile and Lily, returning the direct appraisal, was also smiling; but a feeling of unease came upon the crowd and Mrs. Thorpe silently signaled her husband with her eyes. Mr. Thorpe started his family homeward.

Along the way Easterbrook fell in with them, having been invited to dinner. Mott's manner was lightly agreeable; he was, Musick thought, a pretty complete product of a well-to-do family. There was neither anything cheap or petty in him nor anything very powerful in him; thirty years from now he would be a well-preserved man who had tasted most of the good things without sweating for any of them. Even his courtship of Edith was an effortless affair, as though he recognized that he was the less favored of the two suitors and made a comfortable game of it.

They sat down to dinner, Mr. Thorpe carrying on the kind of conversation he considered necessary as head of the house. Mrs.

Thorpe had an occasional word to say, Grand-mother was silent, and Edith paid Mott more attention than she usually did. She was still displeased, Musick realized, and wanted him to know it.

Dinner done, the group settled in the living room, and at once the dreary prospects of the afternoon appalled Musick. He could think of nothing to say, and wanted to say nothing. All of it became too much — this Sunday dinner, this family circle, this heaviness, this room. The room itself represented the Thorpe family, and the Thorpe family represented a certain group of Portland people who intended to become rich and to build houses which should be permanent in a part of the town which should be permanent. Mr. Thorpe, in common with his kind, intended that he should reach a place in life and crystallize that place for his family and his heirs. They would live generation upon generation in such surroundings, and nothing would change. Front Street would forever be Front and Seventh would forever be Seventh. Mr. Thorpe would walk six days a week down to his office and Mr. Thorpe's descendants would do likewise; and the ladies of the family, sitting in a room whose walls strained out the echoes which came from Front, would pour their teas and live gracefully with their chinaware time without end. Time stopped upon a pleasant and genteel moment in this room and the Thorpes, as others of their sort, wanted to stop the hands of the clock and hold the moment forever.

Grandmother rose and took her alien personality from the room. Mr. Thorpe presently walked up the stairs for his accustomed nap, soon to be followed by Mrs. Thorpe. Their presence had been a constraint. Musick found Edith watching him in the manner he knew so well — formidably serene, with the faintly edged smile and the slight attitude of standing on surer moral ground as she judged him. Mott Easterbrook, who had understood this, looked on with his half-veiled amusement. It was he who broke the silence.

"You were close to a brawl with Ringrose last night."

"A few brawls would be a good thing for this town," said Musick. "If we're all bound for hell, we ought to have a few scars to show for our sins."

"You're rough with your words, Adam," said Edith.

"I am a Front Street character," said Musick. He rose and walked to the window. Edith was outraged with him and let him feel it by her silence. Mott Easterbrook now saw there was a storm blowing up, and rose and departed.

"Adam," said Edith, "you're rude."

"I don't understand what you want," he said. "What do you want?"

"I'm discouraged when I think of the future. Am I supposed to come down to your level to amuse you?"

"What kind of a level am I on?" he asked.

"I can't spend my life being ashamed of the part I play. A woman's supposed to bring gentleness to a home. There are certain right things, and nice things. Am I to have none of them? If I can't make you see them, how can I face my friends? How can we be accepted?"

She was laying her will against him. Was it because she meant to have her way, or was she honestly afraid of him? He was unsure of himself, remembering that Lily had looked at him a little as Edith now did. Perhaps both women saw in him something not to be admired. He stood before Edith and was troubled.

"We're in a tug of war," he said. "That's the way it usually is."

"It's a woman's place to know what a man is. But you're never one thing long enough for me to understand. You change. If you could only be more like other men."

He said: "Does this room please you? Would you like to live in a room just like it the rest of your life?"

"Of course."

"I'd go crazy," he said. "Perhaps that's the difference between us. Perhaps the difference is too much."

It was not part of her rules that a man should concede defeat and withdraw. Men were supposed to be the hunters, inflamed to more aggressive effort by refusal. She sat still and he knew she was trying to discover why the rules would not work with him — this woman with whom he was in love and had greatly wanted for more than a year.

"Edith," he said. "All this is not checkers."

She rose and made a quick turn from him, walking away; she swung around at the far side of the room. "Do other women act differently than I do? You've had experience — you should know."

"Why," he said, "that sounds better." He went toward her, touched by hope. "Your mother's been stuffing you with rules of etiquette she found in the back of the cookbook."

She answered him with a cutting phrase: "Lily Barnes is human, I suppose. Is that the word I want?"

He laughed at her, coming nearer with the

191

intention of taking her and kissing her; but when he got close to her he saw it wouldn't do. There was nothing in her he possessed, nothing she was willing to surrender. She was a stranger set against him.

He had not expected to feel so great a disappointment but he did feel it. This was closer to him than he imagined, this was more important to him than he had thought. He turned and looked for his cap, scarcely wanting to see her face. He got his cap and stood by one of the room's windows. "Everybody's alone," he said. "But nobody wants to be alone."

"You talk queer sometimes. I can't make it out."

"Doesn't matter," he said.

She knew he had tried to say something to her and she knew that he thought it important for her to understand. She was alert, but she was resentful. "Am I to give up everything I want, if it's not what you want?"

"What do you want?"

"Oh, Adam, let's not go into that. It just wears me out to explain things. Can't you just let everything be as it is? Can't you be like other men?"

They were back to the point they always reached. He nodded to her and left the house. He would return the next night, of course. That was part of the routine he couldn't seem to break or change. Why couldn't he change it? Going down the street toward Front, he wondered why he should not stay permanently away, and in a little while he thought he had the answer. He had been attached to her since boyhood; it was a habit he couldn't break. She was his first girl, the first woman he had kissed, the first to slap him and be afraid of him, the first to give him that slow, deliberate glance a woman sometimes used to suggest more than could be decently said. The memory of that time and that rough and wonderful excitement softened the irritation he felt now. She had matured and she no longer thought it proper to be as carelessly frank; but she was still the same girl, she could not change what she was — and when they were married the cloak should drop. He believed this, and the belief consoled him enough to almost cover up the small doubt in the back of his head.

At three o'clock Mr. Thorpe came down from his nap, heavy-eyed and not wholly awake. He went to the kitchen and drenched his face with water; he drank a cup of cold coffee and returned to the front room, opening its door to let in a current of fresh air. "You and Adam have a quarrel?"

"The usual thing, I guess," said Edith.

"Better save your arguments till you get

married," said Mr. Thorpe.

"Do you think Mr. Gorman will freeze him off the river?"

"Adam knows how far to push Gorman and when to stop pushing."

"I don't understand him," said Edith.

Mr. Thorpe broke into a brusque, short laugh. "Nothing serious. He'll be tame enough a year after marriage."

"Mott's not like that."

"Bleached-out bolt of goods," said Mr. Thorpe.

Mrs. Thorpe came down the stairs and the two of them went for their customary afternoon stroll, leaving Edith to herself. She was not long alone. Around four o'clock Mott Easterbrook dropped in and took a comfortable seat. He was cheerful, but the girl knew something was on his mind. She watched him a little while, reading him and guessing at him.

"I rather think," he said, "it's time to decide. I've made my run and I guess I'm out of wind. If you want me, you've got me. If you don't want me, say so. One of us, Adam or I, is entitled to a clear field."

"You say it without much effort. Does it mean so little?"

He said with apparent irrelevance: "I know you much better than he does. You know me better than you know him." He gave her a sly glance. "Much better, Edie."

She looked warningly at Grandmother's doorway and spoke in half a voice. "That's the trouble. The things people do when they are sixteen or seventeen —" She shrugged her shoulders. "You couldn't love me. You don't really want me to accept you, either. But you've been faithful, Mott, and that's been nice."

"Ah," he said, cheerful as a man could be. "I wish you to have what you want. You want Adam. Therefore I supplied competition. Why not? I've done chores for you since you were in plaits. You're a she-devil, Edie, but we grew up together and no doubt we'll die together. I do not know whether I love you or not. But I'd marry you."

"You'd have a dozen affairs," she said.

"They'd never be vulgar," he said. "I'm a sort of gentleman."

"That's not enough."

"Enough for you. You won't break your heart on anybody."

"That's not fair," she said.

"I've heard you say that before. Many times before — clear back to Mr. Doane's Day School. Fair is your side. Unfair is the other. But I like you anyhow and I know you better than Adam ever will. You won't give him what he's after. But you'd give me what I'm after."

"You'll call anyhow, won't you, Mott?"

He stared at her a considerable length of time, slightly more serious than before. "Well," he murmured, "I see it's Adam. You sure you've got him?"

"Yes."

"You're using the wrong way on him. Why be so unapproachable? You were always a little cold, but as for being unapproachable —"

She showed him a bright expression. "Don't say it. If that hadn't happened, I would have taken you."

He rose and looked down at her and when she saw the regret on his face she stood quickly up. "Mott, do you really think that much of me?"

She came to him on a rare emotional impulse and put her hands to his shoulders and lifted her face. He brought her forward and kissed her and held the kiss, the back of his neck growing scarlet. She held him until he lifted his head and broke away; he was through before she was and he saw he could kiss her again if he wished.

"You could always get the worst out of me," she said. "I ought to hate you, but I can't."

"Well, if that's the way you feel —"

She shook her head. "We'd make each other miserable. Neither of us would trust the other."

"You're not giving Adam anything," he said.

"He's in love with me, though."

"You always liked to have the other fellow do the crying and the running."

"That's another reason, Mott. You know too much about me."

"Someday, Edie, your safe game will fall apart and you'll know what it's like to be stabbed."

"How can you know? You've never had anything hurt you?"

"I thought," he answered, very soberly, "I'd get out of here without saying it. The truth is, you've carved me up and that should please you. There's nothing much left of me for another woman. I've watched you play the game too long. I'd always be watching another woman to see her play it the same way. That ruins everything."

He gave her a short nod and immediately left the house.

It did her good to know she had power over Mott. He had come here to make a break in their relations and hadn't made it. He would come back; nothing could keep him away and nothing could make him forget. The knowledge of this restored to her the confidence which had been somewhat shaken by her inability to handle Adam.

"I can handle Adam, too," she told herself.

She had been watching Grandmother's door as she stood with her thoughts, and an expression of concern ran briefly over her face when she thought of what Grandmother might have heard. She moved across the room very quietly, laid a hand upon the knob as softly as possible, and opened the door with a quick shove.

Grandmother stood at her window, one hand parting the lace curtains so that she might have a view of the street, and Grandmother seemed wholly engrossed by what she saw on the street; but Grandmother's short and fast breathing betrayed her. She had been at the door listening a moment before.

"I saw Emily von Gratz just now," said Grandmother, her face to the window. "She's a buxom female. I don't wonder men go to her. Of course, she'll be fat someday, but men never see those things. Men always live for the present. That's why women can manage 'em. Don't forget it, Edie."

"You were listening."

"Of course I was," said Grandmother, turning about. "Don't give me that look. I'm too old to care what's nice and not nice. Well, I never cared."

"You ought to be ashamed," said Edith.

"Oh, foo, foo," said Grandmother. "That's

a very silly word. You were indiscreet. Suppose your mother had been listening? A pretty kettle of fish you'd been in, she weeping and carrying on. Your mother's awfully dull sometimes. She got old so fast."

Edith sought to put a better light on Mott's words. She said: "Mott has always liked to make out there used to be something between us."

"I got a good keyhole," said Grandmother, "and I observed you kiss him. Why don't you kiss Adam that way? Adam's the kind of a man who'd appreciate it."

"He'd think me easy."

"Well," said Grandmother, "what's Mott think of you?"

"I'm not marrying Mott. I'm marrying Adam. A man wants his wife to be above him."

"Sometimes he does and sometimes he don't. You got to be what he wants, when he wants it."

Edith shook her head. "It's not a woman's place to submit to a man."

"You're a dratted fool," said Grandmother. "It is a wonderful thing to submit. Then you got your man tied to you by log chains. Look at your mother. She never gave your father much, and he gave her less — and it is a smell all over this house."

Edith said, "You shouldn't talk that way," and turned to the doorway. She was passing through it when Grandmother's voice turned her back. Grandmother said: "Next time you kiss Adam, make him know you're willing."

"He knows I'll be willing at the proper time."

"No — no," said Grandmother. "Make him feel you can't wait, make him feel you're a naked body lying on the bed for him. That will bring him. It will bring him quick."

10

Musick sauntered down Morrison to Front with a pale sun warming the back of his neck, bound nowhere. The Sunday quiet lay like a weight over this town. Men, as aimless as he, strolled the walks and turned in and out of the various saloons. A young officer from Fort Vancouver came off the ferry and ran his horse through the mud full tilt as far as the Pioneer Hotel, sprang from the saddle and hurried into the hotel's saloon. Ben Crowley sat in front of the Nugget, his legs crossed like a beggar selling trinkets. On the levee a crew of men, superintended by Webley Barnes, worked his freight aboard the *Claire;* beyond the *Claire* lay the *Daisy* and the *Carrie*, and the brig *Bourbon* swung at its anchor in midstream to keep its crew from deserting to the mines. Somewhere on an upper street Musick heard the harking of a strident voice: "Fours left!" At the corner of Oak he saw Captain Corbett's company of very unmilitary volunteer militia at drill, and at the same time Loren Wray stepped from the Knickerbocker Saloon.

"By God," he said, "this has turned into

a tight river when a man can't get a team and a wagon aboard a Navigation Company's boat. Not for a week, they say. Have you got room on the *Daisy*?"

"Yes," said Musick. "I'll take you in the morning."

"Well, let's have a drink on it," said Wray. The two men swung back toward the Pioneer. Loren Wray was a farmer-philosopher out of the Tualatin Valley, a barbed-wire individualist who, looking upon the world from his farm porch, had little faith in Portland's money-changing notions or its morals. He was a short man with a large chest and a white goatee which, when he thrust out his face, stabbed straight at Musick. There was belligerence in him. "I do not like monopolies. I did not come out to this country to see it sold out to the barons. I thank you for taking me aboard."

"You may have trouble getting your wagon around the portage. Both sides of the river are jammed with freight."

"I can drive my own team through," said Wray.

"Both sides are privately owned. You will have to pay your toll and wait your turn."

"Imagine a man paying money to drive across God's own ground. If the Navigation Company gets those portages we shall then have the biggest monopoly of all. No sir, I do not like it. It is feudalism."

Musick let Wray nurse his feelings in silence; for Wray was a member of the state legislature and there was in Musick a forming thought. Elijah Gorman had missed a bet in not accommodating Loren Wray. He walked into the Pioneer bar with the older man, and together they found a place and waited for bottle and glasses. Wray downed his liquor with a puckering of his red lips and turned and hooked his arms over the edge of the bar, thus looking at the crowd in the place. He shook his head. "Too many people. Why do they come here like droves of sheep? Pretty soon we'll be as full of corruption as York state. There's Gorman over there, no doubt drumming up trade. Making people feel good toward his company. A hundred dollars a ton he charges for freight — and forty cubic feet is a ton in the monopoly's language whether it be lead or feathers. Maybe I ought to run my farm the same way and sell wormy apples for the same price as sound ones."

Elijah Gorman, observing Wray, pushed through the crowd. "Loren," he said, "what brings you in?"

"Business," said Wray tartly. "Going up-river."

"With us, I hope," said Gorman.

"Couldn't get aboard your boat," said Wray.

Gorman sensed Wray's temper and became grave. "Always room for you on our boats. I'll speak to Cutter."

"I've got space now," said Wray. "On the *Daisy*."

"That's fine," said Mr. Gorman. "Have a drink, Loren."

"Had mine," said Wray. "Might have another later." He raked Gorman with his critical glance, measuring Gorman for a fall. "Going to buy the portage, Elijah?"

Gorman smiled, "Might as well ask me if I'm going to heaven."

"Well, by God," said Wray, "if that's all the chance you've got, you got a damned slim one. Businessmen don't go to heaven. The bigger the businessman, the more the devil's got him."

Mr. Gorman continued to smile, but Mr. Gorman's face stiffened; he was a dangerous man in any kind of combat. "Well now, Loren," he said, "you buy and sell like the rest of us. Which region are you bound for?"

"I give honest measure," said Loren, "and I got competitors to keep me humble." He had a gathering audience, which he enjoyed; he lifted his voice. "You need competitors, Elijah. You're too big. Nothing big is good."

"The river's free, Loren," said Mr. Gorman.

"Now, my friend," said Wray, "you know you're talking through the top of your stovepipe. You don't mean to let the river be free. If you didn't mind competition, why would you be wantin' to buy the portages out?"

"To give better service."

"Would you let Musick share that service?"

"Why should he share what we have created?"

"The Lord created the portages — not you."

Mr. Gorman straightened himself and was ready to deliver his blow. Mr. Gorman cast a glance around him, speaking to the crowd as much as to Wray. This was a sensitiveness Musick had not observed before, and it came to him that here was Mr. Gorman's vulnerable point. Mr. Gorman did not wish to be ill-thought of by his community.

"Loren," said Mr. Gorman, "small fellows can't grow big. They stay small and fight among themselves. This is a big country. It takes big methods to get anything done. We've got a town and a state started. They'll grow, but do you think they'll grow by accident? No, sir! It takes fighting to make anything grow. I believe in my state and my country and I shall work for them. If the day ever comes when the law of this nation is that

205

no company can grow big, that day this country will cease to be a power. We cannot conquer three thousand miles of space by whittling sticks or sending a one-horse shay from door to door. We've got to risk and push. If the little fellow has got nerve enough to risk, he won't remain little. He'll be big — and then he'll spread prosperity all around. That, sir, is all the philosophy I've got, and if I didn't believe it, I'd quit work and go fishing."

Wray was smiling out his cheerful, friendly cynicism. "Of course you believe it. The prosperous always believe in what makes 'em prosperous. Now we have made speeches enough, ain't we?"

Musick looked at his watch. "Time to go."

"Where?" asked Wray.

Musick glanced around the saloon and lowered his voice, for this was contrary to the laws of Oregon. "Tom Gaween is fighting Lem Considine, a visiting bruiser."

"I'm your man," said Loren Wray and walked out of the saloon with Musick. Mr. Gorman came behind and caught up, displaying considerable interest for so sedate a citizen; and the three stepped aboard the Stark Street Ferry, along with a good many other Portland citizens, and made the river crossing. A trail led around marshy ground, through willows and disappeared in the fir trees; and at the end of the trail stood a barn. They were late. The main crowd had gathered and the fight was about to begin in the barn's half-light.

A rope created a square in the middle of the barn. At one corner of the square Tom Gaween sat on a milk stool, stripped to the waist and wearing skintight pants. He had shaved his head and the bare scalp showed the welting of many an old knuckle mark, and he sat in scowling, furious repose, his vast muscles silent. In the opposite corner was a lighter man with flat ears, a broken nose and a mouth well-crushed. This was Lem Considine, advertised by word of mouth to be the English champion now on American tour. The promoter of the affair, Considine's manager, stepped to the center of the ring.

"The purse has been arranged and we are ready. We have here the heavyweight champion of the continent, never defeated and never knocked out of the ring — Lem Considine. Against him is one of your local men, a Mr. Gaween, I believe. Come up, gentlemen."

The two antagonists rose and faced each other. Gaween had both reach and height on Considine and when the crowd observed this — a crowd composed of men from the saloons and the floating population, leavened by such good citizens as Mr. Gorman — a flurry of betting took place. The referee, again Considine's promoter, nodded and stepped back, whereupon Considine settled himself into a stiff squat, cocked one arm and thrust the other well before him. Gaween followed suit and began a slow side-stepping around Considine.

"The Englishman," observed Mr. Gorman, "appears somewhat less dumb. Ten dollars represents my faith."

"Taken," said Musick.

At that moment Mr. Considine caught Gaween on the shoulder with a solid blow, knocked Gaween off his feet and thus ended the first round. Both contestants repaired to their stools and sat in taciturn silence until called up again by the referee. Tom Gaween had been stung by the blow. Now he made a great rush at Considine, hit him in the belly, turned him and swiped him across the neck with his forearm. It was not a damaging attack but it terminated the round, Considine having dropped to a knee. There was a murmur of approval from the standing audience and Mr. Gorman said, "Good work, Tom," and got from Gaween a knowing nod. Gentlemen circulated to continue their betting and the contestants rose for the third round.

Both men now settled to a watchful shifting,

Gaween's fists revolving before him like a pair of idle pistons, and Considine showing a nimble footwork in his turkey-cock squat. Gaween made a rush and tripped himself and fell; and it went in this manner for ten rounds, a fall ending each. The audience stirred about to see the fight from various angles, to talk business, to drink from the freely circulating whisky bottles. Occasionally the lookout came in from the trail to report there was no law in sight.

At round eleven Gaween dropped some of his early caution. He stepped forward, parried Considine's blow and delivered one of his own into Considine's belly, bringing wind out of the man's throat.

It was the proper place for Considine to fall; instead he circled, recovered his wind and set out to drive Gaween before him. Gaween held his ground and the two men stood chest to chest and sent home their bare-knuckled blows. Considine struck for Gaween's neck. Gaween dropped his head and took the blow on the scalp, this producing a brisk flow of blood. For answer he took Considine on the right cheek, and got back a left fist on his mouth. He bobbed his head and gave Considine a bruised grin. He slid against Considine and used his arms and elbows freely; he back-heeled the visitor and sent him down. Still grinning, he returned to his corner.

He sat on his stool, drawing for wind and splashed with his own gore; he stared around at the crowd with his continued grin, seeking approval. He nodded his confidence. He said to Ed Campbell beside him, "That guinea can't rough me. I'll rough it as far as he wants to go."

It had been a hard exchange and for the next five rounds both men were cautious. Yet the heat of animal antagonism was working its way with both of them, dulling them to pain and prodding them forward to a reckless conclusion. It was to be seen on Gaween's face, and by the beating he took without permitting himself to flinch; it was also to be seen in the brightening and narrowing of Considine's glance. Mr. Gorman, studying both men, spoke to Musick. "Considine's fight undoubtedly. He's cool. Gaween will lose his head."

"Another ten dollars," said Musick.

"Agreeable," said Gorman, as the two fighters came forward for the twenty-third round.

Considine apparently had concluded to end this affair before he left too much of his energy on the barn floor. He came up briskly, feinted and drew down Gaween's guard, and his fist went into Gaween's broad stomach as it would have gone into a pillow. He stepped aside — his motions quickening — and when Gaween started a slow turn Considine delivered the hardest possible smash into the right side of Gaween's face. It sent Gaween back; it stunned him. Campbell sharply called: "Drop, Tom, drop!" But Gaween gave Campbell an unfocused stare and a queer grin, and shook his head. His blood was up. He let out a yell and charged Considine who, foreseeing this, met him with both hands, once to the chest and once to the windpipe. Gaween's rush carried him against Considine and when the latter attempted to step aside, Gaween spread his arms to trap the visitor. It left him open. Considine, a much quicker man, drove in his shortest punches, to stomach, to chin, to heart and low to the crotch.

He threw all he had, and it should have been enough. Gaween had no mind left and not a great deal of consciousness. He was in fact a red mass of instinct moving on; a dewlap of torn skin hung over one eye, his mouth had no shape and his vision could not have been more than a blur. But he had what the smarter and quicker man had not — a savageness greater than his reason. This was the thing Considine had not estimated. Having put faith in his last punches, he had not shifted aside and was therefore enclosed by Gaween's closing arms. Gaween pinned him and laid weight against him.

The audience called up its encouragement and the voices of gentlemen got a little hoarse with emotion. Mr. Gorman bent forward, his dry face lively, "Break it before he wears you out." Campbell cried to Gaween, "Use your knees, Tom. He's spraddled open." There was a shining on all their faces; the kill was near and the scene was good.

Considine escaped, greatly shaken. He wheeled toward a corner and changed his mind and turned back. Gaween, rushing on, started a looping swing with one arm. Considine saw it but was not set to take the chance which was his. He raised his guard, not quite high enough. Gaween's fist landed on the underedge of the visitor's chin; the visitor tipped back on his heels and fell into Musick's arms.

The man's odor was rank with ammonia, blood and spittle; his body was slippery with its sweat and he went through Musick's arms and collapsed over on the barn floor. Gaween watched this, barely aware of it. His arms hung full length and his knees were shaking and his lips — beaten to the breadth of a clown's painted lips — hung wide. He faced the crowd with his drunken smile, asking for the crowd's admiration, and he said in a gasping voice: "I can take anything any man can hand me."

Considine's manager watched his man with

a dismal eye. He stood with his arms folded, waiting; when it appeared doubtful, he crossed the ring, dropped to a knee and rolled Considine to his back. He lifted back one of Considine's eyelids, rose and touched the fallen man with the point of his boot. He said to the crowd sourly: "He's not coming up." Then he reached for a water bucket and tossed its contents on Considine's body. The latter responded with a jumping of muscles.

Somebody presented Gaween with the purse and there was a scattered applause as the crowd turned to leave the barn. Mr. Gorman removed his hat and said: "For the loser, gentlemen. He gave us an excellent afternoon." He went around the audience and collected the consolation money and crossed to the promoter, dumping the contents of the hat in the promoter's doubled hands. The promoter counted it. He said sourly, "Eighty dollars." He stared at the crowd a moment, undecided as to temper, but in the end he made a short bow and said in a growling voice: "I thank you for your generosity."

Musick left with Gorman and Wray, the three of them traveling the path to the ferry. Musick said: "How much of a purse did Gaween get?"

"Two hundred and fifty," answered Gorman and thought of the twenty dollars he owed

Musick. He passed it over with his comment. "You were betting on sentiment. That's all right for a diversion but in business it is a weakness which may trip you."

"There's weakness in anything we believe," said Musick.

The ferry came up and the crowd walked aboard. Tom Gaween stood surrounded by admirers while Mr. Considine and the promoter were by themselves. Mr. Considine appeared shabby in his clothes and his face made a very grisly showing with its cuts and livid bruises; he stood with his feet braced, looking out upon the water with dejection. Impulse turned Musick toward him and impulse caused him to hand over the twenty dollars he had won from Gorman. "You have got a better use for this than I have," he said.

Considine touched his hat — that gesture instantly lifting Musick's dislike. "Very good of you," said Considine. "You're a gentleman. I can see it plainly."

"Let me give you a gentleman's advice then," said Musick. "You've been cut to ribbons in order to give a few men a Sunday holiday. You got eighty dollars for it, which is a bad bargain. You had better get a job with a fairer exchange."

Mr. Considine looked at him with puzzled politeness. Mr. Considine's manager was openly hostile. "We'll take the twenty dollars, but you can keep the advice, my friend."

Musick smiled at the comment and turned away. Mr. Gorman had heard most of this and now drew Musick and Wray along the deck until they were beyond earshot. He displayed a sharp humor. "Do you think you can change a man into something he cannot be?"

"Men are not dogs."

"God made Considine the figure of a man yet without the brain of a man or the sensibilities of a man. Look for yourself. There is a creature who would pound another creature into jelly for two hundred and fifty dollars, or for a glass of beer if nothing better were offered. He fawned over you when you gave him twenty dollars. You can't make him better."

"God didn't put that in him," said Musick. "Men did. They taught him to use his fists and to cringe if he wanted a piece of metal. The gentlemen had the metal and he did not. If gentlemen wished him to crawl, he had to crawl. They taught him to do it when he was no doubt very young. They would let him learn nothing else. He continued to do it, in order to eat. It is a habit with him. Now that he's older he does not like the habit so well — you can observe the insolence in his eyes which comes of knowing that gentlemen have got the best of him. But still he must crawl if he wants to eat."

"Why," said Mr. Gorman, "you're unsound," and stared at Musick as though he had discovered a fatal defect. "You must realize the difference in people if you are to succeed."

"What's the difference between you and Considine?"

Mr. Gorman said tartly: "I will sleep well tonight while he will lie awake with his bruises. It is as good a difference as any."

"Had you muscle, and could make no other living, you would be in Considine's shoes."

Mr. Gorman struck the tip of his cane vigorously against the deck. "Never. I was born to make my own way. Considine was not. Therefore he must take what he can get."

"A comfortable belief," commented Musick. "But only those who are fortunate can afford it. The strong will defend themselves somehow. The weak have no defense. We are masters only so long as the wind runs with our ship. When the wind dies do you think you can blow the ship ahead with your own breath?"

"That man," said Gorman, pointing his cane at Considine, "is a cheap piece of clay, cracking at the first rain."

"We are all clay — and one rain or another

will crack any of us."

Mr. Gorman drew in a brisk breath and stood silent and Musick then realized there was no longer any real friendship between them. This was a strange and sad thing, this shriveling and dying of that faith by which people lived with one another, by which they made life endurable and decent. Mr. Gorman bowed stiffly to him and walked ashore when the ferry docked.

Billy Gattis, that afternoon, was on an errand for five gamblers who had been playing poker for thirty straight hours in one of the Pioneer's rooms. At Front and Stark he saw a group of boys idly collected against the side of Yardley's store, all of them from the upper part of town. One of the boys — this was Joe Ferris — said: "I smell skunk," and the other boys laughed. Billy Gattis gave them a glance without breaking his trot, and hated them because they were different than he was. It never occurred to him to stop and fight Joe Ferris; he had the same feeling about boys of his own age that he had about most of the grown people in Portland — their hands were out to stop him, and to make him do something he didn't want to do; and so he went on with a small dread sharpening his feelings. This was Sunday and Joe Ferris and his crowd had nothing to do but think of trouble.

He went into The Mint and got the particular bottles of whisky requested by the gamblers at the hotel. Leaving The Mint he realized that Joe Ferris's crowd could be at the corner of Stark waiting for him. He stopped a moment, not wanting to go out of his way to avoid them and he made a brief struggle with his conscience; then he put his pride away with a feeling of shame which he tried not to recognize and cut back between buildings toward First Street. When he reached First he looked down Stark and did not see the crowd, and this relieved him; but he was still cautious and after he had crossed Oak he took a rear route through the block, following a small alley. The alley suddenly came upon an open spot in the heart of the block — formed by the back ends of the surrounding buildings. In this open spot Joe Ferris and four other boys waited for him.

"Skunk smell," repeated Joe Ferris. He came forward and the other boys made a half circle around him. They were looking at him as though he were an animal and they had their minds on a fight. He stood with his package of whisky bottles under one arm, wanting to turn and run, and fear made his heart beat fast, and he felt sick. He had always been afraid of these boys, or of other boys. Often at night he had lain wide-awake with his dread of the boys in town who teased and taunted him and wanted to fight him. Often he had thought of scenes such as this one; and here was the scene, and he was trapped.

Joe Ferris came up to him and put out a hand slowly and gave him a soft push. "Skunk smell," he said again. He waited for Billy to strike back. For a moment he was cautious, not sure of the kind of fight Billy would make. But the boys behind him began to sing out: "He's afraid — go ahead — lick him," and that gave Joe Ferris courage and he stuck out his hand and hit Billy in the chest.

Billy still wanted to run, but he could not turn; he wanted to turn but he could not. A wildness went through him that was like drowning; he lost his head and he became almost blind. His face grew thin, his lips pulled back, his open mouth sucked for air. He dropped the whisky package and he jumped at Joe Ferris, hitting but not knowing where he hit, tearing at Joe Ferris's clothes with his fingers. Joe Ferris went down and Billy Gattis stumbled and fell with him, on top of him, and he beat the meaty side of his fist on Joe's face, up and down and up and down, and he rolled over and pushed his knee into Joe's belly; then he reached to the littered ground and scooped up a handful of dirt and threw it into Joe's eyes. He heard Joe crying and he remembered the four other boys ready to jump on him. That made him rise, but he still had his mind on Joe Ferris and he kicked Joe in the side and made Joe cry out. He backed away, seeing the other four boys silently watching him — still watching him again and the sickness was as before. He wheeled, looking around this cluttered open space. A broken bottle lay near him. He reached down with a terrible relief and seized the neck of the bottle with its jagged edge and he held it before him.

Joe Ferris said in a hushed, breathless voice, "I'm hurt." He got up and he put a hand to his side. His face was white and Billy Gattis saw the strange expression on it. Then Joe Ferris began to cry and went running away, the other four following him.

Billy heard their feet scuff along the sidewalk on Washington Street. When he was certain they weren't coming back, he dropped the broken bottle and went to his package. His knees were shaking and he felt sicker than before. He picked up the package. He looked at his clothes and tried to brush off the dirt with his free hand. He said aloud, "Why don't they let me alone?" His nose began to run.

"They'll let you alone now," said a voice.

Billy whirled around and saw Ben Crowley

at the mouth of the alley. Ben Crowley came forward, nodding his head. "Been pickin' on you a long time?"

"Sure," said Billy.

"That's the way it is," said Ben Crowley. "I was afraid you'd run."

"Well," said Billy, "I —"

Ben Crowley cut in. "If you'd run they'd known they could always make you run. That'd been bad. You'd had to run every time one of 'em saw you. When you run, you've always got to run. That's the way it is. But you didn't run. They'll let you alone now."

"I don't know," said Billy. "I wish they would."

"I'm tellin' you," said Ben Crowley. "They'll let you alone because you didn't run. They're afraid now."

Billy continued to brush off his clothes. He looked at Ben Crowley. He said: "That's all I want. Just let 'em let me alone."

"It was a good fight," said Ben Crowley, "but you oughtn't have kicked him."

"It was a fight," said Billy.

"Sure. But you oughtn't have kicked him."

"Why?"

Crowley rubbed his nose and Crowley thought about his answer. His eyes were half-shut as he stared at the boy. "You don't like

Spaniards that draw knives in a fight, do you?"

"No."

"Well, that's it."

Billy Gattis looked at his package. He said, "I got to go," and moved away.

Crowley called at him, "Sonny," and waited until Billy turned around. "When you walk along the street, don't keep your head down. Keep it up."

"You need a quarter?" asked Billy.

"By God, sonny," said Ben Crowley, "don't you offer me money. You look people in the eye and don't get out of their way, see? Don't think like a bum — like me."

"All right," said Billy, and moved on down the alley at his usual trot.

Crowley watched him go, and afterwards turned back to the rear of one of the buildings, which was a stable. He let himself into the stable and climbed to the hay. He pulled a pint flask from his pocket and he sighed and uncorked it and drank a third of it without drawing breath. He sat in the hay a moment, staring straight ahead of him; and then he corked the bottle and lay back on the hay, one hand flung over his face. "By God," he said. "By God, he's all right. By God, he can stand it. Crowley, you're no good. Crowley, you're a bum. But he ain't goin' to be."

11

Musick walked homeward in the late afternoon's dull quiet and found supper ready. Webley ate and returned to the *Claire* for late work and, as so often in the past, Musick was once more alone with Lily.

"You spend a lot of time by yourself," he said.

"I'm agreeable company for myself," she said.

"What happened to Ben Eames who used to call here?"

"I wasn't interested," she said.

"Before him there was Jack Ellencourt. You went to the Willamette with him now and then."

"I wasn't interested."

He stopped talking about it, but he kept it in his mind. He helped her with the dishes and he got a deck of cards and began a game of solitaire on the kitchen table. He could not hold his interest to the cards; he heard her behind him, moving back and forth with the last of the chores, and he watched her go into the living room. She sat down out of sight. He lost his game, and shuffled, and began another. The house windows began to darken and a little later she came back and lighted the kitchen lamp and put it on the table for him. She left the room; in a few minutes she returned with her sewing and sat across the table from him.

"Who won the fight?"

"Gaween."

"Enjoy it?"

"No."

She looked up. "You like a fight."

"I don't like to watch a pair of men cut to ribbons for my entertainment."

She cut a thread with her teeth and met his glance. She laughed at him. "I can't keep track of you."

"Eames was a good man. So was Ellencourt. Why weren't you interested?"

She let her sewing lie and rested back on the chair; her smile disappeared and she gave him a close attention. Her face had the expression he had noticed before and never understood, heavy and strange and vaguely dull. This was the shape of unhappiness.

"Nobody knows about that," she said.

"Think you'll find anybody you can be certain of?"

"Nobody I'll ever be entirely satisfied with."

"That's a hell of a thing to say."

"Yes," she said. "I guess it is. People ought to keep the truth to themselves."

He swept the cards back into a pack and rose and stood by the stove. He put his hands behind him. He locked them together until the muscles of his arms began to tighten all the way to his shoulders. The silence had been an emptiness; now it became a weight. He left the room, suddenly afraid to remain near her. He got his cap, but he stood indecisively before a window and stared upon a street turned dark. A small sound of music drifted forward from some other house and a man obviously drunk dragged his slow feet over the boardwalk.

"Adam — has Edith set the date?"

"No."

He turned to the kitchen. She had abandoned her work; she sat motionless in the chair with the lamp behind her and her face shadowed. He said: "I wonder if Edith is as unsatisfied with me as you are with everybody else?"

"You ought to know by the way she kisses you."

"I've kissed you, but I don't know anything about you."

"That's a good thing," she said. "Will you go now, wherever you're going?"

He left the house. A warm day had lifted

moisture from the sodden earth, and this lay as a crystal haze along the street, beautifully glowing where house lights touched it. Clinging to the haze were the rich odors of spring, of forest mold, of wood smoke from early slashing fires, of the heavy-silted river, of rank decay and the yeasty, unmoral stirring of fertility. In the deep shadows of Second Street he saw a man and a woman walking and heard their laughter; he saw them stop and sway and blend together, and laugh again and move on, and when they came up to the corner he recognized Phoebe McCornack and Perry Judd.

At Front Street he debated going on to the Pioneer for a drink. He decided against it and crossed to the levee and loitered there. Lights burned in the *Daisy*'s saloon where his three partners were probably playing poker and he considered joining them but turned about and returned to First, observing a lone man swing into a building's black doorway. Pacing up First, he had the notion of returning to Edith's and for a moment it was a strong enough desire to quicken his steps. But at Main he slowed down; he remembered the irritation in her eyes and he did not want to see it again this day. He went up Main and turned the corner into Fourth.

A brief blur came to the edge of his vision

as he turned the corner; he took two backward steps and looked down the street he had just left — down Main toward the glow of the gas standard on First. Between him and the gas standard a shape slowly faded away into the shadows. He watched the area for a moment and then, thinking nothing more of it, he resumed his way along Fourth. He passed Emily von Gratz's house. He crossed Yamhill, and in the silence which clung to this part of town the echo of his footsteps seemed to strike both ahead of him and behind him. That interested him; he stopped at once and heard the echoes continue.

When he wheeled he saw nothing behind him. He went on, crossed Morrison and heard the playing of a piano in Elnathan Brenn's house beside him. A vacant lot adjoined Brenn's house, and next to the lot stood an old log shed built in Portland's earliest days and now used by Brenn as a shelter for his milk cow. As he neared this shed, Musick heard a voice across the street lift up a deep, strong, short call: "Here — here!" At once the night's soft stillness was filled with the sound of many boots scurrying up from all quarters of the gloom, and the man across the street plunged rapidly toward Musick. When he came out of the blackness into Musick's view, Musick saw the short stick he carried in his hand.

Others were rushing forward from the various recesses of the night, speechless and urgent and heavy of breath. Somebody came at him from the right, out of the darkness beside Brenn's house, and somebody rushed up from Alder, and these two — together with the man now almost across the street — hemmed him against the wall of the shed.

He had his short moment of thought, his first shock, his first doubt. Then he was warmed by that recklessness which always supported him when trouble came. His mind cleared and he had a good feeling in his muscles, and he swung about and ran at the man who had emerged from the darkness beside Brenn's house. This man, too, had a club which he swung, lifted and brought down. Musick pulled aside and felt it scrape his shoulder as it passed, and heard the man's grunt of effort; immediately he had the man in his arms, and kicked him hard in the crotch with a knee. The man's cry rang in his ears as he reached for the club and tore it out of the other's grasp.

The man dropped and rolled on the vacant lot, shouting his agony as the other two attackers ran at Musick. Brenn's window light revealed them momentarily, then the light died as Brenn, hearing this commotion, cautiously insulated himself from trouble. The darkness made a cloak for these two men; it made a cloak for Musick as well. He retreated toward Brenn's house; he waited a moment and sprang at the nearest man's shadow and brought down his club on an arm. He struck full force and he distinctly heard the snapping of wood or bone, but was too occupied to sort out and identify the sound. He struck a second time, swinging the club like a bat, and felt it find a mark. The two bodies were not now before him. They had dropped, one without a word, the other quietly groaning.

But other men were coming in from the darkness. He heard them running on and he heard a voice say: "In that lot — in there!"

He drew away from the side of Brenn's house and ran toward the shed. He touched it and found the door and stepped inside, blinded by its pure blackness. He collided with Brenn's cow, turned quickly to avoid being kicked, and made his searching circuit of the place, knowing what he wanted. He touched the handle of an implement tilted against the wall, and hefted it swiftly and threw it down; this was a shovel. He came to the pile of hay in the shed's corner and identified the pitchfork impaled in the hay. This was what he wanted. With it, he moved back to the shed's door.

There was a crowd in the lot now — a dozen men more or less. These men had found the three cripples and were softly talking. "In the shed."

"Circle it."

"Might have a gun."

"He don't carry one. I've watched him."

"Beat him down — beat him down."

He waited at the doorway and saw shapes come forward, slow and crouched; he stepped through the door, knowing the darkness concealed him, and he waited a moment until he was able to single out one advanced shape. He walked from the shed and ran at this shape and rammed the pitchfork in the man's legs; the cry he got was higher than any cry he had ever heard. It was a shrill yell sailing all across the tops of the roundabout buildings. He pulled back his pitchfork and rushed at another man frozen in the shadows, and he jabbed the tines of the fork hard into the man's shinbones, and drew another penetrating shout. This man sprang way, and a murmuring came out of the lot.

"What the hell's up?"

"I'm stuck through! Come here — give me a hand! I'm slashed."

The rest of these night prowlers were halted in their tracks. They were listening, they were trying to see, they were made uncertain by something they failed to understand. Musick retreated to the shed wall, leaving no silhouette of himself. He said: —

"I am going to aim this pitchfork higher. Here I come."

He moved forward and scuffed his feet so that they might hear him. A club came whirling at him out of the black and struck him half in the chest and half in the face. He gritted his teeth against the hurt and said nothing. Men's shapes were before him, huddled and still, but as he advanced he saw these shapes break and scatter. He rushed headlong at the nearest man and he thrust the pitchfork ahead, still aimed low, and tickled that man's calves with it, waking another shout. He stopped in the darkness, making a complete turn. There was nobody near him. All over this area, men's boots were rattling the walks in flight, but from a corner of the lot a man called back, "Musick, you're dead," and ran away.

Up Alder Street, two or three blocks distant, was a great deal of shouting from a crowd which seemed to have no relation to the one he had just scattered. A door squealed at the rear of Brenn's house and a voice, Brenn's voice, cautiously called into the darkness, "Who's there — what's the trouble?"

"Nothing," said Musick. He returned to the shed, threw the pitchfork inside and walked on to the corner of Alder. He saw lanterns bobbing through the night, two blocks above him and he heard more voices rise; but he had little curiosity and he continued down Fourth to Pine and turned into Seventh. This thing was queer. He did not believe he had twelve enemies in Portland, yet twelve men or more had sought him out and had intended to beat him to pulp. For a moment he thought it might have been a gang of Eastern thugs wanting a little fun before they went on to the mines; then he remembered that one man had called his name, and he knew that this crowd was not made up of strangers.

He went into the house and found Lily still seated in the kitchen with her sewing. She looked at him and rose and came to him. She said, "What happened to your face?"

He laid a finger to the side of his face and touched a tender spot; he rubbed it and saw blood on his finger tips. Then he went into the kitchen and stood before the mirror. The thrown club had caught him across the left cheek; there was a broken patch from his mouth corner to his ear.

"Got waylaid."

"Who was it?"

"I don't know who. I don't know why."

"Portland is full of thieves. Every boat brings them." She pointed to the kitchen chair. "Sit down." She got the wash basin and filled it partly with water. Into the water she put a few drops of vinegar and a pinch of salt; and she found a clean cloth and soaked it and laid it against the cut. She held it there. She said, hopefully: "Does that sting?"

"Not much."

She added more vinegar and salt to the basin, refreshed the cloth and again laid it on Musick's cheeks, and smiled when he blinked both eyes. "It wasn't strong enough before," she said. He saw the quick motion of her pupils as she ran her glance across his face. Her mouth tightened, and she shook her head. "You like to fight. You always do. What did you use?"

"They had clubs. I had a pitchfork."

"Adam," she murmured, and he saw that he had shocked her. Somebody hurried along the board pathway toward the house and came quickly up the steps and across the porch. Webley Barnes flung open the door in great excitement.

"Some men caught Colonel Delaney up Alder Street and beat him down with clubs."

"Is he dead?" asked Musick.

"No. Terribly cut up. What's wrong with your face?"

"Same crowd went after me," said Musick. "Now I know."

"Who?"

"The Knights," said Musick. "I remember about that club business. They've used it back East. It's just short of murder, which is what they intend."

He rose and put aside the cloth. He felt better for solving the uncertainty. "They're active. It's only a short time until election. I expect we'll have to break a few heads."

She stared at him and her voice dropped and warmth went out of it. "That pleases you, doesn't it?"

It was always like this. There was a time when she drew close to him and he felt her sympathy, and a sweetness came from her to him. But that time was always brief; sooner or later he said a word or committed an act which revived her doubt and made her suspect that something lay within him which was not good. Maybe it was the brutality she once had indirectly mentioned.

He had at this moment a desire which had of late come to him so infrequently that he was surprised at its appearance now. He wanted to see Edith. Swiftly and unaccountably he had remembered a picnic with her up the Willamette. "Three years ago," he thought. Everything had been fine. They had talked of the future, and he had kissed her and she had said, "I hate this waiting, Adam," and in her voice was an impatience which had made him feel he had the world between his two hands.

He got his cap and left the house, walking by Seventh with his hope. "A thing like that can't die," he told himself. "It just gets buried beneath a lot of little aggravations." He came to the porch of the Thorpe house and he knocked, and waited with his hopeful impatience. Edith answered the door.

He said: "I got lonely," and stepped into the room.

She closed the door and turned to him. She seemed surprised to see him and she seemed to be wondering about him, for she studied him closely. A small line showed across her forehead, always the signal of her unsettled thoughts. "Mother and Dad went down to the Applegates' for a visit," she said. "Adam, what happened to your face?"

He told her, watching her eyes move back and forth as she scanned his features.

"You ought to tell Lappeus," she said. "I didn't know things were that serious in Portland. Why should they pick on you?"

"It's Ringrose," he said. But he didn't want to explain it. He said. "You remember the picnic we had up the Willamette? It was the day we passed the big wagon tipped over."

"Yes," she said, "I remember."

He said: "That was a fine day."

"Yes," she said. "I didn't know you'd remember things like that. What made you remember, Adam?"

"I don't know."

"Something must have brought it back," she said. "What brought it back?"

"We've had few days like it lately. Do you recall what you said?"

She was cool and serious and puzzled. She stood silent but he saw that she was not so much interested in drawing on her memory as she was in his reason for being here. "Oh," she said, "I suppose I said a lot of things. I don't know."

"You said you hated to wait."

"Did I?" she said in a small voice. "Well, maybe I did. Maybe that's one of the things wrong, Adam. Maybe we have waited too long."

He stared at her. "What's that mean?"

"Oh, no," she said hurriedly, "I don't mean I'm sorry, or that I've changed my mind. I mean, waiting's so hard. It's not always good for people. I know that people have to be patient, but it can happen that patience turns into dullness, or indifference, or something."

"Has it happened to you?"

"I know I've been cross," she said.

He stepped toward her and put his arms around her. She lifted her face, and this gesture encouraged him. He looked at her a short moment, noticing the stillness of her face. She seemed to be waiting for him to have his kiss, and to let the kiss do whatever it would do to her; she seemed to have no mind in the matter, no inclination. It was as though she drifted without an impulse of her own and was ready to have him change her or stir her. He kissed her and felt the same detachment on her lips. He stepped back.

She smiled slightly but she continued to watch him in her puzzled manner. "A fight always stirs you up, Adam."

He had not moved her at all. He said: "It would be fine to have another day like that day."

"We were pretty young," she said.

"Nothing wrong with that," he said.

"No, I suppose not. Was I a little bit wild then?"

"No," he said, "not wild. Not wild, but —"

"Exciting, Adam?"

"I couldn't name it."

"But whatever it was, you liked it. You liked me that way, didn't you?"

"Yes."

Yet he knew he had not told her what it was he remembered best about her. She was guessing that he remembered one thing — her willingness, her warmth, her open promise of

237

things unmentioned. But that was not what he remembered. It was an expression on her face which held a good many things he couldn't name. He couldn't tell her; he felt the moment die out and he saw that once more he had failed. He had troubled her again.

He said: "Late," and went to the door. As he passed through it he swung back, half hoping to see in her an expression which might put him on the right track. If he saw it he could say to her, "That's what I remember best. That's the way it should be." But he didn't see it. What he saw was the same close and alert studiousness. She said: "I wish I knew what brought it back to you. Good night, Adam."

Ringrose came to Emily von Gratz's house and stopped a moment on the porch, hearing voices inside. He left the porch and walked along the little alley between the house and the adjoining building and got to a window. He grasped the sill and lifted himself until he saw the scene inside, which was of Emily von Gratz seated at a table listening to Billy Gattis. Billy stood at the other side of the table; he had his eyes lifted to a spot on the wall and he seemed to be speaking from memory. Occasionally Emily von Gratz looked down to a book, apparently verifying his words.

Ringrose breathed a disgusted phrase and let himself down from the sill; when he came to the rear door he turned the knob and kicked the door open with a deliberate racket and walked through the kitchen to the living room.

Billy stood where he was, looking toward Ringrose with his prematurely wise face wiped clean of expression. Emily had turned in her chair; she had been startled.

"Floyd," she said, "you've got knuckles. You can knock."

"What's the kid doing here?" asked Ringrose.

"We're spelling," said Emily.

"Do your spelling at school," said Ringrose. "Get on home."

Billy Gattis remained still, but his eyes — eyes that Ringrose disliked — ran quickly up and down Ringrose's clothes. There was a speckling of blood on Ringrose's coat sleeve, and he was dirtied and scummed with a sweat which had not quite settled; an unsteady expression wavered on his face.

"Go on home," said Ringrose, irritably. "You're a weasely little monkey. You know too much. In and out of too many doors."

"I'll do the ordering in this house," said Emily.

"Well, order him out. I won't have him around."

She stared at Ringrose, and got an equal stare from him.

She had the notion of contradicting him but in a moment she changed her mind and nodded at Billy. "We've covered the spelling, Billy. You'll find milk and cake in the kitchen."

"Don't stop for it," said Ringrose. "Keep going."

Emily von Gratz's mouth hardened. "I said I'd do the ordering, Floyd."

"Well," said Billy, "I'm not hungry anyhow." He turned about the table and he walked around Ringrose who stood in his way and made no attempt to move aside. Billy kept his eyes down as he passed the man, but at the kitchen doorway he swung and stared at Ringrose for a brief moment. Ringrose turned his head to meet the stare, whereupon Billy Gattis's glance wavered and dropped and he left the house.

"Rat-faced boy," said Ringrose. "Keep him away from here."

"Why?"

"Don't like him around."

"I like him around," said Emily, "I'm as near a mother as he's got."

"Funny part for you to play," he said.

She said, "Is it?" She looked at him, offended by the remark and hurt by it. "You like to cut people, don't you?"

"Oh, hell," he said. "He's no account. Don't bother with him."

"I get a lot out of having him around. I feel good about it."

"You can forget him. I'm around now." He pointed to his coat. "Wash out these spots in a hurry."

"What's up?"

"For God's sakes, don't ask questions."

She rose. "Let me have the coat. I can use cold water, and iron it dry."

He pulled off the coat and gave it to her. When she started away he took her arm and turned her around and he smiled down at her and kissed her. He stepped back, flushed and more pleasant. "Where's the whisky?"

She went into the kitchen and presently came back with a bottle and a glass. He had stretched himself on the couch and motioned for her to pour his drink. She brought it to him and stood over him, looking down with her thoughtfulness. She was angry at him, but he knew she couldn't stand against him, and the knowledge made him careless of her. She understood that.

He said: "That kid's got sharp eyes. Suppose he noticed the stains?"

She moved away from the couch. She was inside the kitchen before she said: "Probably not."

"I'd shut him up if I thought so," he said.

She put the sleeve of the coat in a pan of water, but she straightened and she looked through the kitchen doorway at him. He didn't see her and he didn't notice the moment of anxiety which came to her face. She said in a carefully indifferent voice: "He wouldn't notice a thing like that. He's a little boy."

"Rat-faced boy," he said. "Hurry up on the coat. I want to get back to the Pioneer saloon and show myself."

The blood, dissolving from the coat sleeve, stained the water. Emily drew her hands quickly from it. She dumped the water and freshened the pan; she finished this distasteful chore and stood by the stove, waiting for the iron to heat. She seemed on the edge of tears.

"Floyd," she said, "why don't we get out of this town? Why don't we go to California? I've been wanting to go."

"My business is here."

She said: "Is it worth it?"

"I told you to stop asking questions."

"Don't always cut me up," she said. "You like to do it, but it isn't fair."

"Then take what you've got and don't ask

for anything more."

The conversation irritated him. He grew restless and he walked around the room. He came to a stop and began to stare at her in a way she hadn't noticed before — in a way that made her both hopeful and afraid. He had her on his mind; he was weighing and debating her.

"What, Floyd?"

" 'What, Floyd?' " he mimicked in an amused, malicious tone. "Have you always got to be boring at me?"

"No," she said, "I didn't mean to. I'm interested, that's all. I like to know what you think about. I'd like not to be so far away from you all the time."

"I'll come close enough — when I want to," he said.

"All right, Floyd."

That answer, too, irritated him. He stood in the center of the room, flushed, discontented and handsome. Rebellion displayed itself on his face, in the sharp light of his eyes, in the pulled corners of his mouth. "I suppose I can expect nothing more. I've never had anything more, in the way of women. I wonder how far I'd have to travel and how high I'd have to climb to get a woman who didn't sell herself or who didn't cheat."

She was curiously unmoved; her answer was

without resentment. "Any woman will cheat, Floyd."

"Any woman you'd know. But not any woman."

"Any woman," she repeated. "It's only a matter of what's important to her."

"No," he said, "there is such a thing as a good woman. I've seen enough of the bad ones to know that much."

"Any woman," she said in her softly stubborn voice. "The best woman in this town will lie and cheat and steal if it will get the thing she wants most. But she wouldn't call it lying or cheating. She'd say it was something she had to do because there wasn't anything else to do. What's a lie if it brings her something she'll have for the rest of her life? Women don't look at things the same as men, Floyd. A man says something is important, and he'll keep on thinking it's important all his life, even if he gives up a lot of other things for it. But a woman will get rid of something she used to believe important the very moment something else comes along which is more important."

"Oh, that's something else," said Ringrose. "Men don't always stick by the things they think important, either. They fall off."

"But they remember what they thought was important," pointed out Emily, "and it bothers them to fall off. They get sick of mind when they thinks they've broken their honor. They're always fighting against that thing. Women don't. When something isn't important any more, they quit worrying about it. Women don't fool themselves much. Men do."

Ringrose looked at her, interested, and skeptical. "Don't you think of what you used to be?"

Emily looked back at him without the least expression to betray her feelings. "That's different, Floyd. I had nothing then. I've got nothing now, Floyd — if something was important to me, I'd never give the past a single thought."

He shook his head and he began to talk as though he hadn't heard her. "When a man's been in the gutter the smell of it sticks to him all his life. Makes no difference where he goes or what luck he has, it is on him, and people know it. That's what drives me crazy."

"You're doing something wrong now," she said. "That's what got you upset. Quit and be straight. Then the past won't mean a thing. You're just lying to yourself, Floyd."

"No," he said, "I'll show these people, and when the time comes I'll have my pick of the best."

"You'll get what you deserve," she said.

"You'll get no more."

He made a gesture of impatience and left the room without answering. Coming out to Fourth Street, he was cautious enough to glance both ways on the dark street before sauntering northward. He was in a turbulent frame of mind, hating the world for its injustice to him and hating himself for weaknesses which had made him what he was. The sight of Emily, so heavy and common, had set him off on a bad train of thought. As he had more or less said to her, she was the only kind of woman he had known. Now and then along the past, he had met women of better quality and, pleased with his discovery, he had skillfully made his pursuit; yet sooner or later he had grown suspicious of his luck, wondering what flaw could be in them that they should find him desirable, and in the end he had found the flaw, or he had created the flaw by his aggression.

He paused to light a cigar and to walk on. He was cold, he was hot; he was self-condemning and he was a boiling compound of bitter ambition. "Well," he thought, "I came here to push my luck and make my change. If I survive it everything will be different. What was any man before he was great? Nothing but cheap stuff. And how did he get great except by taking the chances that came?

There's nothing else to it."

At Oak, on the point of crossing the street, he heard the solid steps of a man rattling the loose boards near by, and he looked in that direction with no amount of curiosity. The man was a shadow, a heavy shadow, but the shape of the shadow or the tempo of the man's steps brought Ringrose slowly around and he had a moment's violent debate with himself — to go on or to stay here. Before he could end the debate the shadow was upon him. It was Musick.

Musick stopped. His face tipped down and the expression upon it, challenging and confident and without courtesy, brought up in Ringrose the full violence he could not halt. He gave back a stare of equal challenge and equal insolence.

"Been around here once before tonight, haven't you?" said Musick.

"That's none of your business," said Ringrose.

"You tried to club me, and that's my business. You want some advice?"

"I want nothing from you."

"You," said Musick quietly, "are headed for a lot of trouble."

"Stay out of my way, then," said Ringrose. "It needn't concern you. I don't tolerate opposition from any man."

"I can tell you something," said Musick. "There's nothing in this town you'll ever get. There's no reward for you in the way of money or politics or friends. Not here. You started wrong and you'll end wrong. You're spotted. Your character's known by everybody, nor can you change that if you lived here a thousand years. You're the kind that needs a rabble to draw on. We don't have that kind in Portland. I'd advise you to pull out."

"That's enough," said Ringrose in his high-strung, end-of-patience tone. "Be done with it and get out of my way."

"But you'll cause somebody trouble," went on Musick. "You might get killed and you might get others killed."

"Keep on bothering me," said Ringrose, "and you may be one of those."

Musick was still for a moment, considering the remark. Then he said: "Let's take care of that now."

"What's that?"

"Now," said Musick. "Then it's done with and a lot of harm's saved. I know what you're up to."

"You'll never lay your hands on me again," said Ringrose.

"Sooner or later I will," said Musick.

"You'll never get that close," said Ringrose.

He drew his breath and once more was locked in violent debate with himself. He was not afraid of this man; he was afraid of no man. But he had felt Musick's knuckles before and he realized he had no more than an even chance. It was not enough; it put too much at stake. "No," he said, "you're the bully boy and you know it. You can push, but I'll wait my time."

"You're a piece of tin with no backing," said Musick.

Ringrose held his ground a moment, wishing to fight yet not wishing it. He said, "There'll be time enough to prove it," and went on across Oak Street without looking behind him. He thought he had acted wisely, but nothing he told himself could quite cover the feeling of smallness — that old feeling he had fought most of his life — which rose within him. "I'll kill him," he thought, but neither was that sufficient reassurance for his unstable pride.

12

At four o'clock of one more Monday morning, Musick followed Pine to the *Daisy*, had his breakfast and took his turn trucking the waiting freight aboard. The *Julia* lay below him and the *Claire* was at the wharf immediately above; thin clouds stood over the town and the cone of Mt. Hood was a beautiful silhouette against the day's changing light. The swollen, restless river carried a good deal of litter — silvered logs hitherto high and dry, chunks of brush from caved-in banks, a chicken coop from some farmer's back yard, a half swamped rowboat.

The town woke and the acrid fragrance of morning smoke drifted upon him, and men began to appear upon the street in a pattern which never varied, each man meeting the day in his particular manner, each with his characteristic motions, each turning the same corners and entering the same doorways. Ben Crowley came down Pine from his night's casual hideout and, with a gesture Musick had seen a hundred times before, looked up to the sky for a brief and blind moment; thereafter he went south on Front with his head lowered.

Musick stood in the pilothouse with his cigar, watching the mate of the *Claire,* Perry Judd, leave his boat and walk toward an angle of the wharf building where Phoebe McCornack waited; she stepped from the building wall and lifted her arms to him, and they remained in this frozen closeness until the *Claire*'s whistle broke the morning with its raw blast. Then Judd turned from the girl and went aboard; he stood a moment on the deck, lifting his cap, smiling at Phoebe and receiving her smile.

Day strengthened upon the land. It was a gentle land which took the sun's raw primary light and blended it into curved green slope, into the river willows, into the great fir masses, into the mist-touched horizons. There was no resistance to this country, no glitter, no fury, no extremes; it was a receiving land and a giving land. The rains fell and all things grew lush. The sun came and the warm mists rose and the air was charged with the reek of growth — and the softness, the everlasting softness, remained.

It was not a country of struggle or of anger. If men struggled and if men grew angry it was of their own making and their own folly. Even then the land whispered to them that nothing they destroyed would remain destroyed. Beside every fallen tree were the hundred seedlings to replace it, and in every gouged-out street was the telltale streak of grass beginning to grow. Men tramped their hard spots upon this land, and the land settled pliantly beneath them; but the ferment of birth remained with it so that when they stepped aside, the marks of their feet were soon lost in new turf. The power of the land was endless, the fertility unquenchable.

The *Julia* sent up her half-hour signal and again the street grew lively with the traffic of gold seekers and the hotel rigs ran along Front toward the Navigation Company dock. The scene was the same, yet this morning something had been added to it. Below the *Julia* lay the *Carrie,* which made the run on alternate days with her sister ship; today was her idle day and she should have been dark, but her lights were on and her steam was up and, from his position in the pilothouse Musick observed that passengers were going aboard both boats. Callahan, coming rapidly up to the pilothouse, brought the news he had already guessed. Bradshaw was at Callahan's heels.

Callahan said: "They've cut the fare in half and they're throwing in a free meal. The *Carrie* and the *Julia* are both makin' the daily run."

"They'd of let us alone," said Bradshaw,

"if we hadn't pushed Gorman too far." Always he had been afraid of this, and now he saw his dream of wealth dying, and it embittered him. He could not get his mind away from it. "We had a million dollars in our laps —"

"Before God," said Callahan, "I'm tired of hearin' you say that. Now shut up. What do we do next, Adam?"

"The next thing, I guess," said Musick, "is to go up the river this morning with an empty boat."

They had some freight, and a few wagons came aboard, Loren Wray's among these. Wray got to the passenger deck and hallooed above him, and came on up to the pilothouse. He saw dissension among the partners but he held his silence until Musick pointed toward the *Carrie* and *Julia*. "Both boats will now make the daily run. The fare's cut in half. You're losing money by traveling with us."

Wray nodded. "I saw it coming. Gorman was unhappy with you yesterday. He made up his mind to do you in. I could tell by the way he walked off the ferry."

"And what's that?" demanded Bradshaw. "What did you do to him, Adam?"

"We got in an argument. A private argument. It had nothing to do with this."

"Didn't it?" demanded Bradshaw. "You shook your shoulders at him, and we lose all we've got in this venture, and you say it had nothin to do with this." He gave Musick the blackest stare and left the pilothouse, slamming the door behind him.

"Ah, the fool," said Callahan, and went out after him. Wray stood still, watching the crowd cross over the gangplanks of both the *Carrie* and the *Julia*. He said nothing; but, looking at the older man's face, Musick noticed a disapproving and somewhat saddened expression.

"They can't keep it up forever," Musick said.

"They can keep it up longer than you. Their fist is bigger than your fist. It's the same old evil we have been fighting since the world began. Too much power."

The *Claire* moved upstream with a last shout of its whistle. Phoebe McCornack, still standing by the wharf-house wall, waved at Perry Judd and he swung his hat a last time at her; and in the background Webley Barnes and Lily watched the *Claire* carry away the cargo on which Webley pinned so much hope. At seven o'clock the *Julia* and the *Carrie* turned into the river, one on the heels of the other; and at seven-twenty, with fifteen passengers and part of a load of freight — the poorest trip in many weeks — the *Daisy* cast off lines. From the pilothouse he saw Lily lift her hand. She knew, and she was sorry for him. He saw it on her face.

"Loren," he said, "Ruckle's portage could be made free to all comers."

"How?"

"It is on the Oregon shore and subject to Oregon law. The legislature could condemn it and open it up as a public road."

Wray said nothing, nor even indicated he had heard the thought. Musick had no way of telling how his suggestion — which he had for two days intended to drop to Wray upon suitable occasion — had been received. A little later, putting the *Daisy* around in the channel, he quietly added: "Of course the Navigation Company has a lot of friends in the legislature. It might not be possible to open a free road."

Wray slowly turned and stared at him. He was a fighting sort of man and the notion stung him. "Well," he said, "the state of Oregon is, or ought to be, above the control of the Navigation Company."

At Rooster Rock the lightly loaded *Daisy* showed her heels to the other two boats and reached Ruckle's portage half an hour ahead. The passengers left the *Daisy* and Loren Wray departed with his team. Ten downriver travelers waited in the soft sunshine but all of them seemed to have through tickets on the Navigation Company. Musick descended from the pilothouse to give his partners a hand with the freight; they were finishing this chore when the *Julia* came up and tied to the *Daisy* and threw her plank over to the *Daisy*'s deck. The *Carrie* arrived soon afterwards and tied outside the *Julia,* the three boats thus fastened abreast and the passengers and freight of the two outer boats passing across the *Daisy* to the landing.

Musick climbed to the pilothouse and stood beside it with his cigar, watching the traffic of the other two boats flow shoreward below him. As soon as the passengers were out of the way the deckhands of both the company boats teamed up — eight of them — and began to hustle freight. Pope and Bradshaw had disappeared but Callahan sat idle on the *Daisy*'s bow, deliberately irritating the men of the other boats by his idleness. These men were loyal to their company and naturally had no love for the *Daisy* which so consistently beat their boats; and now and then Musick heard them ride Callahan with their talk as they went by him. Callahan's continued indifference was enough to goad them.

Bain called over from the *Julia*'s pilothouse. He had a knowing grin for Musick. "Got your tail in the wringer now, Adam."

"They'll get tired turning the wringer," said

Musick. "At half fare it's costing them money."

"They can lose money better than you," pointed out Bain.

"Nevertheless," said Musick, "every lost dollar bothers Gorman and his chums."

"You'll be off the river before it bothers 'em too much."

"No," said Musick, "we can tie up and wait until they get tired of half fare. It won't cost us anything."

"The day you tie up," said Bain, "they'll put the fare back."

"The next day the *Daisy* will go up the river."

"The day after that," said Bain, "they'll cut fare again."

"So they will," agreed Musick, "and pretty soon this up and down business will begin to look pretty raw to the public. You can kick a man in the belly too many times — then people begin to sympathize with the man on the bottom. It'll get under Gorman's skin."

Bain drew a cigar, cut it, lighted it and set it between his teeth. He stared at Musick, thinking about these tactics. He shook his head, and he opened his mouth to ask a question, changed his mind, and appeared slightly embarrassed. Afterwards he said: "Better sell out if he makes you an offer. The man's fair enough. He'll fight longer than you can, but he won't break you flat if you give in."

Musick said: "The *Daisy* runs as long as we can buy wood. I think I'll encourage people to lay their bets on how long the *Daisy* sticks. It ought to stir up the town."

A small crease ran across Bain's forehead. "Actually intend to do it?"

"I have got a lot of uncomfortable little things figured out. If Gorman wants to pick his rose he'll have to take the scratches that go with it." He watched Bain, knowing that this conversation would be faithfully reported back to Gorman. "I know his weak spot, Dave — and I know how your outfit can be licked."

"Licked?" said Bain with a short, challenging tone. "The hell it can." Then he said with a curiosity he could not suppress, "How?"

Half facing Bain and half facing the forward deck, Musick caught a bit of motion in the corner of his vision, and immediately following that he heard Callahan's rough shout. He looked down on the deck and saw Callahan spring up from the deck and jump aside as a bale of sacks fell from a hand truck, bounced on one edge and went overboard. Callahan pointed a finger at the *Julia*'s man pushing the truck. The *Julia*'s man let go the truck and made a swing at Callahan; he missed, and Callahan stepped in with his rising laughter and hit him hard enough to knock him all the way across the deck to the bulkhead.

It appeared to be a plain accident with the usual hotheaded conclusion, but it was not, for the *Julia*'s men and the *Carrie*'s men swarmed over to the *Daisy* too suddenly. They had been waiting for this break; they had manufactured it. Musick had a quick look at them and went tumbling down the ladder to the passenger deck and down the next ladder to the freight deck. He found Callahan, Pope and Bradshaw all engaged in a quick, bitter fight.

Bradshaw was no match for the two company men who presently engaged in chopping at him with their fists. Musick came up behind one of these, pulled him back and hit him as he turned. The man ducked and tried to ram him with his head. Musick cuffed him on the ears and lifted him out of his crouch and, spilling out the deck hand's wind with a short jab to the belly, gave him a heave over the side into the water. Before he could turn about he was caught from behind and a hard arm went about his neck. He dropped to his knee and swung his shoulders and threw his new assailant to the deck. Callahan had one of the *Carrie*'s men overboard and now charged into the tight crowd with his steady laughter. Bradshaw supported himself against a bulkhead, nursing his face, but Pope stood still in his tracks and sparred with one of the *Julia*'s men as methodically as he would have stoked his boilers. Musick stepped back into the engine room and caught hold of a short length of inch pipe lying by Pope's toolbox. He made a club of it and came up to the company's men.

"That's enough of it now."

Callahan found the game too good to stop. "Never mind it, Adam boy." He knocked aside the hands reaching for him, and got his heavy arms around another man, tripped him, and shoved him into the river. "There's another Baptist, Adam."

One of the *Carrie*'s men backed off and got as far as the gangplank. Musick trapped him there and knocked him from the plank. George Pope slowly stepped ahead with his man, slugging at him, making him give ground all the way to the bow. The man looked behind and saw he could retreat no more and he called out: "All right — that's enough," but Pope said in his unstirred voice: "Not enough — but this is," and pushed him off.

One man still lay on the deck and two had retreated to the *Julia,* and that was the end of it. Dave Bain called down from the pilot-house. "All right, down there."

Callahan looked up at Bain and put a thumb to his nose and waggled his fingers. "It looks

260

all right here, don't it?"

One of the men in the river was desperately calling: "I can't swim! Pull me out — pull me out!" Musick walked to the lone company man sitting half-dazed on the deck. He said: "You boys figure this out before you started from Portland?"

"I don't know anything about it," said the man and slowly got to his feet. "My teeth are loose."

"Who told you to start the fight?"

"I don't know nothin' about it," said the man and turned toward the gangplank. Musick stepped in front of him and he saw the man's face lift and show discomfort.

"How much extra were you promised for this little bit of fun?"

"I didn't say that, did I?" said the man. "Come on, now, let me go on to my business. Had your way, ain't you?"

Musick climbed to the pilothouse deck and stood a moment watching Bain. The latter stared back with a poker expression that covered more than innocence. Bain broke off the glance and removed his cigar and searched himself for a match. "Too bad. Boys were itchin' for it."

"Were they now?" asked Musick.

"That's the way it was," said Bain evenly.

"Well," said Musick, "they didn't make it,

but you'd better pay them the bonus any-how."

"What bonus?" demanded Bain. "It was just a fight. You didn't need to throw 'em in the river. Now we'll be half an hour late out of here."

"Didn't hear you call down to pull your men away," said Musick.

Bain apparently thought of an answer but swung on his heel and went back into his pilothouse without giving it.

At four-thirty Musick brought the *Daisy* back, and walked down to the saloon to have his drink. The other three partners came in with their various moods. To Callahan, this search for fortune never had been a serious pursuit and the loss of money was less to him than the losing of a fight. It was the fight and not the money he hated to lose. George Pope was not a man to be stirred greatly by any-thing; if it were not the *Daisy*'s engines he took care of, it would be some other boat's engines. But Bradshaw, long brooding, had nourished his injuries and was in a nasty state. He took liquor and drank it and let his pale eyes touch Musick with their hostile reproach.

"Well," said Callahan, "what do we do now?"

"Go broke," said Bradshaw.

"I was asking Adam, not you," said Callahan. "How long will they keep the rates down?"

"Long enough to ruin us," said Bradshaw.

Callahan gave Bradshaw the glance of a mean horse ready to lash out. Bradshaw ought to have taken warning, and normally would have done so. But his sense of loss made him blind and the desire for money made him brave. He met Callahan's look with one of equal truculence.

"Long enough for that, maybe," said Musick. "It depends on how fast we can think of a way to discourage Gorman."

Callahan grinned. "You'll have to do the thinkin', Adam. It is not this Irishman's long suit."

"And not Musick's long suit, either," said Bradshaw. "His talk got us into this."

Callahan cast a strained glance at Musick, silently begging the latter to stop Bradshaw. He saw nothing encouraging on Musick's face and he quietly closed his fist and looked down at it. He was a man at the edge of his patience.

"Lou," said Musick, "we're not broke yet."

"Fine words — fine words," said Bradshaw and put into the words a pure-distilled contempt. Callahan raised his eyes from his fist like a man dreading what he intended to do but unable to prevent it; and with a ponderous exasperation he swung around with his hand open and shoved his palm into Bradshaw's face. It seemed a slow, soft blow, but it sent Bradshaw backward half across the room. Callahan walked toward Bradshaw, not yet done with his wrath.

"Stop that," said Musick.

"I've had enough of his bellyachin'," said Callahan.

"We're all in this business together," said Musick. "We can't fight about it."

"That's it," said Callahan. "It is like a man listenin' to his wife nag, until he can't listen to any more of it. Lou, shut up or I'll break your damned neck."

George Pope, so silent, so motionless of mind, now slowly stirred on his seat and looked at Callahan. "Shouldn't have done that, Emmett."

"You believe what Lou believes?" demanded Callahan with a mark of surprise. "You believe it?"

Pope put his hands on the table and studied them. "Shouldn't have done it," he repeated.

Musick swallowed his whisky and put the glass on the table. He knew now how fugitively this partnership had rotted away. The thing which had sustained them through their months of sweating and long hours was no longer any good. It was a cement which somehow had gotten water on it and had no more binding power. The affection and the faith of their partnership had disappeared, and this he felt more keenly than any other kind of a loss. Callahan felt it, too. The Irishman was a fighter who loved loyalty; he would have cut off his arm for this partnership — and Bradshaw's sudden destruction of it outraged him. It was a kind of indecency he couldn't stand. Musick turned his glance to Pope, not knowing that somewhere in the man's slow mind a doubt slowly squirmed its way and made its hole. Bradshaw must have talked to Pope quietly and steadily over a long period, for Pope could never have come to his present attitude during this short scene. Musick looked at Bradshaw.

"Do you want me to buy out your interest, Lou?"

"What have you got for money?"

"Make an offer and take my note."

"A piece of paper I'd hold forever," said Bradshaw. "Your offer is worth no more than the suit of clothes you wear. That's all you're worth, the same as the rest of us. We've sweat out our lives on this boat, and you threw us away with foolish words to Gorman. I can't get that out of my head. We were so damned near to what we had in mind."

"Make an offer," insisted Musick, "and

we'll find another partner."

"Who?" asked Bradshaw, reluctantly interested.

"Make your offer," said Musick, "and we'll talk about it later." He left the saloon, Emmett Callahan coming with him. They crossed to the wharf and went along it in silence. It occurred to Musick that the *Claire* was not at her berth where she should have been and he stopped and surveyed the river for sight of her. Phoebe McCornack stood by the wharf building, awaiting the *Claire*'s return. She was in the same place she had been that morning.

"*Claire* must have been delayed at Oregon City," he commented.

"A bad thing," said Callahan. "That, I mean," he added and flung a hand toward the *Daisy*. "It will take a lot of whisky to wash the taste of that away."

"He'll get over it," said Musick, thinking of Bradshaw.

"The want of money is a torment to him, like the want of a woman is a torment to the rest of us. There is something wrong about money. I do not know what — but there's something to it which ruins a lot of people. I stood in that saloon a minute ago, and I thought what fine times we'd all had, but then Lou got to talkin' and I knew the fine times were gone, and that made me mad. There are

266

just two things which are good — what a man gets out of his own self alone, and what he gets from a woman. The rest of livin' is trouble and nothin'. I'm going to get drunk."

He turned north toward that quarter of town which held the cheaper and the rougher saloons. There he would drink and there he would pick a fight, and during the night Lappeus would have a riot on his hands and Emmett would wake in jail. Proceeding up Pine Street in scarcely a better frame of mind, Musick saw Ben Crowley come out of a narrow between-building space. Crowley noticed him, and halted. Crowley was sober but Crowley's eyes were queer; they had a look of begging in them and with that was the small expression of shame which came of his begging. Crowley's glance brushed Musick and fell down. His voice was husky and ragged. He had been sober too long.

"Adam," he said, staring at the walk, "I been a little sick lately. Ate something, I guess. Ain't had much strength to work. I —"

Embarrassment came to Musick. Ben Crowley had begged from others often before, but his victims were men whom he felt no hesitancy in approaching. Somewhere within his mind was a standard, and this standard had kept him away from Musick. Now he had broken it. He stopped Crowley's talk. He said:

"I've noticed it, Ben. You ought to go see Dr. Parris." He dropped a five-dollar gold piece into Crowley's hand and turned away.

Crowley said: "That was tough about the *Claire*, wasn't it?"

Musick wheeled about. "What about the *Claire*?"

Crowley's face brightened when he realized he could give Musick something which the latter did not have. "Why, she struck the reef above Oswego and sunk, carrying everybody down with her except Mike Neal."

Musick remembered Phoebe and he looked down Front, but could not see her because of the wharf building intervening. He had the notion to go back, but he thought: "Nobody can help anybody else's trouble." A moment later he remembered that Webley Barnes's venture was wiped out. He said: "Thanks, Ben, I didn't know it," and continued up Pine.

He walked slowly, hating to enter the Barneses' house, and hating to face Webley. It occurred to him soon afterwards that Webley would not be at the house. Webley would be in the Pioneer drinking himself out of his misery, and Lily would be home alone. He quickened his pace and for the first time he had a feeling of impatience toward Webley Barnes. Webley was a man badly beaten about by the world, neither strong enough to meet misfortune nor buoyant enough to laugh at it; in that respect he was to be pitied. But Webley had reached the point where he was so buried in his own troubles that he had forgotten Lily was a part of them and was equally hurt by them.

He went into the house and saw her in the kitchen. She didn't look around. He hung up his cap and coat and he stood a moment at the rack, finding nothing easy to say. He hated to meet her eyes; it was suddenly harder to do than anything he had before tried to do. But he turned and walked to the kitchen, and he waited for her to swing about. She kept on with her chore, slowly stirring a spoon around a pan; he saw her profile, its tightness, its emptiness — and then he walked to her and laid a hand on her shoulder and brought her around. She looked up at him, refusing to show him anything, and for a moment he could easily have believed she hated him — not because he had any part in her troubles but because her bitterness had to have a target, and he was the target.

"Webley at the Pioneer?" he asked.

"Yes."

"I'll go get him."

"Let him drink it out." She pulled from him. "Supper's ready." She dished it up and put it on the table; she sat down across the table from him, sipping at her coffee. The hardness went easily from her; it had been a passing thing — perhaps it had been something she had used to keep herself from crying when he came in. There was misery in her, but she suffered it passively — and it was at that moment he lost most of his respect for Webley. Webley had leaned on her too long. Webley had hurt her too much with his misfortunes, with his immature helplessness. He had turned her from a carefree girl into a woman carrying troubles she oughtn't to have had.

"He'll never try anything again, Adam. This broke him. When the news came he walked out of the house an old, old man."

"Tough."

She said: "I was afraid of that deal. I felt something wrong about it when he first told me. I think he did, too. But why does it always happen to him? It isn't fair!"

"Nothing's fair," he said.

"Other people who are small and narrow and mean somehow get what they want. All he wanted was to be kind and to enjoy life. It isn't right."

"Nothing's right unless we force it right."

"Adam," she said, "people can't live that way. People can't be fighting and threatening and beating other people senseless. Life ought not to be that brutal."

"It oughtn't," he said, "but it is."

"The clenched fist — you believe in that, don't you?"

"I wish I didn't need to. But I do."

"Do you believe in anything else?"

"I'd like to," he said, "but I don't. Your father believed in gentleness. See what happened to him. Men will push as far as they can. Nothing stops them but a fist."

"It wasn't a man — it was a rock which sank a ship."

"A man or a rock. It's all the same. Men will claw and rocks will rip. Nothing saves us except the power to fight back. We've got to do it. There's no other way."

"Adam, I hate that streak in you."

"Yes," he said, "I know you do." He rose, seeing that dislike in her eyes which he had seen before. He walked into the front room and got his coat and cap and turned around. She was watching him. She had turned in her chair to follow him with her glance, to speculate about him, to leave something with him which always had an effect on him.

"I wish," he said, "I could say that everything will work out in the end. But I'd be a hypocrite if I said it, for I don't believe it. Nothing works out, unless you make it work out. The strongest thing wins, the weakest thing loses. That's not much comfort to you."

"If you were kind or sympathetic with me," she said, "I would have cried. But I'm sorry for you, Adam. I'm sorrier for you than for Dad."

He weighed her remark until he understood it. "No," he said, "I'm having fun. I can make a game out of fighting to survive. It's a good game."

"Wait until you're older and you're no longer able to depend on your fists, and everybody knocks you around. Then you'll be miserable. Then you'll see."

He smiled at her. "Well, we all wish for better things."

She said: "I'm never sure what you really believe. At times I think there's nothing in you but the desire to fight. Then I see other things which are so much nicer. I never know."

13

The Pioneer barroom was always a crowded place; for this town it was a stock exchange, a public market, a lodge hall, a center for the kind of gossip the *Oregonian* could not print, a clearinghouse for public opinion. Musick, entering it, noticed Elijah Gorman deep in conversation with a group of men at the far end of the room. Gorman saw him and made a point of nodding, and an equal point of returning to his conversation. Barnes was at a table and gave him a vague smile when he came up. A good deal of whisky had softened Webley's disaster; the firm lines of the man's face were smeared and the instability of Webley's character lay now close to the surface.

"Supper on the table?" asked Webley.

"Yes," said Musick.

"Nothing new," said Webley. "Supper and sleep and breakfast and work. The same thing over and over."

"Sure," said Musick.

"Failure — that's old, too," said Webley. "Older than anything else."

Webley still had a drink to finish. Musick

went to the bar for a glass and came back to keep Webley company. George Hale drifted up to make talk.

"You cutting rates to meet the company?"

Other men turned, hearing the question and interested in it. He had a ready-made audience, Musick discovered, and he noticed that Elijah Gorman observed the audience and was interested in it. Musick said to Hale: "What would you do?"

"You'll go broke on cut rates," said Hale.

"Suppose we lay up until they restore rates?" asked Musick.

George Hale thought about that a considerable length of time; and the rest of the crowd got interested and began also to think of it. Musick saw something then that heartened him. These men were for him. They were trying to think of something for him. "No," said George Hale. "The company will lift the rates when you quit, and drop 'em when you start again."

"Up one day and down the next," pointed out Musick. "Maybe people will get tired of trying to follow it. Maybe they'll wonder if it is right."

George Hale looked at him and began to grin. "Can you do it? Can you hang on long enough?"

Elijah Gorman had seen George Hale's

amusement. That broke him out of his tracks and brought him over to the circle. There was something here he didn't understand and Musick once more realized how great was Gorman's need to have his company and himself well thought of. George Hale's amusement troubled him more than George Hale's anger would have done. He came into the circle and looked around at these men, searching their faces. He said to Musick, "Hear you had trouble with our deck crews. That was unfortunate. I'm sorry it happened. It won't happen again."

"Your deck crews," said Musick, "are sorrier. You may need a couple new crews for tomorrow. Those boys are beaten out."

Gorman was as much of a fighter as any of his deck hands; fair or unfair, it sat hard on him to have his crew get the worst of a fight and no amount of smoothness could quite hide the wry reaction of his face.

"You understand," he said, "that was their idea."

"I don't know," said Musick. "I can't read minds."

George Hale's grin sharpened and the surrounding men caught the remark and were amused. This was the way he could fight Elijah Gorman, knowing Gorman's careful cultivation of the town's goodwill. Gorman stood

275

still, slowly toughening. He would, Musick knew, be thinking of a way to destroy this sort of opposition.

"Come now," said Gorman, "you're trying to spread the impression that the company will use improper means to do you up. That is unfair. This company is too big a thing and has too much at stake to embrace dishonesty or force."

"I don't know," said Musick. "You squeeze me by reducing rates. That's force. I don't know where you'd stop in the matter of using force."

"A rate is business," said Gorman. "It is fair competition."

"It is fair competition if you keep the rate down when you've lowered it. It is force if you jockey it around to freeze out people and milk your traffic dry."

"It is a matter of competition," repeated Gorman. "Our country is built on it. The moment competition is destroyed our country will be destroyed."

He was talking to the audience around him rather than to Musick. He was driving home his philosophy, he was arguing his case before the town, he was seeking with his words to erase the unpleasant and unpopular thought that his company was Goliath bearing down on David. He did not want Musick to be David in Portland's mind; he was distinctly worried about it. "If you are as valuable to the community as the company is, you will be able to stay on the river. Otherwise you will fade, like any concern which is not strong. Only strong concerns serve a country well."

"Only strong concerns," said Musick, "can play freeze-out. I do not doubt you will serve the community well, on your own terms."

Gorman shook his head. "Naturally you are bitter. You see yourself — you do not see the community. The company makes this land grow. It binds Portland with the inland, it makes a great port of this town. It brings prosperity to everybody."

"It is also so afraid of losing a dollar that it cannot let a competitor operate. If we were too weak to handle business, we'd die off without any force on your part. The point is you are not willing to let us prove whether we can or can't. Your company is a hog with all four feet in the trough."

Gorman squared his jaws. He stared at Musick with all the pressure of his angered will, and then he curtly said: "That was an unseemly remark," and pushed his way through the crowd, departing from the saloon.

George Hale said: "You got under his skin."

"It is his pocketbook I got into," said Musick. "Skin starts there with the Navigation

Company." He touched Webley's elbow, supported the man to his feet and moved him homeward.

Mr. McGruder, having spent the day in discreet research, found himself standing in an alley's blackness across from Ryan's stable. There had been a meeting of the Knights which now was dissolving. Men came from the stable, knotted up to talk, and then in small groups they went down Pine and turned north on First. All of them went in the same direction, which seemed to be a matter of note. After the last one had left Ryan's, Mr. McGruder waited a discreet moment to make sure he was not involved in a trap, then left his hideout and went up to Third. He walked rapidly to Ash, followed Ash to the darkness quite near First, and took stand in time to see these people pass him. They were still moving north and as soon as they had gone, Mr. McGruder hurried to Front, there to put himself against the side of a house.

This was a repetition of his former indirect procedure, based upon a guess; and the guess was excellent, for he soon discovered his party straggling out of Second. He squatted against the building wall and counted them as they passed.

They vanished toward the river. Looking

that way he saw nothing but the outline of a three-story building which seemed to have been abandoned before completion, the upper stories scarcely more than skeleton work. He heard the steps of the men die out and though he watched closely to either side of the building he discovered no shadows passing in either direction; they had gone into the building.

He stepped down B Street, close beside the wall of a brick store; when the wall ended the sidewalk also ended and he came upon a spongy, wagon-rutted mud. The front of the incompleted building loomed over him and its shadows reached out to thicken the ordinary shadows of the night. He struck a shallow pool of water and made a small racket, and he clucked his tongue with self-dissatisfaction and slowed his pace; then he discovered the pool was not a pool but rather the edge of the river which, at flood stage, had climbed out of its banks at this low point. By the time he reached the front of the building — at once placing an ear against its wall — he was in water up to the calves of his legs.

There was nothing to be heard through the wall, though he listened with long patience; and so he stepped gingerly along the wall until his hands found a break which turned out to be a doorway without a door. He stopped and was momentarily doubtful of the wise course to take; and during the next sixty seconds he cast up his chances, weighed them against his hopes, and came to his choice. What influenced him in his decision more than any other thing was a phrase now forming in his mind; it was the phrase with which he wanted to begin his nightly report to his superior in San Francisco: "Tonight I came upon the Conspirators and learned their Intentions. I flatter myself I shall soon resolve this Business favorably." That was the phrase which at last pushed him through the doorway into the building.

He had no knowledge of the building's interior. Spreading both hands before him, he laid his weight carefully upon both feet and pushed his legs through water which now touched his knees. To the left of him he discovered a wall; swinging to the opposite direction he came upon another wall. This, then, was a corridor which no doubt had offices leading from it. Rubbing the tips of his fingers across the wall, and steadily advancing, he discovered a doorway which undoubtedly was the entrance of one such office. He went by this doorway a few feet, then stopped to take his bearings and to listen into the hollowed-out stillness of the place, disturbed by the thought that though there were twelve men somewhere within this place, no sound of them emerged.

He heard only the rubbing of the river against the building's outer wall and only those stray and sibilant sounds which were the breath of any vacant building. He said to himself: "Now, then, McGruder, I do not like this business. They should not be so infernally quiet, and there should be a light somewhere to indicate their meeting. Have I given these animals a smell in the wind?"

Somewhere in the building was a stairway, probably at the end of this corridor, and up there were no doubt a good many other rooms. The whole place was, in fact, a rabbit warren well-suited for the purposes of the crowd he followed. "They will be as high as they can get, and at the front so as to look out on the street and watch it." Pushing forward, he added a sentence to his letter: "I have the Honor to remind you that in my many years of successful Work —"

A thin sound ripped the stillness, and a match burst before him. By the glow of the match he saw three men standing not a yard distant, turned toward him and obviously long waiting for him. One of those faces instantly told him of his own end — for it was the face of Ringrose, and Ringrose was a man whose quality he well knew. He had but one recourse, which was to kill the match light and to make a run back along the corridor.

As he ducked to scoop up water and fling it at the match in Ringrose's hand, he heard the man say: "Hit him," and a club came down on his head, and the impact of it was a flash of light and a bolt of agony down his spine; he felt himself torn inwardly apart — he felt himself die as he pitched head foremost into the water.

14

At the breakfast table these mornings of the past two weeks Webley had said very little; there was a shrinking away to him. His pleasant surface remained — in fact he seemed to take pride in the fixed charm of his old manner; but it was about all he had left to him, this surface which covered a heartbreak which was not too tragically felt, a disillusionment which was not too severe. Webley Barnes's life had been a series of roles — there was that actor's streak in him; and this smiling acceptance of disaster was his new role.

He finished his meal and looked at his watch; he rose, said, "Time to unlock the office," and moved across the living room toward the door. There, with the door open, he turned his head and looked behind him, and for a moment Musick observed the curiosity and the concern lightly printed on his face. It was the slightest of pauses but it left its effect after he had gone from the house.

Lily freshened Musick's coffee and her own; and she did what she had always done — she joined him at the table to finish her breakfast.

"Do you see the difference in him?" she asked.

"No. He's neither happier nor unhappier than he was."

"He's changed."

He reached for the paper. He wanted no argument with Lily; he wanted to say nothing which would touch her loyalty to her father, and he did not want her to know that his own regard for Webley Barnes was thinned by the conviction that Webley was a boy still leaning on a woman. He found himself reading the *Oregonian*'s lead editorial. Election time was nearing and this town had slowly taken on a tenseness and a perceptible anxiety. Men's tempers were shorter, including Harvey Scott's, whose editorial treatment of the Copperheads in Oregon was a slashing, savage bit of prose. Musick read it with pleasure — and then heard Lily call him out of his thoughts. "You're too hard on people. You expect them to be too much. You expect Father to be like you are."

"I've said nothing," he pointed out.

"I know what you think."

He got up from the table. He was disturbed; he disliked what he had done. "Don't pay attention to what I say or what you think I think."

She stared at him and she said something

which surprised him. "You wouldn't be much good if you changed. You'll never successfully change."

"What was Webley thinking when he looked back at me?"

She rose to clear the table. When she wished to hold her thoughts away from him, she usually put on an expression of seeming interest in whatever chore she happened to find for her hands. This was the way it was now. She, too, had known what was in Webley's mind.

"I've been hanging around the house too much," he said. "I've got to find something to do."

"When will you run the *Daisy* again?"

"Soon as the Navigation Company lifts its rate."

"That may not be. What do you think you'd do if you lost the *Daisy*?"

"I've talked to Fisher about his ranch up the river."

"You expect to lose the *Daisy*?"

He grinned at her. "You think we'll lose?"

"The company's too powerful."

"Want me to give up now?"

"You couldn't. You wouldn't be happy. There will always have to be a fight in whatever you do."

"What else do you know?" he asked. He stepped aside as she moved by him with the dishes, and her nearness set off its shocks within him. His vision was like the lens of a camera narrowing down until he saw only the full swell of her lips and their increasing heaviness. She stopped and she turned her head. She saw what was in him. "Nothing else," she said.

"Your father's right," he said.

"Is he?"

These words had a wooden sound, her words and his words. They meant nothing; they were things to fill in a dangerous silence. Her expression was strained and her mouth lost its fullness; it became long and tight and unpretty.

"Adam — no."

He left the kitchen and took his cap and opened the door; but he turned and he found her standing in the same place. She was watching him.

"Next week," he said, "I'll move to the boat."

"It might be wise."

"Your father thinks so."

"I suppose he does. Edith thinks so too, doesn't she?"

"Yes."

She shrugged her shoulders. "Well," she said, and turned away with the sentence unfinished.

He left the house and went along Pine toward Front with the morning air fresh against his face; he traveled with his head down and his mind full of rapid, incomplete thoughts. At Front he paused to fill his pipe and light it. Directly across the street, over Webley Barnes's store doorway hung a sign now two weeks old: —

THE DAISY McGOVERN

We can't make a profit on half fare. Neither can the Navigation Company. We will be back on the run when the company gets tired of taking a loss.

Elijah Gorman had not spoken to him since the posting of the sign, but he realized Gorman would never rest until he found a way of getting rid of that open threat to the company's prestige. Portland would be talking — and that was the thing which Elijah Gorman did not like. Musick crossed to the levee, observing election notices posted on the warehouse wall. He walked the *Daisy*'s plank and discovered the partners in the saloon, idle after their breakfast.

Callahan said: "Anything new?"

"No."

"Well," said Callahan, "we've got an idea.

It ain't mine — it's Bradshaw's, he turned crazy from watching the money slip by."

Pope had not spoken. Bradshaw, still in his sullen and injured frame of mind, gave Musick the shortest of glances. There was a man, Musick thought, who had gone sour and would never again be what he had been. "Well," he said, "I could stand an idea."

"We might pick up a little money," said Callahan, "while we're waiting for the company to come around. We might work the downriver run."

"I don't mind," said Musick. "But what do you want to work for? This is the first rest we've had in two years."

"Oh, hell," said Callahan, "I'm sick of it."

Musick looked at Bradshaw and Pope. "That agreeable?"

"You're the Captain," said Bradshaw sharply.

"Lou," said Musick, "this is bad business."

"Of your making," said Bradshaw.

Musick refused to pick up the quarrel. "Make your offer, Lou, and I'll agree to buy you out."

"You haven't got a damned dime and nobody'd be fool enough to lend you anything. Anyhow, I'll stay in to protect myself. I can think of ways of doing it."

"What would that be?" asked Musick, his interest rising.

"Never mind," said Bradshaw, "but remember it. I'm out for my money."

Callahan sighed, once more outraged at the indecency of a friendship going bad. "Lou, my boy, is there nothing but the want of money in you?"

Bradshaw turned his bitter eyes on the big Irishman. "You're a dumb one, you are. I can take a thousand dollars and buy all the friends I want."

Musick shook his head at Callahan who seemed ready to rise and reach out to Bradshaw with his big fists. "That won't do it, Emmett."

"No," agreed Callahan. "Nothing will do it, I guess. Corruption is corruption — and strange places you find it, too."

"Well, let's pull downriver in the morning," said Musick, "and see what business we can pick up. It will do for a change."

Callahan left the boat with him. Callahan walked on without comment, his long legs striking hard against the boardwalk. He had a thought in him and the thought was hard to express; in the end he never found the proper words for it. All he could say was: "Now there's a good sun shinin' on us — and do we deserve it, Adam? I'd like to know.

What're men so miserable little for? What was born in 'em which is nothin' but brass and dirt, and what of it is of our own filthy makin'? I am not proud of what I know, not a bit."

"What do you think he'd do?" asked Musick, remembering Bradshaw's veiled threat.

"Anything a dog would do, and some things a dog would not," said Callahan.

They were at Yamhill when Edith Thorpe, coming out of Brecken's general store with her market basket, saw them and stopped. She said, quite gaily, "Why, Adam!" and her smile had its sudden brilliance for him. "You can carry this home for me, can't you?"

Callahan removed his hat. He stood aside with his beaming, gallant interest; his face had admiration on it as he watched the girl and waited for her attention. She gave him the slightest side glance and dismissed him very obviously from her mind by turning her glance back to Musick. Callahan's brow creased somewhat and he was uncertain of himself, and uncertainty grew to discomfort. Presently he said, "I'll go along." But before he wheeled away he gave Edith a sharper glance than before, and Musick saw the Irishman's native keenness in the glance and his quick judgment of the girl.

Musick took the basket from Edith, not content with his small scene. He walked beside Edith, down Front to Salmon and up Salmon. She was gayer than she had been; she was somewhat more demonstrative than was her normal manner. She touched his arm and looked up at him, laughing a little. "Do you mind carrying groceries?"

"No," he said.

"You shouldn't. You'll be doing it when we're married, won't you? Or will you be like Mr. Foster whose pride won't let him carry anything in his hands but a cane?"

"I guess I'll have plenty of time to shop," he said.

"Idleness doesn't make you happy," she said. "You have so much vigor that you can't stand it."

He went obediently with her, listening to her and occasionally answering. When they came to the Thorpe house he took the market basket into the kitchen, and came back to the front room. She was waiting for him; she came toward him, her mind obviously made up and her gestures full of assurance. She watched him closely and her smile, so deliberate with its meaning, was the plainest kind of an invitation. She put her arms around him, like a gesture carefully rehearsed, and lifted her mouth. Her eyes remained open when he kissed her and afterwards, done with the kiss, he straightened and saw she had not closed them. They were aroused and no screen of modesty covered their brightness. She wanted him to see this; she was making her offer to him.

A terrible disappointment came upon him and left him both miserable and cold. She remained in his arms with her head tipped back; and as he looked upon her he had a straining wish to see in her lips or upon her face the reflection of some other thing which would give grace to the hunger she showed him. He didn't see it. She was a body and a willingness. That was what she thought he wanted, and that was what she was promising him.

He tried to keep his feelings away from his face, knowing that her glance so frequently caught the shadows which passed through him. She broke the moment with a soft laugh, the laugh of a woman waking from a warm and pleasant dream. She moved away to the far side of the room and put her back to the wall, and whispered a question to him.

"Are you shocked?"

"No."

"Then you are pleased with your conquest?"

"Was it a conquest, Edith?"

"I resisted you, didn't I? I hid from you, until I couldn't pretend any more. You ought to know about me now. Do I suit you? Is there enough of me to keep you content?"

"Yes," he said, "there's enough."

"I think there will be," she said, so smooth and confident. But her smile was tightening; she had seen what was in him. "I do think I've shocked you. You are like all other men. I would never have shown you this if you had not been so plainly disappointed with my modesty. I had to make a choice, didn't I? I had to show you I wasn't cold, didn't I? You wanted to know. You were very urgent. You've found out. Didn't you find what you wished?"

"Yes," he said.

"Well, then," she said and turned gay. "Mrs. Latourell is making my dress. Do you wish to set the time?"

"That's your choice, isn't it?"

"I'll ask her when the dress is to be done. Then I'll set the time."

She came over to him with her smile, and touched his arm. She was almost laughing at him. "Why, you're afraid. I'd think you'd changed your mind if I hadn't heard other men tell me what happens to men."

"What happens to them?"

"Buck fever," she said, and lifted herself on her toes to kiss him. "Go along. Find some of your friends. I shan't mind if you really get drunk tonight."

"Edith," he said, "you're on dangerous ground."

"You like danger, don't you?"

"I don't like what comes out of it sometimes."

"Well, Adam, you're the judge of that. You want a woman, don't you?" The strain lessened on her face, the touch of self-consciousness or disappointment went away. She was excited, she had passed some limit in herself. She murmured, "It's wonderful to be alive."

"Edith," he said, "remember, you can't change back."

She looked closely at him. "How do you mean that?"

"What you are now you'll always have to be."

"What else could I be?"

"The woman you were two months ago."

For a moment — for the briefest of moments — he saw an expression on her which mirrored her old manner, its cool, stiff resistance. He saw it and was warned by it; then it disappeared before her restored cheerfulness. "You'll never entirely know what I am. It would be such a dull marriage if you did. You go along."

He left the house with his self-dissatisfaction growing stronger. How much of this new

Edith was of his making, how much of it was he responsible for? He did not ask himself which Edith, the cool one or the warm one, was the true Edith. There was no solving that puzzle, for every woman was a mixture. But what had he done to her which she had not wanted done? She had put the responsibility on him — and she had asked him if this was not what he wanted.

He reached for a cigar, knowing that he had lied to Edith. He had been shocked, which was a strange thing when he considered he had looked into her eyes for more than a year with the hope of finding what he had at last found. What the hell did he want if not this? Was he so changeable that he ceased to be interested when a woman's resistance faded? He could not answer the question; he only knew that the day had gone wrong, that a moment which ought to have been great had not come off.

Edith stood before the window and watched Musick travel slowly down the street. Her face was pleased, and this was what Grandmother, coming from the lower bedroom, saw. She met Grandmother's inquisitive eyes. "I suppose you heard it all. Did I do it well enough to please you?"

"Ah," said Grandmother and clucked her

tongue. "You made him fight against himself. But —" and she gave Edith a sharp glance, "supposing he hadn't resisted himself?"

"I don't know," said Edith. "I don't know." Then her assurance broke and she shook her head. "It is so difficult. How do I know if he's pleased? He hates me cold — but he's shocked because I'm warm. How do I know what to do?"

"Well," said Grandmother, "it ain't easy. A man's a wonderful animal for dreamin' things. That man dreamed a lot of things into you. He put them there because he wants 'em there. He wants your body, Edie, but he ain't altogether satisfied with that. He wants it mysterious. You got to be Emily von Gratz when you go to him. But you got to be an angel, too. You see?"

"No," said Edith, "I don't."

"Ah," said Grandmother, "neither do I. But that's the way men are. Edie, don't be grieved too much if you don't get him."

"I've got him," said Edith. "He won't leave me now."

"He might."

"He has a sense of honor," said Edith.

"A man can quit a woman after he's kissed her and feel no dishonor," said Grandmother. "I believe I'll heat a pan of milk," she added, and went into the kitchen. She was thinking to herself: "I wonder if he's touched her?" and grew warm and curious over the question. She well knew what Adam wanted but she didn't believe he'd get it. People, Grandmother believed, so seldom did. Mostly they got whatever was at hand and made it do somehow; mostly it was a bed, a baby and a lot of misery.

15

Ringrose came to Emily's house as soon as darkness filled the town. She was in the kitchen when he opened the back door and stepped in. The unexpectedness of it startled her. "Floyd," she said, "I wish you wouldn't do that. I want you to knock."

He grinned at her disturbance; there was that unexplained malice in him. "You'll get used to it," he said. "I'll never knock."

"Then," she said, "I'll lock the door."

"And then," he retorted, "I'll break your damned windows and crawl in and teach you better manners. Don't ever lock a door against me. I don't like that treatment."

Something excited him this night. She saw the pale flickering of it in his eyes. He stood with his hand on the door's knob. He ducked his head at her and said, "The kid around?"

"No!"

He said: "Now, Emily, keep your mouth shut and don't ask any questions," and he opened the door and walked into the darkness of the rear yard, calling quietly to somebody. Emily went to the doorway and saw two shapes, Ringrose's and another man's, paused by the woodshed which stood twenty feet behind the house. One of them drew back the woodshed door and then both went into the shed. A match broke the blackness of the shed and a lantern began to glow; by it she observed there were three men instead of two. Telliver was one of the newcomers but the other she didn't know.

The shed door remained open. Ringrose held the lantern over Telliver who seemed to have brought two or three sticks of cordwood with him. He dropped the cordwood and he reached for some kind of a tool which the third man carried. Ringrose spoke to Telliver in a very low voice and came out of the shed, leaving the lantern behind him, and closed the shed door.

Emily was in the living room when he returned to the house. He came through the kitchen and he looked over the room to her with that bright and dangerous interest which she had once before noticed. "What did you see?" he asked.

"What are you doing?" she countered.

"I said not to ask questions. What did you see?"

"What are you up to in my shed?"

"It would do you no good to know," he said.

"I won't have any dirty business around here. I won't have it."

He watched her with that calculating unsympathetic manner which usually turned her afraid. She meant nothing to him. He had no conscience about her. He could laugh at her, or be kind to her, or kill her; it made no difference to him at all. "Well," he said, "what will you do?"

She stood before him without answering, and he recognized her fear and he suddenly smiled and softened. "You couldn't do anything. You know it, don't you? Don't worry about it. Nothing will happen. Maybe I'll treat you to diamonds one of these days."

"I don't want your diamonds," she said.

"I've heard women say that. But they never mean it. Maybe we'll go to San Francisco. You want that, don't you?"

"Anything," she said. "Anything to get out of here."

"Well," he said, "it won't be long. But don't ask any questions. I'll —"

He whipped around with an astonishing swiftness, having heard something which she had not. Billy Gattis stood in the kitchen; he had very quietly opened the rear door and had come through.

"Boy," said Ringrose, "I told you today to stay away from here, didn't I?"

"Floyd," said Emily, "it's none of your business."

"I have got no use for sneaks," said Ringrose.

"Don't say that," said Emily. "You ought to be ashamed."

Billy Gattis said: "You got somebody prowlin' in your woodshed. That's why I was quiet."

"You worried about it, boy?" asked Ringrose.

"Well," said Billy, "what they doin' there?"

"Maybe we had better go see," said Ringrose. "That's the thing to do, isn't it?" He walked over to Billy; he laid an arm on the boy's shoulder and turned him around and pushed him toward the door. "We'll find out what's wrong."

"Floyd!" said Emily.

Ringrose's hand dug into the boy's shoulder; he opened the door, pushed Billy from the kitchen, followed him and closed the door. Emily let out a labored breath and rushed for the door. She heard the scuffle on the back steps; she heard the sharp crack of two blows — like an open hand against Billy's face — and she heard Billy's brief cry of distress; then a body fell down the steps and the boy's cry came again. Emily's desperate glance raked the kitchen. She saw the teakettle on the stove, the stove lifter, the quart milk can on the shelf — and she saw the filled wood box. She reached down and seized a stick of wood and opened the door. Ringrose was on the porch with his back to her, listening to the running feet of Billy as the latter rushed away between the buildings. Emily, meaning to hit Ringrose on the head, missed her aim and struck his shoulder; when he came about to defend himself she jabbed the end of the wood into his face and knocked him off the porch.

He rose, swearing at her and threatening her, but she hit him again and drove him back. "Emily," he said, "stop it!" and he came up to the porch with a sudden spring and twisted the wood from her hand. He pushed her through the doorway, and by the kitchen's light she saw the blood on his face. He put a hand up to his mouth and drew it away, and when he discovered the blood on his palm he slapped her, first with one hand and then with the other. She drew her arms up around her head, waiting to be hit again. Instead, he shoved her into the living room and walked away from her.

"I don't want that kid near here any more," he said. "You understand me?"

She sat down on the couch. Her face stung from his blows and her ears rang. She bent over and covered her face with her hands and began to cry; she made a whimpering, gushing noise as she cried.

"Quit it," said Ringrose, "you're an overgrown kid, just sloppy with nonsense. You've got to learn."

"Get out of here," she said. "Don't come back."

"I'll do what I want — and you'll do what I say. Then we'll get along fine."

She sat still, not looking at him. She was speaking silently to herself in helpless phrases and her thoughts were stupid and slow. But they grew clearer and they grew more bitter. This was the way Ringrose treated his women, this was the way any Ringrose treated any Emily. She could have forgotten about it if there were any kindness in him, but he was a tiger; he wasn't human. He could kill her and think nothing of it. She had let herself hope that they could stick together and make something of it. That was no use. A lot of other women had known Floyd Ringrose and they had found out the same thing. He used up women and laughed at them and didn't give them anything, and threw them away.

It didn't matter too much. Nothing did, after the hurt wore off. But Billy had been injured enough to cry, Billy who didn't usually cry. That made her thoughts clearer. There was nothing she could do about herself, for she was what Floyd had said she was, a big sloppy fool. Billy's hurts were different and as she thought of this boy, who was the nearest thing to a son she could have, she began to brood protectingly over him and her thoughts toward Ringrose grew scheming and vindictive, and the easy-going looseness left her.

Ringrose said: "I want a drink."

"Get it yourself."

"Come on, old woman, I'm not so bad."

She didn't answer him; she didn't move. He went into the kitchen, saying with a gust of irritation: "If you're a squarehead, too, you can go to hell." He opened the rear door and walked away. She heard voices come from the shed, and then Ringrose returned and came to the couch. He ran a hand under her chin and drew up her head. He was grinning and he was sure of himself. "Can't make a family man out of me." He waited for her to thaw, and he grew impatient of waiting and pulled her to her feet and laid an arm around her and kissed her. She was docile but ungiving, and this disgusted him and brought back his temper. "What's the matter with you?" he said sharply.

"I told you to get out."

"Women don't throw me over," he said. "I'll do that myself when the time comes. You going to get the whisky?"

"No."

"Where you keep it?"

"Bottom of the kitchen cupboard."

He returned to the kitchen and opened the cupboard. He found himself a glass and had his whisky. He came back into the living room, holding the bottle in his hand; he was again smiling, but it was that pressed, narrow smile he showed when his temper was dangerous. "Here's your drink," he said, and brought the bottle down on the living room stove, scattering liquor and glass splinters across stove and floor. He stared at her, turned on his heels and left the house.

When his steps had faded down the street she went to the kitchen door and opened it. There was no light in the shed; the men who had been there were now gone.

Ringrose started to go along the side of Emily's house, toward Fourth Street. Telliver called impatiently to him: "Not that way," and waited until both Ringrose and the third man in this party drifted toward him. Each man had two sticks of cordwood cradled in his arms, and each moved slowly through the black heart of this block. Ringrose murmured: "Watch your footing."

"It's all right," said Telliver. "I've handled

a lot of powder in my time."

He came to Yamhill, gave it a good survey, and crossed over, leading the others into the heart of the adjoining block; by this round-about traveling they came finally to B Street, turned to Front and worked their way back along the levee, using the black shadows for shelter. At Pine another man stepped from the night and stopped them: —

"Callahan's in the Grotto, drunk. Musick's home. Pope and Bradshaw went somewhere an hour ago."

"Stay here and watch it," said Ringrose, and now took the lead along the warehouse edge and across the *Daisy*'s plank. Once aboard he found a ladder going down to the freight deck; at the foot of the ladder one end of his cord-wood struck the ship's bulkhead and for an instant Ringrose, nervy as he was, stopped dead. Telliver had to prompt him. "Won't do a thing. Go on."

The three of them turned into the engine room. Ringrose, going on the strength of his memory, turned to the right and reached a stack of wood ready for the *Daisy*'s firebox; he used his shoulder to guide him along the stack until he came directly before the firebox and he laid his two sticks of cordwood on the top of the pile. "Put yours next to mine," he said to the others. "Be perfect if Pope got all six of these things into his firebox at the same time."

Telliver and the third man laid their cordwood on the pile, and the three of them stood a moment in the engine room's entire darkness. "Plug those holes good?" asked Ringrose.

"Sure."

"Think it will be enough?"

"Plenty," said Telliver.

"Well, let's get out of here," said Ringrose, and led his partners from the boat. Behind them, in the *Daisy*'s engine room, lay the six lengths of cordwood which they had carried through town, each with an auger hole bored into it, stuffed with powder, and plugged.

Musick, having left Edith late that morning, walked back to Front through the day's warm and lazy light. Portland was again crowded with gold seekers deposited by the newly arrived *Brother Jonathan*, and a line of wagons stood by the Navigation Company dock and great freight drays rolled along the street with their cargoes. A Chinaman passed Musick with his heelless slippers brushing the boardwalk; out of Professor Sedlick's came the brassy racket of the town band in practice. These were signs of activity he had noticed a thousand times before, but now he was an idle man outside the stream of action and, like Crowley, he felt alone and useless.

He turned uptown, walking rapidly to sweat the sourness from him, remembering that Lily had said he would never be happy except in motion. It was, he thought, a nice way of telling him he was a collection of muscles without a brain. At Fourteenth he cut through a wood chopper's claim, crossed a creek and came upon the corduroy beginning of Canyon Road which, making a short and climbing turn, passed into the dense, damp, fragrant forest. He took a side trail, presently reaching a grassy point from which he saw the city below him — its hash-marked pattern of streets, its clustered buildings, its edges straggling into the green surrounding hills and into the silvered river.

There lay the town he had lived in so long and of which he knew so little; time always had hurried him and ambition had narrowed his vision until it had no more breadth than the sights of a gun. He lighted a cigar and lay back upon an elbow, realizing that now, cast upon the shore as a spectator, he newly saw that violent, rushing stream of men of which once he had been a part.

Fluffs of smoke rose from the town's chimneys, the sun flashed on south windows, the echo of a boat's long whistle came forward.

Portland was five thousand people in motion; men walked north on Front Street and men walked south on Front, men loaded ships and other men unloaded them, the little waitress in the Pioneer brought filled plates to a table and took empty plates away, the carpenter added board by board to the front of the new Empire Market while a wrecking crew took another building down board by board, the farm boy came into town to make his fortune and the city boy left Portland for the mines to make his fortune, the head-sawyer at the mill cut the great firs into board lengths and then, after working hours, he set out seedling elms around his house for the shade he would get thirty years removed.

It was motion. People died without it. Turning on his side he saw the low spire of the Methodist Church and he thought: "It is hope which makes us move." It was hope that made the young girl wait for a certain man to pass by and notice her. It caused the milliner to work late over the satin pleats of a wedding dress. It kept the tired man grubbing at the stumps in his meadow. It held the shopkeeper on his stool as he added up the day's ledger accounts.

It was hope, when he came to think of it, which bound him to Edith. During these last unsatisfactory months, walking away from the

Thorpe house with his rankling sense of a courtship gone wrong, he had consoled himself by saying: "It will be better. It will be the way it used to be. It will come back." What was it that would come back? He never had known, and did not know now. There was no way of explaining the thing which pulled a man and a woman together and held them together. He knew what part of it was, he knew that savage and destructive and wonderful part of it; but he also knew it was not enough. Some other thing had been with them in earlier days — the same thing which had made Phoebe McCornack's face beautiful when she walked with Perry Judd.

He had lost it and Edith had lost it and now she offered him what was left and believed it was all they needed. "Maybe it will come back," he thought.

He fell asleep and he slept long; when he woke again the sun was behind the western hills and the buildings of the town threw long shadows. "I must have been tired," he told himself, and he remembered that he had been thinking about hope. His cigar had fallen to his chest and a round hole showed on his shirt where it had burned through. He relighted it and sneezed. He tried to pick up his thoughts, but they would not march. Hope was the spire of the church; but eight blocks

310

away stood the square outline of the town's cemetery, and that was the end of hope. The wedding dress was a dream which soon enough would turn into a man and a woman sitting old and strange together, the man in the meadow would spill out his energy on the stubborn stumps and die poor, and the shopkeeper would one day look up from his ledger and whisper: "Why?"

He rose with his muscles stiffened by the damp earth. "Oh, hell," he said, "there's got to be a reason for all this business." The sleep had freshened him. He felt good. The darkness of his thoughts could not hold against the lively hunger and the physical ease within him. He had been down into that darkness before, and would be again; but it didn't matter now because he felt good. Portland was the stroke of a hammer against a board, a woman bending over a fresh cake from the oven, a man and a woman flirting with each other. Portland was five thousand stories; each of these stories would sooner or later end but other stories would come on. Disaster struck this town and death came to it, yet nobody was missed and no place stayed empty. Hope was greater than anything. Maybe it had a meaning, maybe not; it made no difference, for hope was a force like the sun, and its presence was enough meaning for anybody.

The smell of supper was in the town when he returned to it; the quietness of evening was upon it and voices carried far and men came along the streets in their light rigs, homeward bound. He swung into the Barnes house and found Webley and Lily both troubled by his absence. Webley displayed a degree of irritation. "You should not drop out of sight, not when your friends know the Knights are after you."

"Didn't think of it," said Musick.

"You should," said Webley. "McGruder's body was found in the river today. It was down by Linnton, and clearly a murder. You see why you ought to be careful?"

He took his seat opposite Lily. Webley said a hurried grace, and Lily asked her interested question: "Where were you?"

"Just loafing, up on the Point."

"Alone?"

"Yes," he said, and saw her expression change. Webley, listening and watching, observed the change, too, and the effect of it was to turn him silent during the rest of the meal.

The dishes were done and Lily sat by the living-room table with the lamplight falling upon her sewing. Night came to town and the sounds of Front Street rolled up Pine and broke loosely against the house. Musick stood by the window, fed but restless again. The room made him restless. The presence of Lily made him restless. They were silent but the silence was as it always had been — a weight, a pull, a stream of sharp wind.

"Why alone, Adam? Why not Edith with you?"

"Never thought of it."

"You do everything wrong." She stopped her sewing and sat watching her idle hands. "You'd better find something to keep you busy."

"Taking the *Daisy* downriver tomorrow."

"A new run?"

"Just to see what trade we can drum up. Nothing will come of it. Bradshaw wouldn't be satisfied with a small profit. The partnership is done."

"I'm sorry."

"Money's a good thing. Money's a bad thing. For Bradshaw it's like cancer."

She listened to him without looking at him; she waited for him to go on talking. But he had nothing else to say. He stood aside from the window, watching her and presently she lifted her glance to him, made curious by his stillness, and when she saw what was on his face she turned her head away and took up her sewing.

"I'll pull out of here tomorrow night," he said.

"All right."

Somebody came along the walk and turned in; the door opened to show Webley. "Phoebe McCornack drowned herself just a little while ago. She jumped from the levee where the *Claire* used to tie. They haven't found her body yet. I am going to help hunt." He closed the door and went back down the street.

In the distance was the scattered and continuing sound of gun explosions, which would be somebody's notion of bringing a submerged body to the surface of the river. Musick walked away from the window; he sat down in a chair and laid his arms across his knees. He bent over, staring down upon the twined floral pattern of the rug. He was suddenly sick of heart.

"Poor, blessed, tired little soul," whispered Lily.

"Not blessed," said Musick. "She killed herself, so she's damned. There'll be sermons on that next Sunday. Some of our best Christians will not want her to have a church burial. It's not moral to kill yourself, Lily. You've got to stick it out and let yourself be torn apart a chunk at a time. That's the moral way to die. It hurts more, but it's the only way to get to heaven. It will make wonderful stuff for the preachers. All the good ladies of town will file by the coffin to see if they can tell if she was going to have a baby."

"Oh, no."

"She was common clay, cracking at the first rain. Gorman would say so."

"Adam, you don't believe that?"

"I don't believe it, but all good people who have what they want believe it."

"Adam —"

"People are wiggling little things. Water drowns them inside of a minute, a knife lets the blood out of them in less time than that, fire suffocates them in ten seconds. A man stands under a tree and a bolt of lightning kills him, or a mountain explodes and wipes out a whole town. What difference does it make? We're a stream of ants. A foot comes down and some ants die and some live. It's all blind. They'll pray for mercy on Phoebe's soul and beg forgiveness for her sins. What sins did Phoebe have except to want a man? It's just emptiness. We walk to the edge of it, good and bad, and drop into it. Sacrifice and tears and sin and corruption — they both end in nothing. Phoebe was only a little flash of light in a dark place — and the light went out. We're all little flashes of light and we'll all go out, and nobody will know we were here, or give a damn."

"Adam!"

She came quickly up from her chair and crossed to him. She dropped down on her knees and lifted his head up from his hands and saw tears standing against his eyes. "Adam, I didn't know — I didn't know! Oh, Adam —"

She was crying and yet she was smiling. Her hands were around him and her face was close to him, and tenderness came out of her and touched him and went around him. He put his head against her breasts. "Lily — I'm not so tough, not so brutal."

"I know. I know it now. Don't you feel hurt, Adam. Please don't. I don't want you hurt."

Her breath was upon him, and her lips brushed him; she was trying to protect him, she was trying to take his hurt away. He said: "Now what have I done to you?" and tried to look at her.

She whispered, "No," and her arm held his head down.

16

At four o'clock of another gray morning Musick walked down Pine toward the *Daisy*. Since the *Daisy* was going downriver on an unscheduled trip, with neither freight nor passengers, there was no need of rising at this early hour; it was a matter of habit, and habit was a thing hard to break. At the levee he saw Billy standing against the black side of Walling's warehouse. Crowley was with him and in this shadowed air which was half night and half dawn, Crowley appeared old and sick. For all his idleness he was a man early breaking up. He drew back from Billy when Musick arrived. He said: "Mornin' " in a jumpy voice.

Billy had a load of papers under his arm. He gave one to Musick and he said, "Well, I got to go on," and started away.

Musick called, "Hold on." He walked forward until he had a fair look at the boy's swollen lips and the welt standing like an angry boil over his left eye. He said: "How'd you get that, Billy?"

"That's what I asked him," said Ben Crowley. "And he lied to me."

"No," said Billy in a surly voice, "I was in a fight."

"No fight," said Crowley. "I hear about everything in this town, and I didn't hear about no fight. Who beat you, boy?"

"It was a fight," insisted Billy.

"It took a man's knuckles to do that," pointed out Ben Crowley. "A kid couldn't of hit so hard. It was a man. What man?"

Billy Gattis abruptly turned and ran down the dark street with his heavy load. Crowley sighed. "The kid's hidin' somethin'. He's scared. I'd like to know."

"Had breakfast?"

"No."

"Come on," said Musick, and walked with him across the levee to the *Daisy*. The partners were in the saloon and for a moment Musick felt a little of the old comfort come over him; this was the way it once had been. But that went away soon enough when Bradshaw looked up from his meal and showed his changeless resentment. Whatever had been between them was now dead and could not be restored. Musick got an extra plate and cup from the galley for Crowley, and he ate his own breakfast in silence and afterwards went up to the pilothouse, there to smoke his cigar and to watch day come over the land and set up its sharp divisions of light and shadow in the town. Callahan presently climbed the ladder.

"Well," he said with his quick, Irish cheerfulness, "a fine thing to be at it again."

"Yes," said Musick.

Callahan stared at Musick and his smile entirely changed. "No," he said quietly, "we're foolin'. It is not a fine thing."

"The milk went sour," said Musick.

"Well, no use hangin' to something that's bad. Better take Gorman's offer."

"What offer?"

"Lou ain't told you yet? Told me this mornin'. He talked with Gorman. The company will take the boat and give us three thousand apiece."

"Elijah wants a bargain," said Musick. "I'm surprised Lou listened to it."

"Well," said Callahan, "there's more in it for Lou Bradshaw and Pope. More for them but not for us. Pope can go on a company boat as engineer and Lou can be purser. Gorman offered it."

"Divide and conquer," said Musick. "That's the way Gorman does it. He played Pope and Bradshaw against us."

"I don't mind," said Callahan.

"You want to take it?" asked Musick.

Callahan showed embarrassment. "I'll do what you do, Adam. But I'd just as soon get out. There's no fun in it now. We ate the apple and there's nothin' left but the core."

Musick laid his hands on the wheel and looked forward upon the heaving surface of the spring-swollen river. Billy Gattis got into his mind and he remembered the boy's face. Crowley wanted to find the man who struck Billy, and that was odd business for Crowley. But none of this was what he ought to be thinking about. It was the boat that should be in his mind. The trouble was that he no longer thought it important; he was a good deal like Callahan — there was nothing left to this apple. What stuck him was Gorman's offer. He hated to accept it and for his own part he would have thrown the three thousand away and gone on until Gorman beat him down to the last stick of wood for the *Daisy*'s firebox.

Callahan felt Musick's silence to be a criticism of his loyalty and he spoke again. "Adam, am I doin' wrong? I'll stick if you say stick."

"No point to that."

"Point or no point, I'd stick if you feel like it. We're not fightin' for points, are we?"

"What are we fighting for, Emmett?"

"I told you that once," said Callahan. "Just for fightin'."

"No," said Musick, "we'll wash it out."

"My God," said Callahan, "what'll I do with three thousand dollars?"

"Get married and let your wife keep it."

Callahan shook his head. "I'd cause a woman nothin' but misery. It's not for me." Then his cheerfulness returned. "Here I am worryin' about money I ain't got. That's what money does to a man."

The sun rose and Mt. Hood, hitherto a flat, steely silhouette to the east, took on bulk as the rose and purple colors began to flow over it. Smoke and heat shimmered from the *Daisy*'s stack and Front Street grew lively with the traffic of gold seekers hurrying toward the *Julia* and the *Carrie*. Callahan said, "Well," and left the pilothouse to tend the lines. Musick tried his wheel, noting that Lily had come to the levee. She had watched his departure for so many mornings during the last two years, and this constancy made him wonder; it made him think of her, it stirred old impulses and left him unsure.

At seven o'clock the *Julia* turned into the river; at seven-ten the *Carrie* followed. Musick rang down the standby signal and gave the *Daisy*'s whistle cord a quick short pull. Callahan's round voice came up: "All clear," and Musick, sending down a gong and two jingles, put the *Daisy*'s nose into the channel. Lily waved at him and he saw her smile; for answer he gave her the *Daisy*'s whistle.

Lily stood with her back to the warehouse wall, admiring the *Daisy*'s graceful lines. The *Daisy* meant much to her, more than Adam Musick suspected, and the sight of the boat this morning made her unusually sad; for she realized that Elijah Gorman would have his way, no matter how stubbornly Musick and the partners might hang on with the fight. She knew it because she had sensed the admission of eventual defeat in Musick's own manner. He was not always clear to her, but in this matter she understood him. The trip down the river was really a farewell trip.

She watched the boat make its swing and straighten on the far side of the river; she heard the signal jingles come from it and saw the bow wave grow suddenly white as the *Daisy* picked up its speed, and she was about to turn back into Pine Street when she saw the *Daisy* suddenly come upon some kind of an obstruction in the river. The boat seemed to strike, to shudder, to come to a full halt. Afterwards a wall of wind reached over the distance and flung Lily back against the wall of the warehouse, cracking her head on the boards, and a terrible sound struck her and took wind and senses from her, and a moment of blackness came upon her as this sound filled the world and roared through it and tortured it and stunned it. Her vision became distorted. She saw the *Daisy* swell shapeless before her, break apart and become a great fan-shaped mass of bits and chunks and splinters rising and spreading against the morning's sky. It was a nightmare dream, it was not real; and deep in her mind — in the one untouched part of her mind — was the wild thought that it was not the *Daisy* which had changed but herself who was suddenly dying and thus saw the world out of focus. She waved her arms to restore her balance; she had no wind in her, and no power of drawing wind. The force which had flung her against the warehouse wall now suddenly released its pressure and she fell to her knees and got her first breath in what seemed a long stretch of time, and she shook her head from side to side, and saw blood dripping from her nose.

Into her consciousness came a single penetrating scream, one and no more; and about her in swift succession arrived a series of sounds, the rushing of air, a low secondary explosion, the crackling of fire and the pattering echo of something like rain. An object struck her on the back and brought her to her feet and then she saw the air filled with small particles and fragments and fist-sized chunks, dimpling the river as they dropped and clattering upon the wharf. It was no illusion; she was alive and the *Daisy* was no longer a boat. It was a hulk drifting downstream with a great gap torn through its midships and half of its superstructure blown away; it was a gutted scow licked by a rising fire; it was two broken sections loosely tied together and swaying apart, and quickly settling. The forward part slid backward as it sank, bow slanting more sharply into the air, and the stem section went directly down into the water with a ball of smoke puffing out of it and a wave rolling shoreward from it. Debris rolled darkly on the crest of the wave and one broken object, which looked to be a body, came to sight and disappeared. Running her eyes swiftly along the river she saw no men struggling in the water; she saw nothing but these stray and horrible remnants, and as she watched — bent forward and with her hands doubled and half lifted — the *Daisy* vanished.

Musick, bringing the *Daisy* around, eased off on the wheel and sent down his signal for full speed. He checked the *Daisy*'s bow on a point of land well below K Street, and reached into his pocket for matches to relight his dead cigar. He had his chest against the wheel, and he felt a small shuddering vibration come up through the hull and through the wheel to him, much like the shock of the bow against a small floating log. Thereafter the world exploded and emptiness and motion and fury was in him and he had no coherent thought in his head, save one small remembrance of the cigar in his mouth; and some kind of an impulse was in him to reach to his mouth and take out the cigar. . . .

He struck a solid substance and felt pain and cold. He strangled, and he fought with his hands and legs against a substance which pressed against him in all directions, and fire was in his nostrils; and he seemed to wake from a terrible kind of sleep, and realized he was in the river. As soon as he knew it he ceased to struggle; he put his hands above him and swept them down, swimming for the surface. It was still unclear to him how he had gotten into the river, nor did he at the moment recall that he had been on the *Daisy*. There was only one thought in his head; he was in water and he had to rise up through it and draw wind into him; and he rose up and felt air and drew wind.

But he was still not a fully conscious man; he was a living thing going through the primitive gestures of life, swimming toward the surface by instinct rather than by reason, and dog-paddling along the river's surface out of the same primitive reflex. Consciousness came to him later; it seemed like hours but was in fact only a matter of moments. He opened his eyes and felt great heat strike his face and his mind began to function and he realized what had happened to him. He looked around and saw the broken hulk of the *Daisy*, covered by flames, slowly settle. The heat of the fire made him duck under the water.

He did this several times and, when he got up strength, he swam toward the river's eastern bank. The effort tired him and he stopped and rolled on his back to float. The weight of his shoes and clothes pulled him down and forced him to swim again. The *Daisy* went under with a quick lurch and a roller came from it and lifted him up to its fat crest and bobbed him around. A piece of planking teetered on the roller, seemingly at a great distance. He debated going toward it and he thought: "Don't know if I can make it." Over the surface of the water traveled a voice, and the water itself telegraphed to him the sound of oars rubbing against their locks. He turned his head and saw the boat far out in mid-channel and he raised an arm and he called out so that the men in the boat — there were two of them — might discover him, and at once a great problem rose in his mind. Should he save his strength and float until the boat arrived or should he swim for the plank?

He thought: "Boat's a hell of a long way

off. Plank's closer." He was not much of a swimmer. Like most river-men, he never had given much thought to the need of swimming, but now he reached out and started for the plank. When he touched it — and it surprised him how short a distance it really was — he had little energy left. He wrapped an arm around the plank, put too much weight on it, and carried it down with him. He came up, spitting water. A voice said behind him: "Reach out, Adam, and catch my arm." He turned his head and found the stern of the rowboat drifting down upon him with George Pope, dripping wet from his own immersion, bending out to catch him.

He took Pope's hand and hooked himself over the rowboat's transom; he had no further effort to spend, but George Pope, clawing at his clothes like a fisherman hauling in a net, pulled him aboard. He landed head first on the boat's bottom at the feet of the man rowing, Harry March. He righted himself and stared at Pope. Pope's face was pitted and burned. "My God, George, where were you when she blew?"

"Right in front of the firebox."

"I don't see how you made it."

"I don't, either," said Pope.

"Where's Callahan — where's Bradshaw?"

Pope shook his head.

Harry March said: "Must've been a bad boiler."

Pope stared at him. "Nothing wrong with the *Daisy*'s boilers. I took care of the *Daisy*."

Ben Crowley left the *Daisy* as soon as he had his breakfast, well knowing that Lou Bradshaw begrudged him the food. He stood on the levee and watched the *Daisy* depart. Lily Barnes was not far from him but he did not look at her; he pulled his hat down over his forehead, he thrust his hands in his pockets and, having nothing to occupy his time, he remained in this position, seeing the small things around which other men did not see.

The explosion hit him a great blow in the chest and belly and threw him down. He rolled on the ground and reached for his hat and in that dazed moment he thought: "Something's happened to me," and had his moment of panic. But the roar he heard came from the world around him, not from inside him, and then he looked up and discovered the *Daisy* on fire. He squatted on his haunches, watching that scene closely and without much emotion. Once he looked at Lily and noticed that she had not moved away from the warehouse wall. Men ran up from Front Street and one of them — Harry March — put out in a skiff, rowing with all his strength. Crowley watched the skiff grow smaller on the river and reach a point where it seemed to stand still. He swept the river with his glance and thought he saw a body floating on the water; presently the boat stopped, a shape reared up from the water, and March left his oars and hauled this survivor aboard. Then the boat went on and reached another shape. Crowley heard Lily say: —

"Who is it, Ben?"

"Can't see."

He continued to squat while the boat turned back. He put his palms beside his face like blinders.

"Who is it, Ben?"

"Can't make out, yet."

George Pope was the first one he recognized. He said to Lily: "Pope's one of 'em. That's a wonder. He was in the engine room — closest to it." He bent forward, more and more impatient with himself. He saw the other survivor's shoulders and he knew it wasn't Bradshaw, who was a thin man. It was either Callahan or Musick. He got up and went to the edge of the levee and squatted again. "Both the same height," he told himself. "But Callahan's heavier." Then the second survivor turned his head and showed a silhouette against the day's light. Crowley rose and walked back to Lily. He had never seen such strain on anybody's face. "It's Musick," he said and went quickly on toward Front Street, not desiring to look at her face when it changed.

He had something else in his mind as well and walked uptown with more hurry than he usually did. He turned at Emily's house, circled it and knocked at her back door. When she opened the door she said immediately: "What was that big noise, Ben?"

"*Daisy* blew up."

"My God!" she said. "Oh, my God."

"The kid here last night?"

"Billy? Yes. Was he on the *Daisy*?"

"No, that's all right. Was his face swollen when he came here?"

"No," she said. He saw her expression change and realized that she knew something about it.

"Who hit him?"

"Ringrose hit him."

"He here, too, last night?"

"Yes."

"Emmy," he said, "you sure he hit the kid?"

"Yes."

"All right," said Crowley, and turned away. But he swung around and spoke quietly to her. "Oughtn't let that man in your house,

Emmy. He's no damned good."

"Well, Ben," she said, and stared at him.

He continued to watch her, wanting to be angry with her but not quite able to feel anger or to show anger. "I know that, Emmy. But he ain't your sort. He's no good."

"That's funny," she said. "That's funny."

"Wouldn't say it if I didn't think so, Emmy," he told her, and went away.

She returned to the house and closed the door. She stood in the kitchen, staring at a wall but seeing nothing. She ran a hand across her face and brought it down over her mouth and held it there. Presently she opened the back door and went out to the shed. It was a plain shed with a dirt floor on which years of wood chopping had piled up a carpet of splintered wood and bark; she looked at the chopping block, she looked at her own pile of wood, cut into short stove lengths. She got down on her knees, noticing the little mounds of fresh sawdust on the floor, a coarser dust than that made with a saw. She scooped up a bit of it in her hand and returned to the house. She put on her coat and her hat and she looked at herself in the mirror a moment, and went out the front door, going south on Fourth to Pine and up Pine to the Barneses' house.

Coming by the front of the house, she saw

several people inside. She went on to the corner and used the back gate. She knocked at the rear door, and she touched her cheeks and drew a sigh, and grew nervous. It was Lily Barnes who opened the door.

Emily, much afraid that the door would be quickly closed in her face, spoke at once. "You know I wouldn't come here unless I had to. You know it, don't you? Is Adam Musick here? I've got to see him. It's about Billy — it's about the explosion."

Lily said, "Yes, he's here." She paused and seemed uncertain; but her expression wasn't unkind, it wasn't the blank attitude which the women of Portland usually showed Emily. "There are a lot of men in the place," Lily went on. "But come in."

"Oh no," said Emily, "that won't do. Could he come out here?"

"Come in," said Lily.

Emily murmured, "Oh, this isn't wise," but she stepped into the kitchen and followed Lily to the front room. Musick sat in a rocker with his wet clothes shedding their river water on the carpet. He looked tired and pale but when he saw Emily he straightened and cast a puzzled glance at Lily. There were four other men in the room, Webley, Marshal Lappeus, and two townsmen whom Emily knew very well. All four stared at her, and Marshal Lappeus shook his head at her. He gave her a killing glance but he didn't speak.

Lily said — and it seemed to Emily that the girl used a little tone of malice on these men: "Gentlemen, you know Emily, don't you?" Her father looked oddly at her. Lappeus made a distinct effort to compose himself and to erase the disfavor on his countenance; he had run into something he failed to understand and for him the only recourse was to be wholly neutral. One of the other two townsmen, this being March who had rowed the boat to Musick's rescue, managed a blush.

Emily said: "I know something about this that Mr. Musick ought to know."

"All of you," said Lily, "go on."

The men, excepting Musick, departed, and evidently were glad to go. Lily turned back into the kitchen, and was stopped by Emily's request. "No, you ought to stay." She still held the sawdust in her hand, and opened it and showed it to Musick. "Billy was at my house last night. He comes to get a drink of milk, and then we usually do some spelling. Well, Floyd came with two men. They went into the woodshed. They were carrying cordwood. They worked in the shed, doing something. Then they took the cordwood away. Floyd beat Billy. I guess he thought Billy knew too much. I don't know what they did with the cordwood. I found this around the chopping block."

Musick took Emily's hand and spilled the wood dust into his palm. He bent forward in the rocker and he worried the dust around with his hands. "You sure they did it?"

"It wasn't there before," said Emily.

"Didn't hear 'em use a saw?"

"No — no saw." Then she remembered something. "I saw one of those three men. It was Telliver."

The dust was coarse and pieces of it stuck together and made short, brittle curls. Musick stared at his palm quite a long while; then he got up and carried the dust to the living room stove. He opened the stove's top lid and dropped the dust in. "Well, Emily," he said, "thanks."

"Help you any?"

"Yes." He swung around. "Emily," he said, "you know what you're doing?"

"I thought about it last night," she said. "I can't help it."

"You like Floyd?"

"I can't help that either," said Emily.

She was big and overdressed with her cheeks turned red by the excitement she was undergoing; there were moments when she was pretty but now her own private sorrow loos-

334

ened her and made her too heavy and too coarse. She was a woman who had to take care of her appearance if she wished to look well.

"I'm sorry about it," said Musick.

"It's got to be," she said. "What else could I expect? He'd kill Billy if he could. That's what I thought about. Maybe he'd kill me. He's pretty bad. I knew it from the start, but I just hoped it wouldn't be so bad. Then he beat Billy. You watch yourself. He'll kill you if he gets the chance."

"He'll get the chance," said Musick. "I'll see to it. But he won't kill me. You know what he is, Emily?"

"No," she said, "I never did know. What is he?"

"A Copperhead."

"What's he here for? There's nothing here."

"He's out to break up the state." But he still thought of Emily's own personal troubles. "You like Billy a lot?"

"Yes," she said, "I wish I had a boy."

"Or a girl?" asked Lily.

Emily's mouth hardened. "No," she said, "not a girl. Girls —" She looked at Lily and shook her head. "Not the way things are — not a girl."

"Emily," said Musick, "sooner or later people will get to talking. You know. They'll say

Billy oughtn't come to your place."

"I know," she said. "I've been waiting to hear it."

"Well," he said, "don't get too set on him."

"I can't help it," she said. "I know I'll have to tell him to stop coming. I know it. But I can't help liking him. I can't help anything. That's always the way it is." She turned and left the house, closing the back door behind her.

Lily said: "She's nicer than a lot of women. And you were nice to her."

He looked up at her from the rocking chair, covering his regret with a smile. "I'm like Emily. I can't help it."

"What did her story mean? I didn't understand it."

"Ringrose bored holes down the length of those cordwood chunks and stuffed them with explosives. They got on the boat somehow and put the cordwood in the pile. George Pope chucked some of them into the firebox — and we blew." He got up and walked around the room, limping; he didn't know how he got the limp, but his left side was stiff from the shoulder down.

"Adam," she said, "don't do anything alone."

"How did you know?"

"I usually know what you'll do. But not

alone — don't. It's the same old thing again. You can't be your own law. Haven't you learned that yet?"

"Yes," he said, "I've learned it. But I'll kill him if I can."

"Oh, Adam."

17

It was then middle morning. Musick left the house and did not return until supper; after supper, saying nothing, he left again. Webley remarked: "He's up to something. Always easy to tell."

"I wish you'd follow him."

"Not where he's apt to be going," said Webley and departed. Lily washed the dishes with Musick on her mind; the more she thought of him, the faster she worked at the dishes. She never finished them; a sharpening dread sent her out of the house, down Pine to Front. A bonfire burned at the intersection, with townsmen and gold seekers alike standing around it, and other fires lifted their orange flares elsewhere on the street in celebration of the eve of election. Somebody stood on a box in front of the Pioneer, delivering a speech for the Union Party. Billy Gattis trotted past her, unmoved by this excitement as he went about his errands.

She strolled south on Front, never before seeing the town in this restless, darkly carnival spirit. The crowding men touched her with their shoulders as they went by; they were roving, they were excited, they were keyed up by the suspense of tomorrow's vote, and a lot of them were drunk. She had reached Morrison before she saw the man she had set out to find. Marshal Lappeus stood on the corner, calmly watching his town.

He did not like to find her alone and told her so. "I'll walk home with you. It is no place to be unescorted. Where is your father?"

"Have you seen Adam?"

"No. You want him?"

"He'll be looking for Ringrose. It was Ringrose who blew up the *Daisy*."

Lappeus stared at her and she saw on his face the disinterested, polite amusement of one who found it impossible to approve a woman's entrance into the affairs of men. Front Street was not her place at this hour.

She said: "That's what Emily came to tell him. They bored holes in some cordwood in her woodshed, and carried the wood to the *Daisy*. Ringrose and Telliver, and somebody else."

He watched her with his unstirred countenance. "Adam tell you this?"

"Yes."

"Well," said Lappeus, "don't worry. Nothing will happen. I'll take you home."

His lack of interest irritated her. She said: "Will nothing happen, or is it that you'll take care not to see anything that might happen?"

She swung away from his offered arm, but she noticed the change on his face, and the change shamed her. She came around. The Marshal's eyes displayed anger, but there was unsureness in them too. "I should not have said that," she told him.

"Oh, well," he said, "I know how it is. You're worried, ain't you? People say funny things. I've seen a lot of that. It's all right. You want me to take you home?"

"No," she said, and retraced her way along Front. She had never ceased to think of Musick, but the memory of Lappeus's eyes remained. It was that moment of uncertainty which clung to her. Lappeus was the law and there shouldn't be any uncertainty in him. Did he wear a mask, like so many other people? She remembered then what Musick once had said in a moment of bitterness. "Nobody knows anybody else."

She turned up Oak instead of Pine to avoid a fist fight half down the block. The saloons were brimful and the air of tenseness seemed greater to her; it got into her and increased her fear for Musick. She crossed First Street and continued toward Second, but she stopped and swung back and looked down First. A man stood against the wall of a building, half in and half out of the light of the adjacent gas standard, and motionlessly watched something across the street.

It was Crowley. She walked toward him and watched his head come slowly around, as though he were reluctant to take his eyes from the object in which he was interested. "Have you seen Adam Musick?"

He said, "No," but he said it after too long a pause.

"Tell me —"

"Ma'am," he said in a way that rebuked her, "this ain't no place for you. Go home."

She followed Oak with an increasing awareness of the tension around her. The town had turned from a pleasant place to a jungle in which men dangerously prowled, in which men hunted and were hunted, and waited to strike. Lappeus knew something and Crowley knew something, and at once she realized that all the men of Portland probably knew what was in the wind; some kind of a word had been quietly whispered around. A group came out of a space between buildings ahead of her, crossed the street at a shuffling run and ducked into another space. She saw the vague shadow of their low-bent bodies, she heard their boots scudding along the soft earth of the rear lots, she caught one swift low word from the distance. At Seventh she turned from Oak toward Pine, but for an instant she looked behind her and saw the big bonfire burning down at the intersection of Oak and Front, and the color of the flame was — with this new feeling upon her — the color of fresh blood.

She reached her house and stood a moment on the porch, more and more fearful for Adam Musick who moved somewhere within the jungle. She thought: "It would be Ringrose and the Knights." She hated Ringrose, she hated the lawlessness which lay upon this town tonight like a river fog, and she was angry at Musick for being in it. She was afraid of what might happen to him and she was afraid of what his own unloosed impulses might do to him. When he had cried at the news of Phoebe's death she had observed gentleness in him, but now that gentleness was lost and his old roughness was upon him — that blind, unkind self-confidence which she so greatly distrusted.

She stepped into the house, and came face to face with Edith Thorpe who stood in the front room waiting for her.

Edith said: "I thought it better to wait here than to go away without seeing you. Do you know where Adam might be?"

"No."

"Lily," said Edith, "he ought not be living here. People are beginning to talk."

"What are they saying?"

Edith seemed reluctant to repeat what she had heard. She enacted a silent struggle for Lily's benefit, in which modesty overwhelmed her and embarrassment came upon her. It was, Lily thought, a part nicely played. "You know," said Edith, "what unkind people would say."

"Why should they be unkind?"

"There are people like that. A woman has to watch her friends. I mean the kind of friends who'd love to talk about her. They don't really mean to be malicious, but women have to talk about something when they meet, and they'll pick anything exciting. It doesn't take much in a town like this to ruin a reputation. I worry about that sometimes. A woman can so easily do something to make tongues go. We have to be so careful. And, of course, all of us have a few enemies who'd love nothing better."

"What are they saying?" pressed Lily.

"Oh, you know. Hints. Just little things. He's a man, and you're pretty. And he lives in your house, and you see a lot of each other."

"That's true," said Lily.

A bit of the charm evaporated from Edith's face; her lips tightened as though she gathered her strength for some physical effort. "What's true?"

"We do see a lot of each other."

"Don't you think that unwise?"

"You see a lot of him, don't you?" asked Lily.

"Oh, that's different. We're engaged."

"Does it allow him more freedom?"

Edith stared at Lily. "I wouldn't permit freedom if he wished it, and certainly he doesn't wish for it."

"Do you think I'd give him any greater freedom? Do you think he'd wish for it with me and not with you?"

"People talk," said Edith, shading the phrase with greater suggestion than before. "People think things."

"What do you think?"

"I think it would be much wiser if he didn't stay here."

"He'll probably leave. We've decided that."

"I think it best," said Edith. Her indifference broke and she stared at Lily with a glance of almost brutal suspicion. "You should have decided it long ago." But that was not enough; she could not let it alone. "What caused you to decide?"

"We thought it best."

"Did somebody say something that made you decide?"

"No."

Edith bent forward in her chair, not realizing the intensity of her body or the sharpening and darkening of her expression. "He's been here for months; and you didn't think about it. Now you think about it. Something must have happened."

Lily shook her head, which was a tantalizing answer. Edith rose from her chair with a strained gesture of her hands. "You've put me in a bad light." That was not what she wanted to say; it did not convey the full force of her wounded pride. She continued her stare and she made the attempt to hold the manner with which she had started this interview; she had meant to be charming, to be clever, to stand above Lily and to speak down. But she had been thrown from that position. "It's nice of you," she said, "to hand him back. You hate me, don't you?"

"No," said Lily.

"Yes, you do. You always have. You never belonged to our crowd. You knew it, too. You knew you couldn't be one of us. That's why you hate me, and that's why you've involved Adam. You've done what you wanted with him and you hand him back like a secondhand coat. I can have what's left. Everybody will know about it and laugh at me or talk about me. I can do nothing but swallow my pride and make it appear I'm happy."

"Edith," said Lily seriously, "nothing's happened."

"You're lying. Something's happened. It

had to. You wouldn't send him away after all this time, if there wasn't something between you."

"If there was something between us," said Lily, "I wouldn't send him away. But you're wrong. I didn't send him. He decided to leave."

"Why?" demanded Edith. "He wouldn't go without reason."

"I don't know his reason."

"You know," said Edith, "but you hate me and you won't tell. You'll let me think the worst. You know I'll keep thinking of it. You know it will spoil every day we're married. You mean it to be like that."

"No," said Lily, "I don't. Why should you think anything wrong's happened? He's in love with you, isn't he? Don't you believe him?"

"You think I don't know about men," said Edith. "Because I don't hang around Front Street you think I'm innocent of things. He's moving out of here too late. Something caused it."

Lily stood silent. She knew the reason for Adam's leaving, and he too knew the reason. It was no longer safe for both of them to be together within this house, and he, still faithful to Edith, was running from temptation. It ought to reassure Edith to know this much about him and she wanted to say it to Edith; but she realized it would be as great a source of discontent to the girl as her present suspicions were. It would be a different discontent, but it would hurt her pride as much, and would feed her suspicions as much.

"I wish," said Edith, "I could pay you back."

"I suppose I'll get what I deserve," said Lily, "whatever that is to be."

"You can always make a living by running a boarding-house," said Edith, turned wholly cruel. "It would have been so much better if Adam had never seen you."

"Yes," said Lily.

Edith searched Lily's face to know what that admission meant. It freshened her jealous anger, and it renewed the vindictive and quarrelsome streak within her. "Then there was something between you," she said, and showed satisfaction. "You wanted him and you weren't careful. Now you can remember you were common and got thrown over. I hope you never manage to forget it. It makes me happy to know it."

"That's a terrible kind of happiness," said Lily.

Edith gathered herself together and turned to the door. She cast a glance behind her. Her face was flushed and square and unlovely. She showed Lily her triumph, but it was a triumph mixed with the bitter and malicious expression of a woman who had been hurt in the exchange of blows and could not forgive. Out of her head she drew one last remark. "Your mother was some sort of a dance-hall woman, wasn't she?" as she left the house and slammed the door behind her.

The distant sounds of Front Street came quietly into the room, and one shot sounded from some dark areas of this town. That explosion took the thought of Edith quite out of Lily's mind; she remembered Adam.

Webley came home and went to bed, but she stayed up with her sewing. It was past twelve when Musick returned. He put his cap on the hall rack and he stopped a moment to watch her. His shoes were wet and his hands were black with dirt and by the lively shining of his eyes she saw the excitement steadily churning within him.

She said: "Want me to make you coffee?"

"No," he said. Then he added, "Good night, Lily," and went to his room. She wanted to stop him and argue with him; she wanted to ask him if this kind of life — crawling through the dark in search of a man and intending to kill that man — satisfied him, if it answered those questions she so often noticed on his face. But she didn't stop him. He would not have listened. His misfortunes, his outraged feelings, his sense of injustice had come to a focus on Ringrose; it was too powerful a thing for her to change. She sat long and thoughtfully with her sewing untouched on her lap, and wondered about him.

The voting had begun early. Standing in the line, at ten o'clock of the morning, Musick heard somebody say: "Two hundred and fifty people already voted."

Somebody else said: "How's she stand?"

"Hundred ninety-five Union. Sixty Democrat."

The line was long, running from the end of the block in serpentine looseness forward to the courthouse door and through the door. People came out of the courthouse, having voted, and the line inched forward. Lily was behind Musick standing with her father to keep him company, and to watch this scene with her interest. Mr. Gorman's stovepipe bobbed in the crowd somewhat to the rear. Adam caught Mr. Gorman's eye accidentally as he turned to Webley and he received Mr. Gorman's steady, chilly stare.

"Why," said Webley, "that's a good vote. A comfortable majority. What made us so worried about the result?"

"We'll have to roll it up heavy," said Musick. "The rest of the state is not so firm. Jacksonville will go Democrat. Baker may too. Curry also, I hear."

"Curry!" said Webley. "There's not fifty votes in the whole county — and they'll have to swing by their tails to get from the timber to the voting booth."

The remark was confidently delivered and woke a nearby gentleman's protest. "By God," he said, "I come from Curry. Monkeys, are we?"

"Uncurried," said Webley and thought it clever.

The gentleman said: "We live free down there, my friend. We shoot our dinner half an hour before we cook it, and we don't grub and bend and beg for our bread. A thousand square miles for each family — that's room for proper livin'. What have you got here? It is a mudhole full of corruption. Even the Siwashes wouldn't have it."

"Now," said Webley amiably, "I suppose we're even."

Ringrose and Telliver were a dozen places ahead of Musick. When he reached the courthouse doorway and commanded a view of the room, he found that Ringrose had reached the clerk. Lappeus was in the room to watch the scene officially, and representatives from each party were present to observe the proceedings. There had been challenges during the morning, Musick heard, and Lappeus had taken two men to jail — both of them having caused trouble on being denied their voting privilege. Ringrose stood up to the clerk. "Ringrose, Floyd," said the clerk.

Another gentleman tallied the name. "Eligible," he said.

"How do you vote?" said the clerk.

"Democrat," said Ringrose.

The vote was recorded, and several watchers tallied it as well, and stared at Ringrose.

"Step aside, Mr. Ringrose," said the clerk. "You have voted. Telliver, Anson."

"Eligible," said the man with the registration sheet.

"How do you vote?" called the clerk.

"Democrat," said Telliver, and made a flourish with his hand and stepped aside. "And you see to it that you damned well put it down."

One of the Union poll watchers said: "We'll damned well put you down, brother."

"Walk outside, both of you," said Lappeus. "No electioneering in here."

"Nothing was said about that," stated Telliver, and pointed a finger at the Union man. "Want your tail feather pulled, little turkey cock?"

"No fighting either," said Lappeus. "Do I tell you again? Get out of here."

Telliver turned out with a confident flourish. He saw Musick at the doorway. He swung his shoulder and struck Musick's shoulder as he went by; when he reached the sidewalk he looked back and gave Musick his stare. Ringrose also saw Musick, his face showing its little lines of pressure as he passed from the courthouse. Both men, Ringrose and Telliver, strolled down the street side by side, giving no room.

Lily said: "Adam —"

Musick shook his head. She saw the light again dancing in his eyes, she saw the excitement roughen his expression. He was quick to head off whatever she might have said. "We'll know about the two near-by precincts tonight. Sandy, St. John's, Multnomah, Sauvies, Powell's Valley — not until tomorrow. The rest of the state will straggle in all week. But two days should give us a good enough answer."

"Musick, Adam," said the clerk.

"Eligible."

"Union," said Musick.

Lily waited for her father to vote and meanwhile observed that Musick had gone over to speak to Lappeus. She saw Lappeus's face grow smooth and she saw him draw his watch and look at it, and nod. Everybody in the room watched this scene — the people in line, the Union poll watchers and the Democratic poll watchers. Then Musick grinned at Lappeus and came across the room to Lily; they returned to the street and stood there in the day's bland sunlight to wait for Webley.

She said: "Will you be home for noon?"

"No," he said. He had his glance on Ringrose and Telliver now going down the block; he had his thoughts on them and the narrow, heated and calculating expression was once more visible on his face.

She touched his arm and drew him around to her. "Adam," she said, "listen to me."

"No," he said, "I won't be home for noon."

"Listen to me. Is this what you want? Is it right?"

"I don't know, Lily — I don't know if it's right."

"Suppose you do what you want to do? Will it please you?"

"It's not a thing anybody'd find pleasure in."

"Will it end your troubles if you're successful? Will it pay back the people who've been hurt?"

"The hurt's been done."

"Then why," she asked him. "Why, Adam?"

He looked at her and his mind came away

from Ringrose. She drew his full, close attention and she had a moment of hope. "I couldn't tell you why I do most of the things I do," he said. He continued to watch her, and he added: "Do you want to tell me to give it up, Lily?"

She wanted to tell him exactly that; for twenty-four hours she had tried to find a way of saying it — a way which would sound right, which would be something he could grasp and agree to, and which would not offend him. But, looking at this man whose character was a blend of things she both admired and distrusted, she found herself unable to say it. He had thought of this business too long. "No," she said, "I don't want to tell you anything."

He said, "Well, that's the way it is. Maybe I'm wrong. I guess I'll find that out later. We always find out what's right, later." Webley walked from the courthouse toward them. Musick stepped nearer Lily and dropped his voice. He said, "What I wanted to tell you that night in the ice cream parlor —" but he stopped there and showed her the quick flash of his embarrassment. He swung away the moment Webley arrived.

He crossed Yamhill and went on to Morrison, and at the entrance to the Pioneer's barroom he stopped a moment to search the stray traffic of men ahead of him on the street.

Ringrose and Telliver both had disappeared; down at the corner of Alder he saw Crowley standing with his back to the wall of Marryat's store. A moment later Crowley turned the corner out of sight.

Musick moved into the saloon and found the trade brisk. He had a beer and stood by the counter with it, his mind traveling from one odd thing to another until he happened to think of Callahan. The taste of the beer brought Callahan's face directly before him; he saw the Irishman's face show relish at the thought of beer and he heard the Irishman's lips smack gustily over the beer. This was Callahan who loved the plain sensations of life as few men did, who loved them so much that there was always in him a fear of growing old too soon and losing the zest which gave his life its final moments.

"Well, Adam," said a voice.

Musick turned to discover George Pope. Pope had on a new suit to replace the one damaged by the river; and the suit lay stiffly on him. He looked at Musick, not with much sentiment — since he had little sentiment in him — but with a vague expression of wonder.

"Have a drink," said Musick.

George Pope took his beer when it came. He tipped back his hat, rested one elbow on the counter, and drank the beer straight down.

He wiped his lips and he stared at the floor. He said: "Well, what now?"

"Nothing now."

"I guess that's right," said Pope. "What you goin' to do?"

"I don't know. What you going to do?"

"That I can't say," said Pope. He turned from the bar, but arrested himself. "You know," he said finally, "I been thinkin'. Maybe Bradshaw was too sharp."

"Well," said Musick, "he's dead."

"That's the funny thing," said Pope. "Him wantin' so much and gettin' nothin'." He went out of the saloon.

Musick finished his drink, he said a casual "Hello," here and there and moved to the door. He stopped to talk a moment with Ray Cannister, and gave the door a push and stepped to the sidewalk. Elijah Gorman was at the moment coming down from the courthouse; his hat stood straight up and he swung his cane ahead of him, like a man of considerable age. He saw Musick and wheeled in. It was an abrupt, decisive gesture — it was Elijah Gorman meeting an unpleasant chore head-on.

"Adam," he said, "I regret the loss of the *Daisy*. I do regret it."

"What's done's done."

"Why, I suppose so," said Mr. Gorman.

"Though nothing is ended if a man has got the push to start it again. You have got push enough. Always believed that about you. I should not like to see you drifting in shallow water. It would be a waste. If it is any help to you, I'll stake you to a new venture."

"Another boat?"

"No," said Gorman, "I never give a man chips to play poker against me. But any other venture."

"Expect me to take the offer?" asked Musick.

"I judged you wouldn't," said Gorman, "but I felt obliged to make it, and I'm sorry you refused it. It is a personal feeling on your part, I believe. I regret it. You're not cold enough for business. Not nearly cold enough." But there was a question in him which he had to ask. The question was on his face in the shape of an expression which shadowed his self-assurance. He was, and Musick had never noticed this in Elijah Gorman before, troubled by unaccustomed doubts. "Adam," he said, "do you believe I am not a just man?"

"If you were to go to put the question to the town," said Musick, "the verdict would be that you were personally honest and that you would not stoop to injustice or indignity as you saw those things to be." He paused to make himself clear and to divorce from his judgment the sense of wrong which he knew would sway him. "The verdict would also be, I believe, that bigness has done to you what it would do to me or any other man — it has made its own excuse and its own set of morals. A man with a million dollars at stake will forgive the sin committed by that much money where he would never forgive the same thing done by a ten-dollar bill. I think that's the answer you'd get, Elijah." He was not wholly satisfied with what he had said; he had to try again, to be fairer if he could. "I don't say it is your fault, so much as it is the money. You looked at men in one way when you were poor, but you can't ever look at men that way again."

"I am aware of some resentment," said Gorman regretfully. "Men do not understand. They do not see the bigness of this country. They do not see what must be done. If they were in my shoes, they'd understand."

"If they were in your shoes," said Adam, "they'd think as you think. The million dollars would let them think no other way."

"It disturbs me to be thought unjust. But I cannot go around with a sign painted on my back for people to read. I should not care to have you believe me small. You are an excellent pilot, and I should be happy to offer you a job on the middle river at four hundred dollars a month. If you are wise you will take it. Five years will give you a substantial capital to start another business."

Musick said: "Would you have offered me this job last month?"

Mr. Gorman considered his answer with more than usual care, meanwhile studying Musick's face with his pressing glance. "No," he said bluntly. "Can't say that I would."

Musick had been deeply angered, but that feeling left him. It left him completely, and all the harshness of his judgment of Elijah Gorman went with it, and he no longer had any desire to hurt this man. For now he knew Mr. Gorman, and the knowledge relieved him and made him smile.

"Let me share the humor," said Mr. Gorman stiffly.

Musick said: "I am sorry for you." Mr. Gorman was as common and decent as any other man. It was Gorman's tremendous energy and his sharp mind which had made him a power in this state. But the power which created him was a thing which also had at last imprisoned him. He was no longer a free man. The company, in which he had so large a part, now dominated him and made its demands on him. He could make no decision without thinking of the instrument which he had helped to create. He grew great with it but also he became more its prisoner, surrendering his vigor and his freedom to it. He had no waking hours of his own and his leisure was the incomplete leisure of one whose thoughts were never entirely away from his desk.

Mr. Gorman's situation was worse than that. He had a conscience but his corporation had none. As it moved ahead, it destroyed what lay before it, and this could only bring to any honest human being certain moments of troubled wonder. Mr. Gorman was honest enough, yet the company's destiny was his destiny, a thing he had to defend. Mr. Gorman's defense was to create the philosophy that business was one thing and human relations another; on this thought he took his stand and made his speeches, and convinced many a man — yet never wholly convinced himself. He knew what things were said beyond his hearing, things which reflected not only upon his company but upon himself. As an honest man this knowledge greatly hurt him, and left him helpless. He could not apologize or admit error, he was whatever his company was and could never be anything else and the animosity and suspicion which the company drew upon itself was also his to bear.

This was Mr. Gorman as he stood before Adam Musick, a man troubled by the consequences of his philosophy. The offer of a job had been as much an admission of error as he ever could make.

"I couldn't work for you," said Musick. "But I hold no feelings against you. I did hold them. I don't now. I shall tell you something. I am better off than you are." And then he had one of those rare moments in which, looking upon a man, he saw the shape of that man's private troubles; he had a quick sympathy for Elijah Gorman and he put a hand to Gorman's shoulder and he said: "Elijah, I'm sorry for you."

Gorman reared back, tremendously offended. He lifted a hand and struck Musick's arm away and he gave Musick a glance crowded with affront and turned on his heels and went away.

Musick found a cigar in his pocket and lighted it. He watched Gorman march down Front with his outraged pride. Gorman was a strong man possessing a strong man's faith in himself, and this expression of sympathy was the most galling thing which could happen to him. Musick had not intended it that way; he had spoken without malice, and had roused a furious resentment. It was one more demonstration of something he strongly believed: No man truly knew another man.

He looked beyond Gorman and noticed

Crowley come into view on Front Street, down by Stark, and he watched Crowley until the latter disappeared. A woman came beside him and spoke, and he turned to find Edith Thorpe there.

"Want to walk home with me?" she asked.

He took his cigar from his mouth and lifted his hat, and he swung beside her, walking back along Front to Yamhill, and up Yamhill. She said: "We're winning, aren't we?"

"In the county," he said, "we'll win. I don't know about the rest of the state." Then he corrected himself. "No — I'm sure we'll win. Oregon's got good people in it. We're a little slow, but we're faithful. We stick. There's a lot of fun we miss, a lot of excitement we pass by, not being the kind of people to see it or feel it. But we stick."

"Adam, would you rather live with a different sort of people?"

He smiled at her. "If I went somewhere else I'd miss what was here. That's it, isn't it? I mean, we all want too much."

"Losing the *Daisy* was a terrible blow, wasn't it?"

"I shouldn't tell you this," he said. "You'll think I'm a fool. The loss of the boat doesn't mean anything to me."

She gave him a surprised glance. He wished he could tell her more, but he realized he could not trace out his reasoning and make it seem very real to her. He was saddened by Bradshaw's death, and the passing of Callahan was a hard blow. He missed Callahan. Callahan meant something to him. The *Daisy* did not. It had ceased to mean anything the day Bradshaw had faced him with anger.

They reached the Thorpe house in silence. She paused there, looking up to him and trying to read him. He saw that she wanted to please him and that she was worried about him. Unsureness was on her — that he also saw. She knew there was something wrong with him and suddenly she took his arm and swung away from the house. "It is probably stuffy inside," she said. "Let's walk around the block."

She fell in step with him and the light weight of her hand was on his arm, and for a little while he felt quite close to her. They turned the first corner, the Gatewood's spotted dog joining them and trotting ahead of them. Across the street, opposite the Gatewood house, was the empty half block which Edith had wanted him to buy; on impulse he turned her, crossed the street and went past the lot. She had wanted the usual half-moon driveway before their house, and she had wanted a house much like her father's house. She had talked about that house more than of any other thing;

it meant a great deal to her.

He turned the next corner, recrossing the street. He noticed that she had not glanced at the vacant half block. She stared ahead of her, very little to be seen on her face. What was she thinking, and what was she feeling? Was it time for him to speak, was that what she waited for? The closeness remained, the unusual feeling that he understood her and that she understood him. It was sad to think that after the contradictions she had shown him and the uncertainty he had caused her, they were now at peace with each other. Quietness was with them; he felt no demand from her, no bold warm insistence, no antagonism. In the very beginning of their courtship it had been like this, but soon had passed into a silent clash of wills; now it was as it had been in the beginning, except that the glow of that early courtship was gone and could not be restored. He brought her around the last corner and stopped by the Thorpe gate. She went through it and turned to look up at him. Her eyes were large, the corners of her mouth made sharp down curves. Suddenly she touched the gate with the point of her finger and closed it between them. The latch dropped home with a dry, brisk sound — and that was when he knew.

She said: "Have you anything in mind?"

She had decided, and this was her way of telling him; it was up to him to tell her that he understood and to say it in the same casual manner she used. She had set the scene and would want him to keep it. "I'm going ranching," he said. "Up the Columbia at Fishers Landing."

She nodded. "You always had that in the back of your head. You will be lonely, Adam. You will miss Portland more than you think. I think I should tell you something, Adam. I am accepting Mott. We know each other so well."

He looked beyond her to the scrollwork decoration at the peak of the Thorpe porch, greatly stirred by the hurts they had caused each other, by the memories and moments of warmth, and by the inexplainable way a great desire died and left so little behind. He brought his glance back to her, wishing he might say something about this; but he saw a look in her eyes which stopped him, a fear that he might say too much, a wish that he say nothing at all. She put her hand out to him and murmured: "Good luck, Adam." As soon as he touched her hand she withdrew it.

He nodded and turned away. At the street corner he glanced back and saw her still at the gate, her head lowered as she watched him;

then he went down Salmon toward Front. She would be in this town the rest of her life, and he would probably be somewhere near it most of his life. They would now and then meet. They would say the things that people ordinarily said, and pass on; yet for both of them would be an old feeling softly stirred. These were the things most treasured by people — these little bits of wistful sentiment, these recollections of events once so crowded with meanings. For a woman it was like opening a vanity box and seeing there the rings and pins and brooches once worn, once favored — each with its association of a man or a night or a dance or a kiss or a few tears. Now they lay loose and jumbled in the vanity box; some, formerly so precious, were now cheap and some no longer had meaning and some were to be laughed at; but all of them together in their pile made a woman's life.

He was well down Yamhill, at Third, when Crowley called to him from a space between Kittridge's cabinet shop and Mellick's Hall. Musick came around. He said: "Where now?"

"Ringrose's playing poker at the Miner's Rest. Telliver and some others went to their old meetin' place in the stable."

"They won't stay there," said Musick. "They'll collect by the river. But they'll wait until night. I'll see you here as soon as it gets dark."

"Lappeus got it straight?"

"Yes."

18

He turned from Crowley and went down to
Front. A man stood on the corner of Front
with his face bent toward a copy of the *Oregonian*. He was a little man, Musick idly noted,
with a miner's red double-breasted shirt and
a woolly, rusty beard. Adam turned the corner
and moved on to Lay White's Restaurant. He
stepped in here for a meal and afterwards returned to the street with a cigar. It was then
two o'clock, with nothing more to do until
darkness came. A line still stood before the
courthouse and from the stray townsmen
moving he got the odds and ends of their gossip. The vote was still strongly Union. At
Alder he saw a familiar face in the crowd, and
remembered that this was the fellow who had
earlier been reading the *Oregonian*. Turning
up Pine he looked behind him for no particular
reason and discovered that the man was half
a block away. He knew then that he was being
followed.

"Stranger," he thought. "Ringrose has got
some recruits."

He went home and found Lily cleaning the
house. She had a towel wrapped around her

head and on her face was an expression both determined and harassed — the expression of a woman who intended to clean a room. The chairs were piled in the kitchen, the sideboard pulled away from the wall; all the windows were open and the smell of dust was in the air. She stared at him. "You'd come back at a time like this," she said. "I thought you meant to stay away."

"I'll get out of your road."

"You'd better. I'm not a happy woman now."

He let himself out of the rear door, and stopped in the woodshed. He took off his coat and he removed the revolver he carried beneath his trouser band and laid it on the coat. He got the file from the joist, gave the ax a dressing and began to chop wood. He remembered Edith's eyes, he remembered the short and strained and dry way she had spoken to him. He had bruised her with his roughness, as he seemed to bruise so many people; and for that he had his self-condemning regret. Yet he was a freer man at this moment than he had been two hours before. He felt that freeness and he felt an unaccustomed quietness. Callahan would have said: "Now, Adam, lad, go get drunk and wash the memory of it away."

He thought of Callahan, whose life was a

letter which, once meaning something, was now a thing torn to bits and thrown to the wind so that nobody would read it again or know what it meant. Callahan's life was like most lives — a few episodes to remember, a woman, many chances lost, a year of work here and a year of work somewhere else, a drifting, a tragedy, a fight, another woman. That was the story of most men; and as they told the story, when they grew old, there would be a smile, a shake of the head, a shrug; the heat and the pain alike had faded out of those scenes which once had meant so much to them.

He said to himself, the hell with it, and was irritated at the pessimism of his thoughts. He knew better. Whatever the disillusionment, no man could cease to hunt for what he wanted, or to hope for great things. Great things existed. It was men who destroyed them or made them seem hopeless.

He had enough of chopping. He straightened out the cordwood pile so that it was moderately flat, laid himself on it, drew his hat over his eyes, and fell asleep.

Lily said: "If you can sleep on that wood, you could sleep on spikes. Do you want supper?"

He rose up and saw her smiling at him. "Just

took a little nap."

"You've been snoring like a horse for three hours," she said. She took his arm and walked him back to the house. She had hot water in the basin for him, and laughed at him and went on to the kitchen. When he came in later he found Webley waiting at the table.

"I do not understand this town," Webley said. "The vote is going well, yet the feeling is tight. Reminds me of a swarm of bees. It is an angry sound. I hear it."

Musick said nothing. Excitement slowly ran its warm, fermenting sensation along his nerves and tight spots began to form here and there within his body. Webley watched him and Lily watched him, and he saw the question which was in both. But he was slowly pulling away from them; the impulses which governed him now made him a stranger to them. This was why Lily distrusted him; the world he slowly went into was black, it was not her world. He rose and walked to the front room. He stood by the window to watch the clear sunless light perform its changes. Pearl shadows came upon the eaves of houses and the dusty road took on soft, silver shadings. Evening's peace magnified distant sounds, and for a moment the hour stood still and he felt the closeness of the town and the closeness of its people.

Webley went away on some sort of business. Musick swung back to the kitchen to wipe the supper dishes, watching Lily and wondering what was in her mind. He had the notion to speak of Edith, but found nothing in Lily to encourage him. She was remote from him; her guard was up. He finished the dishes and once more went back to the front room to watch day go. He jingled the loose silver in his pocket; he traveled to the rear porch and put on his coat, and slid the revolver underneath his trouser band; he returned to the front room. Now the eaves of the buildings were darkening and lights began to wink out of windows, and the voice of the town, vitalized by supper, began to growl up from Front Street. It was time to meet Crowley.

He turned to the door. He saw Lily standing in the room's corner, so still and so greatly troubled. She had been there a long while. "Adam," she said, "it's a nice evening for walking. Would you like to walk with me?"

"Tomorrow night, or any other night. But not tonight."

"All those men will be dead someday. Why should you worry about them?"

"They mean to make trouble."

"That's not why you're doing it. They hit you, and you mean to hit back."

"You want me to stay?"

She shook her head. "It has to be your idea, not mine."

"I don't want to stay," he said. Then he thought of Edith and a fresh current of excitement washed through him; he felt it spread through his chest and go out to his fingers. "I saw Edith today."

"Does she know about this?"

"No."

"You ought to tell her."

"I've had my walk with her."

"Are you on some sort of a schedule?" she asked in a discontented voice. "What is it — once a day at a certain hour? Can't you see her whenever you please? Don't you want to see her any time, don't you want to be near her any time?" She checked herself. "I shouldn't have said that."

"We walked around the block. I said nothing. She said nothing. When we got back to the gate she said good-by and I walked away."

"A quarrel?"

"Nothing left to quarrel about. We just gave it up."

A stiff, desperate expression came to her face. He saw it change her mouth, and he watched tears make their bright points in her eyes. "What's that for?" he asked.

"Why do you have to tell me now?" she

asked. "You always do things at the wrong time."

Night squeezed the last streaks of day down against the silhouetted hills to the south, and he knew he should be on his way. He opened the door. "I'll be back in a little while," he said, and shut the door behind him. He went up Seventh Street to Yamhill and down Yamhill to Third. He stopped by the building space and he took a step into it. He called down its wholly black slot: "Crowley?"

He had no answer. He walked the length of the little alley, and walked back. Then he thought: "He got restless. He's already started." He reached Second and moved north on it rapidly, bound for Yamhill Street.

Crowley never reached the rendezvous on Yamhill Street. During that long afternoon he moved in and out of the town's saloons, he strolled the streets, he sat at the edge of the walks and seemingly soaked up the pale sunshine. In this way he collected his information, saw Ringrose at one place or another, saw Telliver, saw men he knew to be Knights. Toward sundown he observed that these men disappeared and he guessed they were somewhere meeting. He checked the stable wherein they had formerly collected and did not see them, and he cruised the town once more and had no trace of them.

He began to have a fear that he had failed to do the thing which both Musick and Lappeus expected him to do, which was to keep those people within his view during this one day; for this was the day when, as Musick had said, "They'll hit now if they intend to do it at all."

Shortly before dark he stopped at the corner of Front and Stark and waited there. Presently Lappeus came along and slowed down. "Anything?"

"I lost track," said Crowley. "They been out of sight for three hours."

"Then they're all in a bunch," said Lappeus. "Where's Musick?"

"I'm meetin' him pretty soon."

Lappeus stared at Crowley with more than the usual gloom. "Dirty enough business. I can see it comin'. You got a gun?"

"I got one, but it ain't what I'll use. I still got strong arms — if I can get 'em around that man."

"Why?" said Lappeus curiously. "It ain't no affair of yours."

"He beat the boy," said Crowley.

Lappeus stared at Crowley with a narrow, full-grown interest. "Crowley," he said, "what about that boy?"

Crowley shook his head and went away. But

a thought halted him and brought him back. "I don't know," he said. "A fellow of my kind is here today and gone tomorrow. It happens quick and there's nobody to know the difference, or care much. When I was younger, I never wanted to be tied down by anything. I wanted to do just what I pleased. So I did it. What was fun then is hell now, Lappeus. I'm a bum with nothin' or nobody. I made it that way and I've got no claim for better. If I'd done it square, I'd had something to claim. Nobody can duck nothin'. We get paid back for everything. You know a lot about people around here, and you don't say what you know. Put this in the back of your head. I oughtn't tell you, but I'd like somebody in the world to know it. Don't let it get any farther. Billy's my son."

He wheeled and went away fast. At Washington he turned toward First. At First, in the growing shadows, he saw a man traveling north rapidly; the man passed him and gave him a brief, close glance and walked on. Crowley, knowing Musick would now be waiting for him at Yamhill, nevertheless drew back against the wall of a building and watched this man continue on. When the man crossed Stark and still seemed bent in the same direction, Crowley suddenly thought: "He's late and he's goin' to wherever they're meetin'."

It was a question of whether he should follow this fellow or go find Musick; he solved it by turning toward Front.

Halfway down the block to Front, Crowley thought to save himself a little time by leaving the street and running back through a lumberyard. The yard stretched halfway through the block. Beyond it was the rear end of one of the town's newest business buildings, with the scrap piles of lumber and brick still lying on the ground. Crowley made some noise in finding his way through and around these piles. He grew careless and he swore when he struck his knee against a board; he reached a gap between buildings and, still trotting, he followed the gap to Oak and came out upon that street.

He came out also directly before a group of men waiting for him. He could not distinguish them; what he saw was the shape of their bodies semicircularly placed in the darkness and he heard their hard breathing — which told him they too had been running, and then he realized they had played a game of fox with him and had caught him.

"Crowley," said a voice, "what you doin' here?"

Crowley hesitated briefly, knowing there was no hope for him, and with all the force of his body he plunged directly against the nearest shape, locked his massive arms about that man, rammed him hard with a lifted knee, laid an elbow against the man's neck and gave it a great twist. The man dropped without a sound, but the rest of these waiting figures now closed upon him and reached for him with their fists and with their clubs. He was hard struck and knocked half out. He bent his head and got one more man within his arms and he slid his arms upward, jabbing at the man's eyes with his thumbs. He was struck again in the spine and felt himself paralyzed. Somebody coarsely whispered, "Be careful what you hit!" He was seized at the waist and hauled back. He had enough strength in his arms to cling to his victim, and he heard his victim crying. After that a club came roaring down upon his skull and when he started to fall another club struck him — but of this second blow he had no knowledge.

The group drew back. Somebody whispered: "That's Nick on the ground."

"No time now."

"Where we go?"

"The warehouse."

The four remaining men went across Oak at a run and disappeared in the adjoining block.

19

Musick, moving down First Street, thought to himself: They've been watching Crowley and maybe they've caught him. He lengthened his stride until he traveled at a soft run. One block below him, on Front, the sounds of night were livelier than usual; this was the beginning of election celebration, since the results of the town vote were now pretty well known. At Oak he saw a party of men coming up from Front Street, rapping at doorways with their sticks, and he heard a voice say: "Copperhead, come out of there!" Every Southern voter now was known, and there would be fighting before the night was done.

He swung south when he reached B Street and went directly to its foot. When he reached the edge of the floodwater, he slowed himself and moved quite cautiously through it. The doorway of the unfinished building was somewhere before him but he avoided it, came to a corner and moved along the building's side. The ground sloped away and the water rose around his legs until he was hip-deep in it. There was another doorway to this place — a wide arch meant for freight wagons — and when he reached it he walked upward along a ramp into the building's blackness. Here he stopped.

The smell of the place was rank with dead fish lodged here, and the dampness of the place was like a fog coming down upon him. The river, at this high stage, softly rippled against the outer walls and the water standing on the lower floor made its own small, uneasy sounds. He heard feet press against the weather-warped boards of the floor above him, and he heard voices.

He closed his eyes a moment, visualizing the building and his own present location. He moved to the right. His hand touched a wall and he followed the wall forward, shoving his legs gently through the water, and came upon another wall; he followed this and he discovered a doorway, and he passed through this doorway with the recollection that it ought to let him out near a set of stairs. He walked on, guided by his memory until his foot touched a stair's riser with force enough to waken a subdued echo which soon spent itself in the darkness. Looking upward along the opening of the stairway he made out a coffee-colored stain of light.

The hallway in which he now stood ran directly forward through the middle of the building to the front doorway, beyond which other men appeared to be moving. He heard the sound of their feet in the water, and that sound suddenly woke a guard who stood secretly by the doorway. The guard's voice said: "Well?"

A voice came at the guard. "Porter," and the outside party moved into the building and ceased to be cautious.

"That you out there a minute ago?" asked the guard.

"We came straight on, just now."

"Somebody else out there."

These men came along the hall, rolling up short waves of water which made racket enough to cover their talk. Musick stepped away from the stair's foot and listened to them as they searched for the rail, and swore, and moved upward. He came after them, and rose behind them, using the sound of their tramping to cover him. He was halfway up when somebody at the head of the party — there were four of them — halted and spoke. "Porter."

"Yes."

"You go back and watch the door."

A man swung about and started down the stairs. Then he stopped and he said: "What for?"

Musick pulled himself to one side; he flattened himself against the inner wall of the stair well. "Because I said so," answered the first man.

Porter slowly descended. He murmured: "No time for this stuff now." Two steps above Musick, he stumbled. It was a well-established reflex which made him swing himself toward the handrailing, away from Musick, as he came down. He struck the railing, and swore again, and kept going. "Time to quit bein' careful," he said.

The other men reached the second floor landing, walked along it and opened a door. Light brightened along the upper hall and died as soon as the door was shut. Still pressed against the wall, half up the stairs, Musick waited for Porter to continue on toward the front door. He didn't hear the man. Porter had stopped wherever he was.

Men were moving around the upper room as they talked, and the sound of their words grew stronger. He thought: "They'll come out pretty soon — I can't stay here." He made a move to descend, but he remembered that Porter was somewhere at the foot of the stairs, and he changed his mind and started upward, laying his weight cautiously on each foot. One small report broke from the stairs and made a definite sound throughout the building. Heat ran through him and he felt its stinging on his face. At the top of the stairs he swung and saw light coming through the cracks of a door near by; he slid on, he passed this door, he heard Telliver's voice, rank and quarreling, and he heard the colder tone of Ringrose.

This second floor was also partitioned into office rooms; crowding the wall as he stepped on, his arm discovered another doorway and he swung through it into one such room, at the same moment hearing Porter's voice rise from below.

"Who's up there?"

The challenge silenced the talk in the adjoining room. Somebody moved over the room and flung open the door, calling down. "What's that?"

"Somebody moving around up there?"

"Sure," said the man in the doorway. "We are."

The door stayed open. Musick heard Ringrose say: "That's all of it anyhow. We'll meet there in fifteen minutes."

Men began to leave the room and to follow the hall to the stairway. Musick dropped flat on the floor and put his head around the bottom of the door, in this manner looking along the hallway and seeing these men as they passed through the yellow beam of light. He watched them turn when they started down; he saw their faces shine for a moment in the light and then sink into the lower darkness.

Telliver and Ringrose were still in the room with three or four remaining men; but in a moment Telliver came out with these others. Telliver turned on the threshold and looked behind him. "When you coming, Floyd?"

"We'll string it out," called Ringrose. "I'll meet you there."

"Don't make it long," said Telliver and went down the stairs with his group.

Below Musick was the scuff and splash of their careless departure. In the adjoining room Ringrose paced slowly back and forth. Outside the building Musick heard the mild rumor of voices and the softened sound of feet pushing through the river's spilled-over water. He listened to that carefully. He listened and he waited, and he wondered: What the hell is the delay?

He had a quick answer for his question. Out there somebody said: "Pull in there!" and instantly the watery racket grew into a sound like the ripping of sheets, and men began to cry, and a gun broke the night. As soon as he heard it, Musick rose from the floor and stepped into the hall and moved toward Ringrose's room.

Ringrose killed the light; he came from his room quickly, murmuring to himself. He reached the hall, swinging toward the stairs; and he was still swinging when Musick got both arms around him and pulled him to a stop. Ringrose let out the sharpest of breaths. He asked no question, he made no challenge, he said nothing. He whirled, he got away. He bent down when Musick searched for him and he rose and his fist rushed out of the blackness on a wild aim and caught Musick high on the head. Then he broke for the stairway.

"Coming after you," said Musick.

"Goddamn you," said Ringrose and made a full halt. Musick whirled against the hallway wall and felt the floor's loose boards jump beneath his feet when Ringrose's gun exploded. Air swelled and everything around him rattled and the gun's muzzle light made its sharp flash and vanished. Musick left the wall, rushing on. He wheeled, fearing the second shot, and he fell before it came and felt the breath of it. He was on his knees, and from this position he made his jump and caught Ringrose by the legs and capsized the man down the stairs. He was on his feet even as he heard Ringrose roll and strike and shout all the way down; he got a hand on the railing and he took the steps recklessly and caught his heel and plunged to the foot of the stairs shoulders first into the knee-deep water. Ringrose was beneath him. He had his shoulder on Ringrose's chest and his head was under the water, and water poured into his nostrils and stung and strangled him. He pushed himself away and got his head above the surface, gagging for wind.

Ringrose rolled and rose. Musick caught the man by the coat; he got to his feet and received the muzzle of Ringrose's gun on his cheek and felt the gun sight lay open its furrow of flesh. He heard the hammer strike on its damp cap and he laid his arms around the man and started to drive his back against the wall. When he put weight on his boots he slipped on the water-slick floor and fell, bringing Ringrose down with him. Both of them went under again.

Ringrose was beneath him, his arms pinned and his feet off the floor. He had nothing solid to support him and so he sank under Musick's weight and touched bottom. He shoved his buttocks against the floor and rocked himself in order to capsize Musick; he let out a big bubble of air which, breaking surface, seemed like a considerable explosion. He butted his head at Musick never able to put force into his blows, and his efforts were all in the rhythm of his desperation, frantic and shuddering and rising to a last terrible convulsive struggling, and falling away as little by little hope went out and strength was spent.

Musick let his weight work for him. He lay atop Ringrose and hoarded his own energy.

Being also under the water, he paid out his wind in miserly little bits; he thought of Phoebe and he thought of Callahan and Bradshaw, and he knew he intended to kill Ringrose. Everything he hated was below him, in Ringrose's body. Ringrose was the evil which men so seldom could get their hands on, but he had his hands on Ringrose now and he meant to do away with him.

Yet, letting the last bubble of wind seep through his mouth, he knew he could not do what he wished to do; and, in deepest reluctance and with greatest regret, he lifted his head above the water, got to his feet and pulled Ringrose to the surface. Ringrose was unconscious. Musick seized him by the hair and held him up, feeling the man's body sway to the short waves rolling back and forth through the hall. Outside was a shouting and a crying and an occasional shot breaking the night, and lanterns made their twinkle through the doorway of the warehouse building and he heard Lappeus call his name.

He was exhausted and he was empty of whatever had been in him; his anger was dead, his sense of injustice vanished. Ringrose had done evil and would, if he escaped hanging by law, do evil again. Yet even the thought that he might live to do evil again could not bring back Musick's anger. Ringrose was one more fragment blown through the world by a great wind; and the wind blew everybody, and nobody had power to prevent it. How could he change anything by holding Ringrose under the water until he was dead? He felt disgusted with himself; he felt like a man coming out of a long drunk. Ringrose was a straw dummy which he, Adam Musick, had been kicking around to satisfy himself — and the thought wasn't good. "This is not business," he thought. "I can't be doing it. Lily's right."

The sound of voices grew nearer the warehouse. He pulled Ringrose along the hall and reached the door which now was lighted by lanterns swinging forward. Lappeus came up with his crowd of men gathered from Front Street. All of them had guns and all of them were excited, pointing the guns upon the lantern-illumined shape of Ringrose.

"Put those damned guns down," Musick said.

Lappeus said: "Anybody else in there?"

"I guess not."

"Some of those Copperheads got away," said Lappeus, "but there's a crowd on their heels now, and they won't get far. Hear 'em?"

Musick heard them; from this distance it was like the brisk yapping of a pack of hounds. He swung Ringrose over to Lappeus's hands and started on. He called back to Lappeus.

"Better get hold of your men before they shoot the wrong people."

He turned into Front and went along it to Pine. He had started up Pine when he saw men trotting out of Front into Oak, and heard a shouting over there. He swung about and continued to Oak. Halfway up the block a group of lanterns bobbed and a crowd made a circle on the street. He broke through the circle and saw Ben Crowley lying dead on the boardwalk. Billy Gattis stood within the circle, staring down at Crowley.

"That's too bad, Billy," said Musick.

Billy looked up. The thinned, overwise expression was gone from his face; he was sad enough to cry, had he known how to cry. He was loose and lost.

"Too bad," Musick repeated. Then he said to Billy in a lower voice: "Maybe you ought to tell Emily about this."

"All right," said Billy.

Musick dropped a hand on Billy's shoulder; he was puzzled that this boy, so centered on himself and so aloof from other people, should feel so strongly Ben Crowley's death. "Liked him, didn't you?"

Billy shrugged his shoulders. "Yes," he said. "He liked me, too," he added and turned away.

Musick continued up Oak. The night had

furnished this town with the kind of a stimulant it seldom got, and little groups of men tramped the walks and went Indian-file down between-building alleys, and came rushing out of these alleys; a sound or a call or an impulse brought them around corners at a full run, their voices rough and high.

There were still some of Ringrose's men at large and the main chase now appeared to be above Seventh Street; he heard gunfire in that direction. At Fifth, five men sprang suddenly out from a vacant lot and challenged him. A gun touched him urgently in the back and a lantern swung up to his face. They were all strangers to him; they were Easterners off the *Brother Jonathan* who had joined the hunt for the fun of it. Somebody said: "That's one of 'em! He's been in the water! What's your name?"

The lantern light turned their faces sallow; the shadows lying in their eye pockets gave them a sightless, hungry expression. He saw their lips stirring, he saw the wildness on them. He said: "None of your damned business. Put the gun down."

"Clip him with it," said one of the crowd. "He's too smart. Clip him with the butt."

But another party came down Pine at the run, drawn by this scene, and a man called out: "Never mind. That's Musick."

"Well, why the hell didn't he say so?"

Musick turned to face the man who had the gun at his back. He reached out and pushed the gun aside. "Your mistake, wasn't it?"

The man seemed offended that it should have been a mistake. "Nervy of you to be walkin' around the street alone. Get off the street if you don't want to be shot for a Copperhead."

Musick dropped his arm as far as his chest; he put one leg back and tipped his body a little and delivered his short, slugging blow to the man's chin. The man's mouth flew open and his hat bounced from his head; he went down at the knees, straight down, and collapsed on the walk. Musick wheeled to face the intent crowd. He stepped ahead and put the flat of his hand against a man in his road. He pressed gently on this one's chest, but the man braced himself. Musick bowed his head and flung his weight into his arm and knocked the man away. He went on up Pine hearing the growing murmur behind him. He was eager to hear somebody call him back; he was restless — as he always was when something touched him.

The door of the Barneses' house was open, with Lily in it. She stepped out to the porch and laid her hand on his shoulder. She drew him inside and closed the door. "Have you been in this?"

"They were down at the unfinished warehouse at the foot of B. Lappeus has got Ringrose and the rest of that crowd will be picked up."

"Dad's out there."

"The whole town is."

"Want some coffee?"

"Yes."

"I saved some."

He climbed the stairs to his room. He stripped and scrubbed himself dry and got into a dry outfit. He put the wet clothes over his arm and returned to the kitchen with the clothes stitching a wet seam on the floor. Lily took them and hung them on the back porch; she returned to pour coffee for him and for herself. She sat down across the table, watching him over the rim of her cup. "The devil gets possession of you when you're idle. What did you hit with your knuckles?"

"A fool man who put a gun in my back because he thought I was a Copperhead."

"Then you felt much better."

He said, "Yes," and added with some surprise, "why yes, I did."

She had her elbows on the table and her chin in her hands; and when he saw her this way, the lamplight making her fair and hopeful, he thought of Phoebe McCornack. He would, he believed, see something of Phoebe McCornack in every woman he ever met; he would always see in them a little reflection of that faithful tenderness which was so vulnerable to the cruelties of the world.

He was more and more restless; excitement worked at him — a tremendously growing excitement. He rose and went into the front room and stood at the window. "Well," he said, "Phoebe had a few good hours and so did Perry Judd before the big wind blew them out of the world. They were lucky to have had as much as they did."

"That's what you'd like to believe. But you can't quit hoping things will work out. That's why you get so angry when something isn't right. You want to fix it up. If you can't fix it, you want to destroy it and get it out of the way."

"Well," he said, "I had a chance to kill Ringrose tonight. If I'd held him under the water another twenty seconds he'd been dead. I wanted to do it, but I couldn't manage it. I guess you're right after all. It's not up to me."

"That's nice to hear," she said. "I hoped that you'd someday see it." She rose, walking toward him, and he turned and saw the uncertain expression on her face. "You feel badly

about Edith. You wanted her. You saw everything in her. But you didn't find it — and
it's not good."

"I didn't want her after I kissed you."

"You can't fall out of love with a woman
whenever some other woman kisses you."

"I did. But it goes back a lot farther than
the kiss. I've not left this house during the
last six months without wanting to return to
it."

She listened to him so closely that he felt
that if he spoke a careless word she would
quit him and never believe him again. "Six
months? Did it take you that long to break
with her?" She shook her head. "Were you
trying to be honorable?"

"I don't know."

"What a waste of time," she said. "Honor
is for business, or playing games. It's not for
this — not for a man and a woman."

"Well," he said, "do you expect me to leave
you flat when I no longer love you?"

Her smile had a hundred variations. She put
her arms around his neck and laced her fingers
together; she settled her head against him with
a motion of luxurious relief. "You won't fall
out," she said. "Not with me. I'm not that
careless."

"I never understood," he said, "why you
let me kiss you that night."

"There wasn't any reason," she said. "I'm not mysterious. I just wanted you."

He thought she was smiling, but she had her face against his chest and he couldn't see. He pulled up her chin and saw that she wasn't smiling. She was waiting for him. She lifted her mouth quickly when she knew he wanted it.

The *Julia* let them off at Fishers Landing and the deck hands wheeled their freight onto the little dock — their baggage, their supplies, their implements. Dave Bain called down from the pilothouse: "You won't stay long, Adam. You'll be back to the river." Then the *Julia* pulled clear and McNulty gave them a long blast; that scene was a pretty one — the *Julia* standing on the smooth surface of the river with her smoke trailing up to the blue sky and the waterfall of her paddles very bright against the sun.

Musick looked at Lily, fearing this moment in particular, this sharp break when the *Julia* went away. If she were only being kind to him, if she were just another wife suppressing her own hopes and her own fears, it would show on her no matter how good she was at concealment. But he discovered no wistfulness on her face. She seemed happy.

"If you ever get lonely," he said, "if you

395

ever get tired or discouraged of this, you'll let me know about it, won't you?"

She had at times an indirect way of answering. "The day you tire of it," she said, "will be the day I tire of it."

"You talk like a Chinaman."

"What Chinese women would you be knowing?"

"I mean the way they're supposed to talk."

"Adam," she said, "that reminds me, you can get me a pair of jade earrings some day."

The river was their front door, along which the *Julia* would come once a day; and Portland was thirty-five miles downstream from this landing. On the other side stood the south wall of the gorge, black with timber and rising to its sharp rim two thousand feet above. Between river and gorge wall lay the long meadows in which the hay lay newly cut and cocked, and the half-frame, and half-log house which Fisher had built ten years before when the Indian wars made it dangerous for a man to live in this country. There was a barn and some fencing; and a few cattle and two indifferent work horses browsed near the river's edge. Back in the timber, behind the house, would be the twisting, difficult trail which ran from Portland to Eastern Oregon. Once in a while there would be travelers on this to break the solitariness of the location; and there were neighbors within five miles. Otherwise they were alone.

"Do you think," he said, "you'll be happy here? Can you raise your children here — not feel you've passed the good things by?"

"You'll be home nights, won't you?"

He smiled. "Days and nights, from the looks of this country."

"Well, then, what do you think a woman's life is?"

He faced the rough ground to the rear of the house and his eyes lifted along the massive carpet of fir running up the wall, running downriver, running upriver; he had not paid much attention to this before, but now he had a thought about it, and the thought interested him. "It wouldn't be much of a trick to put up a one-horse mill here, stack the lumber on the dock and let the boats pick it up. Lumber's always good."

She put her arm through his arm and watched him with her strengthening smile. "Well, Adam, you'll probably start a mill."

"Is that what I am?"

"Always be struggling with something."

That was as close as he would ever get to himself — that appraisal by his wife who knew him better than he knew himself, and seemed to like what she knew. He had some kind of a dream of contentment, and thought it was to be had at Fishers Landing. Yet here he was thinking of a mill. He could not honestly say that Fishers Landing would be contentment, or that the mill would quell his restlessness. About all he could make out of it was that a man was meant for motion; he was meant to hope and to struggle, to be wrestling always with some sort of chains binding him. It was true of Gorman and Phoebe and Ringrose; it was true of himself. Not any of them knew how the struggle would come out. They could only hope. Some would wear themselves thin at it, some would grow corrupt, some would — by chance or talent — make a go of it; but the ending, good or bad, didn't seem to matter.

"Adam, come back a moment."

"I'm here."

"No — you've been over the hill looking at tomorrow. You like to go there, and it's good for you. But just you remember — there's today to enjoy."

He would never cease to marvel at the range of her spirit; he had seen hurt stain her eyes, he had heard bitterness in her voice, he had seen the shades of loveliness come upon her, he had responded to her heated wanting. At present she was smiling, she was sure of him and sure of herself, and he realized that whatever his own capacities were, he would be pushed to keep up with the varied nature of this woman.

She said: "I'm the only thing on this earth you'll ever feel sure of having. I am the one thing you'll never lose."

Ernest Haycox during his lifetime was considered the dean among authors of Western fiction. When the Western Writers of America was first organized in 1953, what became the Golden Spur Award for outstanding achievement in writing Western fiction was first going to be called the "Erny" in homage to Haycox. He was born in Portland, Oregon and, while still an undergraduate at the University of Oregon in Eugene, sold his first short story to the OVERLAND MONTHLY. His name soon became established in all the leading pulp magazines of the day, including Street and Smith's WESTERN STORY MAGAZINE and Doubleday's WEST MAGAZINE. His first novel, FREE GRASS, was published in book form in 1929. In 1931 he broke into the pages of COLLIER'S and from that time on was regularly featured in this magazine, either with a short story or a serial that was later published as a novel. In the 1940s his serials began appearing in THE SATURDAY EVENING POST and it was there that modern classics such as BUGLES IN THE AFTERNOON (1944) and CANYON PASSAGE (1945) were first published. Both of these novels were also made into major motion pictures although, perhaps, the film most loved and remembered is STAGECOACH (United Artists, 1939) directed by John Ford and starring John Wayne, based on Haycox's short story "Stage to Lordsburg." No history of the Western story in the 20th Century would be possible without reference to Haycox's fiction and his tremendous influence on other writers of stature, such as Peter Dawson, Norman A. Fox, Wayne D. Overholser, and Luke Short, among many. During his last years, before his premature death from abdominal carcinoma, he set himself the task of writing historical fiction which he felt would provide a fitting legacy and the consummation of his life's work. He almost always has an involving story to tell and one in which there is something not so readily definable that raises it above its time, an image possibly, a turn of phrase, or even a sensation, the smell of dust after rain or the solitude of an Arizona night. Haycox was an author whose Western fiction has made an abiding contribution to world literature.

The employees of THORNDIKE PRESS hope you have enjoyed this Large Print book. All our Large Print titles are designed for easy reading, and all our books are made to last. Other Thorndike Large Print books are available at your library, through selected bookstores, or directly from us. For more information about current and upcoming titles, please call or mail your name and address to:

THORNDIKE PRESS
PO Box 159
Thorndike, Maine 04986
800/223-6121
207/948-2962